T0356887

FOUL PLAY

CAROLYN RIDDER ASPENSON

SEVERN RIVER
PUBLISHING

Severn River Publishing
www.SevernRiverBooks.com

This is a work of fiction. Names, characters, businesses, places, events and incidents are either the products of the author's imagination or used in a fictitious manner. Any resemblance to actual persons, living or dead, or actual events is purely coincidental.

ISBN: 978-1-64875-621-4 (Paperback)

ALSO BY CAROLYN RIDDER ASPENSON

To find out more about Carolyn Ridder Aspenson and her books, visit
severnriverbooks.com

To Jack
Forever and Always

1

I had guzzled half a pint of Duke's finest—a brew so local you could taste the sweat of its employees in every sip—when I spotted Rob Bishop, my partner in crime-solving, deep in conversation with Hamby detective Justin Michels, our recently married friend, grinning at me like he had pulled one over on the whole department.

Dukes was the bar that made every night feel like a high school reunion, with a class composed entirely of cops, their significant others, and the occasional brave civilian. Police badges from all over the state plastered the walls, and the jukebox played more country than Nashville on a Saturday night.

"What?" I asked. I'd nursed that one pint for over an hour, and it had truly tasted like sweat. "What are you saying about me, Bishop?"

He smirked. "Nothing I wouldn't say to your face."

"Let it rip, baby." I guzzled the rest of the warm beer to get it over with. I wasn't much of a drinker, though one would think that after having been a cop in Chicago for too many years, I would be. Nope. I'd moved to small town Georgia, where drinking wasn't a pastime. It was a way of life. One I'd chosen only to dip my toes into, not soak my feet.

Lauren Levy, my good friend and the fourth and last Hamby detective, parked on the barstool beside me and elbowed me gently. "Don't let him rile you up. He's only sore because you outshot him at the range last week."

Bishop scowled. "Hey, even Michels missed a few in his time, right?"

"Yeah, but he's out of practice since he got back from his honeymoon," I said, the corner of my mouth twitching upward. "And his target was moving. Yours was stuck to a wall."

"Ouch," Bishop clutched his chest and feigned a heart attack. "Just wait, partner. I'll be back on top in no time."

"Whatever you say, partner."

Kyle, my significant other, walked up behind me and rubbed my shoulder. "Cut the old timer some slack, will ya?"

"Old timer?" Bishop said in a jokingly defensive tone. "Want to put a little wager on my old timer status?"

Laughter bubbled up from our group. It was those moments—the easy camaraderie and the unwinding after long shifts—that kept us all sane in a job that had dragged us through the mud more often than not.

Kyle laughed it off. Bigger and younger than Bishop, I doubted he perceived him as a threat, but given how Bishop had morphed into a younger version of himself a while back, he probably figured better safe than sorry.

"So, Rach, got any big weekend plans?" Lauren probed, her tone light but her gaze piercing. She always had a way of reading people, knowing when to dig a little deeper or change the subject.

"Kyle and I are going riding, but that's about it. You?"

She shrugged. "You don't like to talk about it." The smile stretched across her face.

"Garcia's coming to town? That's great. Y'all should come over for dinner tomorrow."

"You did it again."

"Did what?"

"Said y'all," she said with a smile.

"Hell. I think I'm turning southern. Shoot me now."

"I mean, I will, but you'll need to sign a waiver or something first."

I laughed. "I'm serious. Come over for dinner."

"Can I let you know? I'm not sure we'll have the time."

I cringed because I knew what that meant. Garcia had been my partner in Chicago for several years. A while back, he left the department and hung up his private investigator's sign. So, we'd used him for an intense case, which led to a long-distance relationship with Levy. Garcia was never good at dating on the daily, and I suspected Levy wasn't either, so I was happy they'd found each other. I just didn't want to hear about their sex life.

"Come on folks," Bishop said. "A round of pool says I'm as good as you children."

"As good as us at what?" Michels asked.

"Everything, but let's start with pool," Bishop said.

I dug into my pocket and flung a fiver onto the table. "I'm in."

The rest of the group followed.

"Watch and learn, Agent Olsen," Bishop teased Kyle, lining up a shot that looked more hopeful than skilled. "Let's rip it out of the ballpark."

"That's baseball," I said. I glanced at Kyle and jokingly added, "Is he too old to remember that?"

"Bite me, Ryder," Bishop said.

Kyle leaned against his cue, watching as Bishop wildly missed his target, only to sink a different ball. "I'm watching, I'm learning," Kyle said, his voice rich with mock seriousness. "Is that the secret technique you used to catch that fence-jumper you chased down a few weeks back?"

"You mean the fly-by-the-seat-of-his-pants technique?" I asked, laughing. "I think it is."

Bishop laughed. "I was breaking. I didn't call a ball. You must have assumed something and been wrong." He cleared his throat. "And I thoroughly and professionally executed a take down with that runner, regardless of what it looked like."

Michels pointed at him and said, "Yeah, sounded like it when you dropped, what? At least fifty f-bombs while chasing the guy."

Bishop flipped him the bird.

The game heated into an intense match. Bishop was an excellent pool player, but Kyle was good as well. As one ball after another made it into the pockets, I rooted for them both and held my breath every time one of them shot.

Being in love with someone you would die for and having a partner you would die for, too, was tough when they competed, so when Kyle gave me a look, I kept my support to myself.

The TV on the side wall clicked back to the late-night news and caught my attention with a picture of a familiar face.

Former baseball superstar Ryan Hicks, who captured hearts in Georgia and the rest of the country on the field, is now moving forward in making a big hit in education with his latest endeavor.

Ryan Hicks is no stranger to giving back to the community, and since stepping up to the plate with a grand slam plan to support future generations, after months of delays, his school is finally moving forward. This Friday, Hicks will host an auction here at Lanier Tech Center in Cumming, featuring memorabilia donated by himself and other renowned players from the National Baseball League.

The auction's goal is to raise funds for scholarships that will help interested students attend the new private school Hicks is in the process of building in Hamby. This auction promises to offer top-notch education and opportunities to students who qualify academically but might lack the financial means to attend.

Some of the items up for grabs include signed baseballs, bats, jerseys, and even some unique experiences like training sessions with the players themselves. It's not only an opportunity to own a piece of sports history, but also a chance to make a real difference in the lives of young learners.

All proceeds from the auction will go directly towards these scholarships, making it a win-win situation for bidders and beneficiaries alike. So, if you're a baseball fan, or you want to support a noble cause, be sure to head down to the Lanier Tech Center this Friday. The event kicks off at 6 p.m. and is expected to draw a crowd of sports enthusiasts and community supporters.

For those who want to help but can't make it in person, online bidding will also be available, details of which can be found on the event's website listed on the screen. Don't miss your chance to step up to the plate and help Ryan Hicks hit this one out of the park for the kids in North Fulton County.

"He seems like a great guy," Levy said. "Too bad he didn't play for Philly."

Levy came from Philly, and her loyalty remained with its sports teams.

"I've talked to him at Cooper's place a few times. He's a good guy." A local, Ben Cooper, owned a farm in town and, a while back, we had become friends. After we'd cleared him in a murder investigation, to be exact.

"Seriously?" Levy asked. "Next time he's there, let me know. I'll come by and see your horses."

"Right. That's not at all obvious."

"Hey, with a hot former MLB player, I'm not picky about who he played for."

"I'll make sure Garcia knows that, and isn't Hicks married?"

She laughed. "You understand Garcia. He'd congratulate me. The paper said Hicks is getting divorced. Apparently, it's a nasty one too."

"That's right," I said. "Probably why I never see his wife at the stables."

"Shocking," she said. "All-plastic celebrity baseball wife doesn't want to step in horse dung with her stilettos."

"Isn't it always that way with the celebrities?"

She was right about Garcia. Her hooking up with Hicks would have thrilled him. He never let things like commitment impede a good time. Kyle would have used Hicks's bat to beat the hell out of him. I smiled to myself at the idea. Not that I wanted Kyle beating anyone with a baseball bat, but because I understood how much the guy loved me.

"Whoa!" Michels said. "The old timer just wiped the table with Kyle's shirt."

Levy and I laughed. I glanced at Kyle, shrugged, and mouthed, "Ouch."

He patted Bishop on the back. "I let you win."

∽

"Did you really let him win?" I asked Kyle on the way home.

"Hell no. He kicked my butt."

I chuckled. "Guess he's not such an old timer after all, huh?"

"It's all those bench presses he's doing and those new contact lenses he wears. He's got tools now."

"Right. That's it. Except he's not working out like he used to. He's even eating more sugar. Yesterday, he downed four donuts in a minute straight."

"Everything okay with him?"

"He hasn't said otherwise, but I'm worried there's trouble in paradise."

"With Cathy? They're perfect together."

"We make things look easy, but some people can't handle being involved with someone in law enforcement."

"Are you saying they might be breaking up?"

"It's probably growing pains, but it doesn't mean it's not stressing him out."

"Poor guy. Glad I let him win."

I laughed. "You just said—"

"Pretend, Rach. It's pretend."

We pulled into the driveway. Kyle had insisted we leave our outside lights on every time we left the house. Too many things had happened at that place, and he wanted our security cameras to have a good view in case something else did.

I glanced at the front door. "Hey, let me out. There's something on the door."

He looked over and put the car in park. "Looks like an envelope. I'll get it."

I flashed him a grin. "If you've forgotten, I'm a cop, and I'm pretty damn good at investigating a scene. I can handle something as simple as an envelope from my door." Inside the envelope, I found a note scrawled on a ripped-out page from likely a journal. There was a pile of pumpkins printed in the bottom corner, but the words were chilling and blunt: *Find my killer*, followed by someone signing Ryan Hicks's name.

"What if it's really from him?" I asked Kyle.

"It's a prank," he said. He headed straight upstairs. "I need to get out of these clothes. They smell like beer."

"You reek of beer," I shot back. I sidled over to Louie, my beta fish, and threw on my best Irish accent. "Top of the morning to ya, Louie." He bobbed up to the front of his glass castle, clearly unimpressed. I dropped a few pellets into his bowl to sweeten the deal and hopefully buy his love. Louie always had a way of calming my nerves, but he was too busy eating to help. Prank or not, something felt off with the note. Why would Ryan Hicks prank me? Was it one of those shows where they did stupid stuff to unassuming people? If so, why me? I barely knew the guy. Was it even his signature in the first place? I grabbed my phone and searched the internet for something signed by the famous baseball player. A quick look at a signed photo showed the signature matched, but I wasn't a writing expert.

"Check the camera," Kyle said from upstairs.

"On it," I replied, thumbing open the app on my phone and flicking to the front entrance cam. As I scrutinized the grainy footage, my heart pounded—there was Ryan Hicks, unmistakable even in the dim porch light. He glanced over his shoulder, his movements jittery and uneven. Every few seconds, his head would abruptly shift to one side, followed by the other, as if he were anticipating a sudden appearance from the shadows. I almost sensed the dread clinging to him as he hastily placed the note on my door. Despite the chill in my living room, a bead of sweat trickled down my back. What on earth had Ryan so spooked? I switched to the garage to check those videos.

Ryan Hicks pulled into the driveway. He climbed out of his vehicle, his eyes scanning the surroundings with frantic intensity. He looked left, followed by a quick glance to the right, his gaze sharp and cautious, as if he expected trouble at every corner. Finally, he rushed toward my front door. His every step seemed hurried, desperate. What was making Ryan so nervous?

I sank into our leather sofa, the video of him leaving played on my screen, but my mind raced a mile a minute. I dialed dispatch. "This is Detective Ryder. I need a welfare check on—" I paused, my brain screeching to a halt—I didn't have Hicks's address. "Ryan Hicks's place. It's off Providence Road, but I don't have the address on me."

"Ten-four," the dispatcher responded, her voice calm and collected. "I believe everyone in town is aware of the spot. I'll send someone."

"Appreciate it," I said and disconnected the call.

I watched the side cameras videos but saw nothing out of the ordinary and immediately hit up Ben Cooper.

"Hello?" His voice was all gravel and Texas, as if he'd gargled with the state itself.

"Hey, I know it's late, but I need Ryan Hicks's personal cell. You got it?"

"Sure thing. Something wrong?" Cooper's drawl was heavy with concern.

"Not sure yet."

He rattled off the number.

"Thanks," I said and killed the line. My call to Hicks dumped straight to voicemail. I texted and called a few more times, but nothing.

Following that, the officer sent to Hicks's house contacted me, his tone revealing everything I needed to know prior to his words. "No answer at the door, and the place is all dark, like they're sleeping or gone."

"Great. Thank you," I said. "Monitor the place, will you?"

"Sure thing, Detective."

I bounded upstairs two at a time to fill Kyle in.

He stood in the bedroom with only a towel wrapped around his waist. My eyes traveled up and down his body for a quick second or five.

"You like what you see?" he asked.

"It's distracting, but yes." I gave him the 411.

He pulled on a clean pair of jeans, which meant he was getting ready to rumble if need be. "Are you sure it was him on the camera?"

"Unless he's got a twin, yes."

"The house is dark, right?"

I nodded. "That doesn't mean everything's okay." I handed him my phone. "Check the cameras. He's scared, but there's nothing around him."

"No, I understand that, but it's strange. Why didn't he call you? I'm sure Cooper would have given him your cell."

"Right?" I asked. "Doesn't make sense, which is why I think this is for real."

"You want to run by there?" he asked.

"Yes, but let me call Jimmy. See how he wants to handle it." I dialed the Hamby Police Chief's cell. Jimmy and I had established a strong relationship when I'd first started at the PD, and his wife, Savannah, had become my best friend. Though we were nothing alike, it worked.

He answered on one ring. "What's up?"

I gave him the 411.

"The slick sleeve said everything appeared okay?" he asked. Slick sleeve was standard law enforcement slang for a patrol officer, though usually only those above them used it.

"He said it appeared no one was home. No one answered the door."

He grumbled under his breath. "And you're sure it's him on the video?"

"Have you seen him? He isn't hard to recognize."

"Hey, now," Kyle kidded.

"Call Bishop. If something's happened to our resident celebrity and we're not on it, the mayor will can the entire department. I'll get with dispatch. See you there in fifteen."

I cut the call and contacted Bishop.

"Holy hell," he said.

"I'll get the exact address from dispatch and send it to you," I said.

"I'll meet you there."

Hicks had his slice of paradise staked out on ten acres along Freemanville Road, not Providence, and a mile past the guy who'd built himself a mini-Tombstone, Arizona, right inside his already massive house. Kyle had come along for the ride because he'd gotten to know Hicks at Cooper's ranch and because we always appreciated his input.

Most of the department, including Michels and Levy, arrived around the same time, meeting up with the two cruisers who had originally made the welfare check. The fire department brought three trucks, the chief, and two EMT trucks. Preparation for anything was key when we had no information.

"Call him again," Jimmy said.

"I tried on the way. Still no answer, and my texts say delivered." I looked for security cameras and found one above the garage and another above the front door. "We need copies of the videos on those cameras."

"Already noted," Bishop said.

"I called Cooper," Kyle said. "He said Lara Hicks moved out last year when the couple separated."

"Yes, nasty divorce according to the news," I agreed, recalling what Levy had said earlier.

"Do we have her number?" Jimmy asked me.

"No."

"I'll get someone to call Bubba and ask him to check," he said. "Hate to wake him, but if anyone can locate it, it's him. I've got men monitoring every exit, inspecting every window on the main and terrace levels. If someone's entered through one of them, we'll find out."

Bubba, our IT genius, could find anything hiding in the ether.

"We need to go in," I said.

"Cooper said he's got a key if we need it," Kyle said.

"We can't wait to get him here," Jimmy said.

Levy hurried to the door and knocked on it again. "Ryan Hicks, this is the Hamby PD. Tell us you're inside or we'll have to break down this door."

Still no response.

"Chief, the four of us got this," Michels said. His yawn didn't help him win his case. "I've got my battering ram in the truck."

"Get it, and you all get inside," he said. "Now!"

Kyle helped with the ram but then, since he wasn't part of our department, he stayed outside while we did our jobs. He would lend a hand if Jimmy requested.

Three minutes later, the heavy oak door groaned on its hinges as it swung open into Ryan Hicks's mansion—a fortress of understated elegance that smacked more of classic tastes than celebrity flash.

Michels's jaw dropped. "This place is a hell of a lot bigger than it looks."

"Right. We need all these officers out of here," Bishop said into the radio. "Keep five but send the rest home. We can't have them screwing up a potential crime scene.

"On it," Jimmy replied.

When the five arrived, we stationed three at the door so no one else could get in unless they had to. We divided the rest of us into groups of two, with Michels and Levy patrolling the upper level, the two slick sleeves on the terrace level, and Bishop and I on the main floor.

Not long after, Levy reported on the radio, "We've got a 10-54 on the bed of the primary bedroom."

A body. Bishop and I shared a look.

"It's Hicks," she added.

We ascended the stairs two at a time, with Bishop leading by a few.

Luxury clashed with violence where Ryan Hicks's body lay face down, sprawled across a king-sized bed, expensive sheets crumpled beneath him. Levy crouched beside him, her attention focused on the gunshot residue. She checked her watch before gently moving his left index finger. "He's not in rigor yet, so it's not even been two hours."

"He was at my place at 10:30, according to the videos."

"So, maybe he came home, decided to head up to bed, and someone shot him," Levy said.

"Isn't that weird?" Michels said. "If he was paranoid in the videos, would he be going to bed right away?"

"Paranoia and fear are exhausting," I said. "Have you considered he felt it was all he could do?"

Levy continued to check the body carefully but didn't touch it. "See the stippling here?" She gestured to the pattern around the wound. "Tells us the shot was up close and personal. Probably didn't even wake up."

"This is bad," Michels said. "The person had to have been here before he got home and hid in another room or something."

Jimmy stood behind me, dropping F-bombs like candy from a pinata. "Ryan Hicks." He shook his head. "Hell. We need to keep this as tight as possible. The media's going to be on us like white on rice."

Michels had flung open the balcony doors and was inspecting the lock with a detective's precision. "Lock's clean," he announced, his voice bouncing around the spacious room. "No signs of a break-in. Looks like my theory is getting warmer."

"Levy, Michels," Jimmy said. "You two secure the scene." He pointed to each of the two slick sleeves. "I want you at the bottom of the stairs. No one, and I mean no one, without a badge or with the fire department, gets up the stairs. You understand?"

They both nodded and rushed out as Jimmy issued more orders.

Nikki burst into the room, hauling a hefty nylon bag. Her entourage, a pair of eager interns from the University of Georgia, followed her, equipped with cameras and kits for evidence gathering.

She stared at Hicks lying face down on his bed. "Oh, wow. It's really him."

"Dude," Taylor Crowe, one of her interns, said. "It's totally him."

The other, Carl with a last name I didn't remember, stared at him in a weird awe. "Dude."

I caught Jimmy's glance—a pair of sharp knives couldn't have cut deeper into that intern's sick.

"Remember, what happens here stays here. Clear?" he snapped.

"Yes, chief," she mumbled.

"It's a no to dinner," Levy said to me. "And to Garcia coming to town as well."

"Sorry about that," I said.

She shrugged. "It's part of the job."

Like a mother hen with her brood, Nikki orchestrated the search with military precision. "Taylor, take the left side, log everything. And by everything, I mean even a ball of dust. Got it?"

"Yes, ma'am," Taylor said.

"We'll sort it at the precinct." Her gaze swung to Remi, her other intern. "You're on the right. Same drill. Report back when you're done, and we'll sweep the next area." We made eye contact. "Carl, you do a sweep of the property with whatever slick sleeves are out there. If they give you grief, tell them to get me on the radio."

"You rock," I said.

"There's a safe in the closet," Bishop said. "It's locked."

"I found keys under the bed," Nikki said. "Let's try them."

The safe key was on the key chain, but the safe was empty.

"Theft?" I asked.

"Why would he instruct you to find his killer if someone had already robbed him?" Bishop asked. "Did someone give him an advanced warning?"

"Good point," I said.

"Not everyone puts valuables in their safe," Bishop said. "Often it's just important papers."

"Could be for jewelry, but the wife moved out," Michels said. He looked out the window. "The vultures are circling already."

I peered out to see the growing swarm of fire and police personnel, their voices a dull roar behind the mansion's thick walls. True to Michels's prediction, the press had begun to gather, hovering, even starving, for any sensational tidbit. "They're clawing for a slice of scandal," I said.

"I'll handle them," Jimmy grunted, frustration lining his words.

Dr. Mike Barron, the coroner, showed up at that time, as always, his stride full of pure Southern grit. Despite the accent that might fool some into underestimating him, he was sharper than a tack. "Looks like you dragged me into a crime scene right as I was kicking off my boots for the night," he said, eyeing the body before his gaze landed on me and Bishop. "It's him, isn't it?"

Bishop simply nodded.

He checked for a pulse but found nothing, calling the time of death at that moment. His chest rose and fell with a heavy sigh. "A legend, gone too soon." He eyed us curiously. "So, what's the story?"

I relayed the details of the note.

He whistled, his mouth rounding in awe. "Predicting his own death, huh? The man could knock a 250-mph fastball out of the park, but calling his last shot like this? That's downright eerie."

"Or genius," Levy said from behind me. She handed me a journal with the same pumpkin photo as the paper on which Ryan had written the note. "Is this the paper?"

Nikki's radio beeped. "Yeah?"

"We may have found a footprint," Carl said.

2

We rolled back into Hamby PD after leaving the scene as the first hints of dawn were trying to shove the night aside. Exhausted and over-stimulated already, Bishop and I, in sync as always, lugged in a box of Dunkin' coffee each that we bet would disappear faster than dignity in a strip club.

I yawned. "I'm more tired than a stripper working a double shift in a night club."

"A stripper in a nightclub?" He laughed. "Where do you get your similes?"

Feigning shock, I asked, "You know what a simile is?"

He flipped me the bird, his favorite comeback.

Looming down the hall, the investigation room waited for us, stark and unwelcoming, with its soul-sucking metal chairs and whiteboards. Though on the newer side, it had seen better days.

"Any word on the footprint?" Jimmy asked as we walked into the room.

"Nikki's making a mold of it. We'll move on it when she's finished," Bishop said.

"Bubba's here. He's been on a Zoom call with the surveillance company checking the cameras."

"Anything yet?" I asked.

"Let's check." He used the landline phone on the table and hit Bubba's extension. "Anything?"

"Nothing's showing up on any of the cameras, Chief. Looks like whoever did this found a way around them."

"Not surprising," Jimmy said. "Thanks for coming in for this."

"Sure thing. I'll stick around if you need me."

Jimmy tossed a file on the metal table. It echoed with a thud when it hit. "I wouldn't have thought someone as famous and important to the community as Ryan Hicks would simply leave a note instead of approaching us directly," he grumbled.

"If not for the video," I chimed in, leaning against the cool wall, feeling every hour of missed sleep weighing down my eyelids. "I wouldn't have believed it either, Chief."

Levy, cutting to the chase, frowned and said, "So, why? If you honestly believe someone's out to kill you, why play games? What stopped him from coming to us directly?"

"Fear?" Bishop suggested.

"Blackmail?" Michels added.

"He's hiding something," Bubba piped up from his corner, where he nested among various tech gadgets. Our very own wizard with anything that beeped or blinked, Bubba had started to dip his toes into the murky waters of detective work from a tech angle—and we were all better for it.

"That's it," I snapped my fingers, the idea crystallizing into something logical in my head. "He saw it coming, and he'd rather face a bullet than the public's scorn."

Bishop raised an eyebrow. "Not dramatic at all."

Michels, leaning back with a smirk, added, "Sounds more like a soccer player than a baseball star. You know, the whole acting hurt when someone barely brushes past them thing? Baseball players are tougher than that."

Levy shook her head, like me, not buying her partner's lighter mood. "This is heavier than a fabricated injury. Drugs?"

"Drugs, embezzlement, fraud, money laundering," Bishop rattled off plausible scenarios from a list in his mind. "Take your pick, and we'll start digging."

He wasn't wrong. Ryan Hicks could have had reasons aplenty to dodge the cops and they all funneled into our dark reality. "He didn't think he could be saved," I said.

"Probably," Michels said. "So much for trusting law enforcement to do their job."

"But he wants his killer on the hook," Levy noted, crossing her arms. "Even if it means dragging his own dirt into the light."

"After he's dead," Michels added. "That way he doesn't have to face the music."

"It's possible," I confirmed, feeling the case's weight already sitting on my soul. The media was already all over it, and the last thing we needed was Jimmy hiring another liaison who leaked too much information and compromised us. "Whatever mess Ryan Hicks got himself into, it's up to us to wade through the muck and uncover the truth, no matter how ugly it reveals itself."

"The next question is where do we start?" Michels asked. He yawned.

I gestured toward Bishop as I settled beside him. "The list in Bishop's head sounds like a good place."

"Add blackmail to it too," Bubba suggested. "I got a feeling."

I'd take a feeling over a guess any day.

Jimmy's cell phone rang. "It's the mayor." He quickly answered the call while exiting the room.

"I have an idea." I'd recently taken a class in mind mapping for law enforcement at the Department of Public Safety in Forsyth, Georgia. Jimmy asked me to check it out and see if it was worth its salt. It wasn't awful, but we did practically use it already. "We can mind map it," I offered. "I know the chief here has been waiting for me to use what he so graciously sent me to bumble Georgia to learn."

"How 'bout we work this like normal?" Bishop asked. "The old way, process of elimination?"

"That's basically what mind mapping is, old man."

He flipped me the bird again. He needed a better response. That one had no effect on me, ever.

I grabbed an erasable marker and dragged myself to one of our many whiteboards. "This is our stage, our canvas, our crime scene."

I scribbled Ryan Hicks in the middle of the board and circled it. "Okay, let your thoughts branch out like the routes you chase leads on and give me something. I'll draw lines from his name to your ideas. These are our clues, our suspects, our leads. Every new idea gets its own line shooting off from the center or branching from another idea. Look at it as a web made by a spider high on espresso."

"We're already doing that," Michels argued.

"Come on guys," Levy said. "All it'll do is organize our thoughts. Ain't nothing wrong with that."

"Thanks, Levy," I said. "She's right. The goal here isn't to create a neat, orderly map. It's letting our ideas run wild. We're mapping the terrain of our minds, and sometimes that terrain is a wild jungle of possibilities." I smiled at Bubba. "Especially yours."

"And what happens after that?" Bishop grumbled. The guy got seriously prickly with no sleep.

"Let's start there and see where it leads." I didn't want to tell him we would keep adding to the ideas until something felt right for fear he'd quit right there. "Bishop, it's the same thing we always do. We're just doing it in an organized way." I felt like a kindergarten teacher trying to teach the alphabet. Say it and repeat it over and over.

"We're always organized," he said.

"Jeez." The man was impossible. "Go with the flow."

"I can flow," he said. "Extortion." A smile stretched across his smug face.

I pointed at him and shook my head. He was a pain, but a smart one.

"Right," Michels said. "He's getting divorced, right? Is it possible he had incriminating information about the wife and used it as a threat to force her to comply with his demands?"

"Or she had something on him," Levy suggested.

I jotted down extortion. Bishop did the same in his small notepad.

"Or his lawyer," Bubba said. "Lawyers have information most don't. His could have used it against him."

"Or hers," Levy added. "Business associates, friends, his publicity manager. Former players. His coaches. The guy that runs the leagues. Scorned lover. The list is endless."

"Hell," Bishop said. "This sounds worse than trying to find Hoffa."

"You'll never find him. He's buried under a skyscraper," Levy said.

"Blackmail," Bubba said again. "I think that's the best one. Either Hicks tried to blackmail someone, or they blackmailed him and failed, so they killed him."

We spent the next three hours coming up with scenarios for a murder in which we were clueless, but it was a place to start.

Jimmy's assistant knocked as we were about to break for some much-needed shut eye. The caffeine buzz had fizzled too quickly.

"The wife's here," she said. Susan was an older woman Jimmy had hired to replace his previous assistant who had left to have a baby. Not discounting the expertise of the previous one, Susan had snapped the department and the chief into line like that same kindergarten teacher but with an unruly class. It was genius. "She wants to know what we're doing to find her husband's killer. The chief would like everyone to meet with her in his office."

Bishop peeled himself out of his chair. "I need a breath mint."

"Copy that," I said.

I paused at the women's locker room to freshen up and rewrap the bun at my neck's base before going to meet the wife of one of the biggest celebrities in the state, if not the country. I didn't care about making a good impression for her sake, but I did for Jimmy's. Also, my bun had all but collapsed and it needed a refresh.

Savannah had their baby, a son named Carter on the bench, waving a diaper over his head. "I don't care how cute you are. If you pee on me, we're going to throw down."

I smirked. The kid had the aim of a sniper.

With planned precision, she detached the used diaper and ripped it out from under him and set the clean one on top of his sprayer.

I golf-clapped. "Impressive moves there, Mama."

"I'm the stupid one who wore a new outfit."

"I was going to say."

"Hush, Ryder," she said jokingly.

I covered my mouth and walked over to Scarlet, her older child and my goddaughter, who was in her stroller pretending to read a book. "Hey, sweetie. How's my girl?"

She ignored me. I'd be lying if I said it didn't bother me.

Carter smiled at me. The kid was Hollywood gorgeous and not even eight months.

"It's not as hard as it looks." She secured the fresh diaper, finished by pressing the snaps of his adorable overalls together and said, "I'm glad you caught me. I ran into Lara Hicks. Are you heading her way?"

"I am," I said. "Give me the 411."

"Oh, honey, prepare yourself. That woman is a lot to handle. She's got it in her head she's going to eat all y'all alive." She laughed. "I have no doubt she has no clue what she's walking into, in there demanding answers like she's someone special. It's not even been twelve hours." She zipped her diaper bag closed and hitched it over her shoulder. "I have half a mind to shove this right where the sun don't shine."

I bit back a smile. "I'd pay to see that."

"I don't get what people see in her," she said as she checked herself out in the mirror. "Looks are one thing, but if the soul's as dark as a storm cloud on Sunday, you best believe the heart's just as muddy." She smiled at herself. "And that woman's got a storm cloud brewing inside her."

"Got it," I said.

She continued her rant. "Bless her heart, every speck of her, from that diamond-studded watch to her Jimmy Choo's, just screams in her own head she's the very pinnacle of baseball wives." She'd picked up Carter before her bag and placed him in the double stroller.

Scarlet looked at him and cried. She wasn't a fan of her little brother.

"Which of course, she's not," Savannah said, completely ignoring Scarlet's cries which usually passed in a matter of seconds.

"Nope. She's not," I said. "Thanks for the description. Now I understand what I'm working with." Walking out, I already didn't trust Lara Hicks. Savannah's intuition bordered on psychic. If she didn't like the woman, neither did I.

Jimmy's gaze sliced through me the second I walked in. I understood the meaning of that look well, warning me to keep my words tight or my mouth shut, whichever would get him in less trouble. Was he psychic like his wife?

"Mrs. Hicks," I said, introducing myself. "I'm sorry we have to meet under such terrible circumstances. Your husband and I were acquaintances. He was a good man."

She sniffled and moved a tissue from her nose to dab her eyes. As a child my mother told me I'd get conjunctivitis doing that. "What's going on? What happened to my sweet husband?"

She'd really played it up for us. Innocent or guilty, genuine or forced, they always exploded with emotion as did I after my husband Tommy's murder. "We're in the beginning stages of the investigation, but your coming by is very helpful." My eyes shifted to Jimmy's, then back to her. "Are you able to answer some questions?"

She sniffled again and nodded. "Yes. Yes, of course. Ryan and I didn't work being married, but we were still very close friends." She sniffled again but was yet to shed an actual tear. "I can't understand why any of this happened."

Police Academy 101: The survivor of a recently deceased family member rarely referred to the victim in the past tense. It only happened when they had consciously accepted the death or caused it. Had Lara Hicks murdered her husband? That divorce they were going through. All that money? It could bring anyone to murder.

"Okay," I said. "Let's go into a private room. One where we won't have to worry about prying eyes," I said, glancing out into the pit full of law enforcement officers.

"Mrs. Hicks," Jimmy said. "We will do everything we can to find out what happened to your husband."

"Are you saying someone murdered him?"

"The coroner hasn't given us a definitive just yet," Jimmy said.

"Wasn't he shot in the back of the head?"

Great, someone leaked the news. It always happened that way with celebrities. People couldn't keep their mouths shut.

"Yes," Jimmy said. "But until the coroner provides a definitive, we call it a suspicious homicide."

"Oh, okay." She fiddled with the tissue again. "Don't I need to identify the body or something?"

"Along with Mr. Hicks's celebrity and other factors, we've determined his identity, but if you want to see his remains," Jimmy said, "I can set up a time with the medical examiner."

She sniveled. "Oh, no. I trust you."

Good friends? Right. If she cared at all, she'd demand to see him, if for no other reason than to convince herself he was dead.

"Very well, please let me know if you have any questions."

"Of course," she said and followed us out of his office.

Susan made eye contact and motioned for me. I excused myself, letting Bishop take the lead getting everyone into an interrogation room.

"What's up?" I asked.

"The wolves are close to breaking down the door. Regardless of our feelings about a communications liaison, one might be best."

I exhaled. "I hate to say this, but I agree."

She nodded. "I'll talk to the chief and make sure we pick one you won't want to whip a slipper at."

I laughed, knowing at her age, she understood I understood that concept. "Anyone you pick is good with me."

"I'll keep you posted."

A symphony of cuss words burst to life inside Jimmy's office.

"Guess who just found out the media is already outside?" she asked and hurried to him.

Better her than me.

The interrogation rooms at the Hamby PD were stale, uninviting places. Intentionally. The high temps, harsh fluorescent overhead lights, and metal chairs about as comfortable as a bed of nails were all part of the décor to pressure suspects to talk. Lara Hicks was a person of interest, though she'd arrived of her own accord, and not because she was summoned to be questioned. She'd realize that soon enough, say, as her makeup melted down her face. God knew it was thick enough to leave indentions.

Bishop and I had been partners long enough to read each other and formulate a plan of attack without speaking a word. He leaned against the wall, his arms folded, his face unreadable to the average person. Bad cop mode face, but since he wasn't flat-out grimacing, I knew he'd handle her with a touch of grace, likely because she was the estranged wife of a celebrity, and all eyes would be on us. One bad media report could destroy not only the case but our careers.

I placed a glass of water in front of Mrs. Hicks and sat across from the widow with a semi-sincere, sympathetic look on my face.

She sipped the water. "Thank you." We didn't know if she'd murdered Hicks. Though we were there to figure that out. My gut always played a big role in my work, and it said she'd killed him. I'd consider it correct even if I liked the woman, but I didn't. Playing good cop wasn't easy for me. My Chicago and Italian demeanor often showed itself at the wrong time, but I gave it my best shot.

Lara looked every inch the estranged celebrity wife—pristine makeup, not a hair out of place, dressed in a simple but expensive blouse and slacks. She folded her hands neatly in her lap with her right hand's ring finger sporting an obnoxiously enormous emerald and diamond ring. She wore a square blue stone with diamonds on it on her left ring finger. All the stones were nearly the size of a tater tot. If you just glanced at her, you might see a picture of a grieving widow. But I'd been a cop long enough to understand that appearances were often deceiving.

"Mrs. Hicks," I began, trying to keep my tone sympathetic but professional. "We understand this is a difficult time for you. We appreciate your willingness to speak with us." I glanced at the one-way mirror, knowing everyone stood behind it listening and watching.

She nodded, dabbing the same tissue delicately at her eyes. "Anything to help clear up this awful situation."

Bishop straightened from the wall, stepping forward. His voice was gentle, but with a steel edge. "It must be hard, being a celebrity in the middle of a divorce. We're subject to the scrutiny of the media, of course, but I suspect they're worse for you."

"Oh, you have no idea. I have no privacy, and poor Ryan, he was always dealing with reporters, paparazzi, and fans. It was terrible. He was always polite, but it frustrated him."

"Can you tell us about your relationship?" I asked.

"Our relationship? What about it?"

"You must have had problems," I said. "Divorces don't just happen."

The question caused her shoulders to stiffen just slightly, but it was a definitive crack in her poised demeanor. "People grow apart," she said flatly. "It's as simple as that. We wanted different things. It's nobody's fault."

"Was it amicable?" Bishop asked.

"Of course. We were still best friends. We just weren't in love anymore."

My intuitive red flags waved all around the woman. I wanted to call her out, but I tried a different technique. "I'm almost embarrassed to say this," I said. "I'm from Chicago. I'm a die-hard Cubs fan, but since moving here, I've learned to like the Braves as well. I just don't pay attention to the personal lives of the players."

"So many people do," she said. "It can be exhausting."

"I'm sure. How long were you married?"

"Twelve years."

"Wow," I said, impressed. "I'll be honest, that's a long time for a celebrity."

"We loved each other."

"So, the rumors about affairs were just rumors, then?" Bishop asked.

Ouch.

Her reaction revealed volumes. She sat with her back arrow-straight, projecting the illusion that she wasn't messing around. With her hands clasped neatly in her lap, she embodied control and poise, but my gut warned me she either withheld something or was lying.

She held Bishop's gaze without flinching. "Ryan never cheated on me. It wasn't his style," she declared, her voice steady. Each word came with a slight, confident nod that tried desperately to underscore her certainty about the man she married.

"Was it yours?"

Dang, the man tossed out passive aggressive insults like Halloween candy.

"I stayed faithful to Ryan."

"Until one of you filed for divorce," Bishop said. He walked the short distance from one wall to the other. "I'm not a gossip reader by any means, but my lady friend loves to read the magazines while waiting at the register in the grocery store. She mentioned you'd begun seeing the head land-scaper at your home. Or was it the pool guy?" He shook his head. "I'm sorry, I don't remember."

"That was just a rumor. Jerome owns the company that services our pool, but it wasn't what it looked like. Reporters get on the property and take photos out of context. I wasn't hugging Jerome because we were sleeping together. I hugged him because his dog had died. Jerome and I were good friends. Ryan traveled a lot. Jerome helped around the house. It was so big, and impossible for me to care for while raising my children, but it wasn't an affair."

"Jerome?" I repeated. "Does he have a last name?"

She hesitated but said, "White."

I felt like I was sitting on my grandmother's plastic wrapped couch watching her stories, what she called the soaps. Sullen widows, big houses, pool boys. The stuff that flooded daytime TV. "Helped?" I pressed. "In what ways?"

"Maintenance, errands," she blurted, her gaze darting between us. "He was reliable and supportive of my situation."

"Supportive how?" I asked. "Did he ever discuss Ryan with you? Any plans or concerns he had?"

Her fingers tightened around the tissue. "It wasn't like that. He just listened."

"Did you have any ongoing disputes or conflicts? You and Ryan?"

"Detective," she said, "are you married?"

The pain in my chest hit me like a nine-millimeter bullet. "I'm a widow." No sense in sugarcoating it. "I watched my husband get murdered in cold blood."

She blanched. "I'm sorry. I didn't—"

"Thank you," I said before she finished, and meaning it.

"We had our issues, obviously. Otherwise, we'd still be married."

"Who filed?" I asked.

"It doesn't really matter anymore," she said, dipping her head down so her eyes wouldn't meet mine. "He'd threatened to do it multiple times, and I just couldn't take it anymore. As hard as it was for us both to walk away, we weren't in love, and it was the right thing to do."

Bishop looked at me, then back at her. "That suggests you did."

"Yes," she said.

"How did Ryan handle that?" I asked.

"He was angry, but not that we would get divorced, that I'd filed before he had the chance."

"Did you have a pre-nup?" Bishop asked.

"His attorney made one, yes, but I never signed it, and neither did he. We began our marriage expecting it to be forever. We weren't like other celebrities. I came from a small, let's say, lower middle-class family, and Ryan was a local boy who'd done well in baseball. We just wanted our happily ever after."

Nothing in her voice or body language said they wanted the same things. Pull my left leg, sweetheart. It does a tap dance. "Are you familiar with Ben Cooper?"

"The guy with the farm? Yes. Our horses are there." A tear slid down her cheek. "I guess I'll have to handle them now."

"I have horses there too," I said. "I'd talked to Ryan multiple times. We'd become friendly." I hoped to see her flinch, but she didn't.

"He loved those horses. I am not an animal person."

"So, you two are friends?" I asked. "You and Ben?"

"Only enough to recognize him in town. Ryan once dragged me to Ben's ranch to see the horses. We chatted, but it was nothing important." Her eyes narrowed. "Why? Are you saying he murdered my husband?"

I ignored her question. "When was the divorce supposed to be finalized?"

Bishop spoke before I had a chance. "Where were you last night?"

"At what time precisely?" she asked.

"Between six and midnight," he said. Giving a bigger timeframe allowed us to get more information such as, 'I stopped by the grocery store then to the gym,' instead of something like, 'I went to the grocery store.'

She looked at the glass of water on the table, but not at us. "I was otherwise engaged."

"May we have his number?" Bishop asked.

She finally looked up. "Why are you talking to me as if I've done something wrong? I came here this morning to discuss my husband's murder, not to have the police interrogate me."

"Consider it a bonus," he said.

"Mrs. Hicks," I said, trying to get her to talk more. "We're just gathering information. We're not accusing you of anything."

"I don't care. I'm a celebrity. This could get me cancelled, and I can't ruin my future over this."

Over her husband's murder? She'd rendered me speechless.

She stood. "I'm leaving now."

I kept my cool. "Sit down, Ms. Hicks."

She blanched. "It's Mrs. I am not divorced yet."

"Which is why we're questioning you," I said. "Did you know that most murders are committed by someone close to the victim?"

A tear finally fell from her eye. "I want an attorney."

And there they were. The four words that shut us up faster than a sucker for a crying baby.

"You're not under arrest, Ms. Hicks," Bishop said. "But if the preliminary autopsy report comes back saying someone murdered Mr. Hicks, your request for an attorney just put you on the top of our suspect list." He gave her a slight nod. "Have a nice day."

I exhaled as Bishop walked out. Standing, I said, "The more we know, if warranted, the sooner we can eliminate you as a suspect and find your husband's killer."

"Wait," she said. "I'll answer any questions you ask. I didn't kill my husband."

Once spoken, even if the suspect retracted their statement like she had, anything we learned would be dismissed by a good defense attorney. I would have gladly accepted her offer if she hadn't uttered those four paralyzing words. Given the celebrity element in the situation, I had to play it by the book. We'd approach her again once her frustration diminished. If she'd secured legal representation by then, we'd likely get nothing, but we'd still give it a shot.

I handed her my card. "Get an attorney and give me a call."

After escorting Lara Hicks to the lobby, I returned to the interrogation room and, using a tissue, grasped her water glass and carried it to the investigation room. Bishop sat in a chair examining the crime scene photos Nikki had arranged. I passed the glass to Nikki. "This has Lara Hicks's prints on it."

"Oh," she said, smiling. "The old sip for print trick. Good work, detective." She left the room with the glass.

"Nice job acting there, partner," I said to Bishop.

"I wasn't acting. That woman yanks my chain. She feels she's better than us."

"She's a celebrity. She worked hard to marry for that. Cut her some slack."

He turned and rolled his eyes. "Lack of sleep softens you."

I laughed.

Jimmy slammed through the door. "I said talk to her, not interrogate her." He glared at me. Not Bishop. Me. "What the hell is wrong with you people? She'll be the star of a special report disrupting my mother-in-law's soap operas for sure now." He glimpsed the crime scene photos and lowered his voice a notch. "He was doing good things. The school would have been great for the community. We were considering sending Scarlet and Carter there, eventually."

"It'll still happen," Bubba said.

"How do you know?" I asked.

"I did a little research last night. He's not the only owner. There are several investors. If they're smart, they'll capitalize on Hicks's murder and twist it to their benefit." He paused, adding, "Like the school is still opening in honor of him or something."

I nodded. "It's possible."

"I'm hiring a temporary communications liaison," Jimmy said. He pointed at me as he walked toward the door. "Don't scare her away." He opened the door and bumped into Nikki.

"Carl made the mold of the footprint we found on the scene."

3

"Size thirteen," Nikki said. She thrust a stack of photos into my hands for the team's review. Jimmy snatched one for himself and vanished through the door. "There were no signs of forced entry at the window or any other entries," she said, "but we did an entire search of the grounds, and there were no other footprints that close to a possible entrance."

"Except for law enforcement," Michels said.

"Yes," she replied. "The print looks to be from a sneaker or some type of athletic shoe, not a boot or dress one, so it's unlikely to be one of ours, but we'll still check. Carl is currently looking into brands with the same sole."

"Is Remi helping?" Bishop asked.

"Remi is no longer with my department," Nikki said. "She decided she preferred a desk job over dead bodies. She switched to administration."

"Better to figure that out before she graduated," I said.

"I'll send the print out to the local departments," Bubba said. "Someone might have the same one from another crime."

"Which means more possible suspects," I said.

"Part of the job," Bishop said.

"It's doubtful we'll get any response," Michels said. "Take it from a recent former sleeve. Research like that is almost as bad as being assigned to cold cases."

"I agree," Levy said. "Not about the sleeve comment. About the unlikelihood of us getting any response."

"Still worth a shot," I said.

"We found no evidence of drugs, legal or illegal."

"Thank God," Bishop said. "I'd hate to see his legacy destroyed by something like that."

"Agreed," she said. "Someone recently mowed the lawn, and the print was in an area of fresh soil. It's possible it belongs to someone from their landscape company. If they're any good at their job, they'd cover up their prints after they finish a job."

"My question is, what would a landscaper be doing at their house after dark?" Levy asked.

"Not the wife," Michels said.

She whacked him on the arm. "Shut it, Michels."

He acted like he hadn't practically called the victim's almost-ex-wife a slut. "What'd I do?"

"That was rough," Bishop said.

Michels sulked in his seat. "Geez. Nobody's got a sense of humor anymore."

"Can we hope Lara Hicks will give us the name of their landscaper?" Levy asked.

"Good luck with that," Bishop said.

"She's not going to give us anything anymore," I added, my eyes glued to Bishop. "Prince Charming here made sure of that."

"Just doing my job, ma'am." He added the ma'am knowing it was one of my least favorite things to be called.

Call me any word in the book, even the ones hated by most women, and I was fine, but call me ma'am, and I could spit nails. I got that it was a southern manners thing, but it rubbed me the wrong way.

"Whoever did this had a way into the house," Levy said.

"That list could be long," I said.

"Cleaning people," Bubba suggested. "Assistants, lawyers. Friends. Family. It could be anyone."

I exhaled. "Thanks for the fifty-pound dumbbell to the chest, Bubba."

He cringed. "Sorry."

"No, he's right," Michels said. "We need to find out who's got access to the house."

"He had cameras," Bishop said. He looked at Bubba.

"I'll get on that."

"What about his manager?" Levy asked. "Or his agent? Someone's got to be managing his money and his time, and whoever does that would be close to Ryan."

"That's right," Bubba said. "I've seen his assistant on TV with him. Rutherford or something?" His fingers pounded the keyboard of one of his computers. "Colin Rutherford. He's tagged in Hicks's social media posts."

"I doubt Hicks was posting his own social media," I said. "Can you get us Rutherford's contact info?"

"Shouldn't be a problem." His fingers danced on the keyboard. If the guy played the piano, he'd be the next Beethoven. He said, "Here you go," as the printer came to life.

"His attorney," Bishop said. "He could be involved in every aspect of Hicks's life. We need to get on him pronto."

"I'll look into him," Bubba said. "Give me a sec."

"What about his partners in the charter school?" Levy asked.

"Oh," Bubba said, "I'm already working on that. I also have the team list from when he played and the first year after, and all the employees for the stadium. I can get contact information, but that's going to take some time."

"Great," Bishop said. "Let's leave the players and employees with the shift commander. If need be, he can get a few guys making calls, but I don't want him taking men off their assigned duties for it yet. Let's work our options first. If something leads to someone on those lists, we'll have them check others."

"They'd love to do that," Michels said.

I looked at him. "Sarcasm?"

"Hell no. I loved doing that stuff. It made me feel like a detective."

"You're such a dork," Levy said.

"Am not."

I chuckled. They acted like brother and sister, but in a sense, they were family. "Let's start with his manager."

"This is interesting," Bubba said. "Colin Rutherford is his manager and attorney."

"He's wrapped like a tight bow around Hicks's life. He would have a key to the house, and it wouldn't be odd for him to stop by any time, day or night," Bishop said.

"We'll talk to him," I said.

"We'll take a business partner on the school," Levy said. "Slider Johnson. I just read something about him pulling out last week."

"That's my partner," Michels added, "always following the money."

"I heard about that," Bishop said. "Looks like they had a falling out."

"And you're just remembering this now?" I asked him, only half kidding.

"I heard it in passing is all."

"I saw it on the news a few days ago then heard it on sports talk radio on my way in," Michels said.

"I'd prefer to take him as well," Bishop said. His tone came out slightly higher than normal.

"You want him because he's a former MLB player, don't you?" I asked.

"Is that a problem?"

"Fine with me," Michels said.

"Ditto," Levy said.

"They could talk to Mason Reinhardt," Bubba said. "He's another investor that pulled out." He tapped on his laptop. "Said they had a disagreement about the plans for the school in general."

"Oh," Michels said. "I haven't heard about that."

"I know how to deep dive the internet," Bubba said, smiling.

"Sounds good," Levy said. "Got his info?"

Bubba cocked his head to the side. "Do you really need to ask that?"

"Let's get a move on this," I said.

Levy shook her head. "One day I'll get a tip for my leads," she said.

"Doubtful," Michels said. He looked at Bishop. "Meet back here in a few hours?"

"With the media on us, we're non-stop on this until our eyes shut on their own."

"I'll take that as a yes," Michels said.

"Oh, Bubba," I said before leaving. "Can you run a check on a Jerome White? He owns the company that services Hicks's pool."

He saluted me. "Will do, boss."

Colin Rutherford, Hicks's jack-of-all-trades business manager, attorney, and agent, operated in the King tower on Concourse Parkway in Sandy Springs. The King and Queen Towers dominated the Sandy Springs skyline, their distinctive crowns one of the first things visible from the suburbs around Hamby. Back before I'd moved to town, they were proof that Atlanta had begun to encroach into the suburbs, and how the area was desirable for those who escaped colder states. Since I moved to Hamby, though, Atlanta's expansion had skyrocketed, stretching out farther than ever expected, but the crowns on those towers were still key figures in the skyline. The cities were still catching up. Depending on the whims of the traffic gods, we could reach our destination in a breezy thirty minutes or find ourselves aging together over several hours. State Route 400 had undergone a midlife crisis a while back, beefing itself up with extra lanes, but it still wasn't enough. Instead of making the highway manageable, it just transformed into a wider parking lot. One minute, you're a NASCAR hero hitting eighty miles an hour, and the next, you're crawling at five, contemplating the existential meaning of brake lights. Most of the drivers had all the savvy of a carnival goldfish, making accidents the norm.

Bishop navigated us through some convoluted route, exiting the highway too early and heading down streets unfamiliar to me. Not that many in that area were familiar to me, but he must have known what he was doing because it took us less than thirty minutes.

"Not bad," I said.

"There's two accidents showing up on Wyze," he said, waving his phone like it held the secrets to world peace. "Better safe than sorry." He whipped into the parking garage, sliding into a spot reserved for law enforcement with the confidence of a man who believed rules were mere suggestions, and speed limits didn't apply to him.

I raised an eyebrow. Between the two of us, Bishop was the one who followed the rules. I considered some of them suggestions if I wasn't outright breaking the law. "What's up with you today? I think this is meant for Sandy Springs law enforcement."

"Then the sign should say that," he shot back without missing a beat.

"Good point," I conceded.

We hadn't given Rutherford a heads-up, but I had our bases covered. A quick call pretending to need his signature for a fake delivery confirmed he was in. Bubba's impeccable research had dug up that Rutherford ran RPM, Rutherford Professional Management, out of the tenth floor of the King building.

As we strolled in, the young receptionist flashed us a smile that was pure customer service gold. "Welcome to RPM. Are you looking for representation?"

I unhooked my badge from my belt and flashed it. "We're looking for Colin Rutherford."

Her smile collapsed into a panicked expression "Yes, of course." She stood up, her hands trembling just a bit. "Please give me a moment."

"Why so nervous?" I whispered to Bishop as she walked through a closed door.

"Guilty by association?"

I shrugged. "Could be."

She returned quickly. "Please follow me."

Rutherford's office was either proof of his success or a sign that he was exceptionally good at fleecing celebrities. I hadn't determined which. The place was a sprawling corner suite with double-sided windows that offered a panoramic view of Sandy Springs all the way to downtown Atlanta. Morning light flooded in, reflecting off the sleek, modern furniture and the array of framed accolades adorning the walls. Rutherford himself embodied the part—a man in his late fifties with silver hair combed to perfection, a tailored suit that shouted professionalism, and an air of controlled authority, even though the distress on his face was hard to miss. He stood as Bishop and I entered, extending a firm handshake toward first me, then Bishop, his eyes clouded with grief and suspicion.

"Thank you for coming," he said, his voice strained. "This has been a difficult time, and I was hoping to have discussions with the police."

"Why is that?" I asked, taking a seat in one of the plush leather chairs opposite his massive oak desk. Bishop settled in next to me, his notepad ready.

"I'm not just Ryan's manager. I'm also his friend."

"And agent, and attorney," I said. "One stop shop for it all, it seems."

"That's certainly a way to describe it, but Ryan trusted me. Trust was important to him." Rutherford sat back down, clasping his hands on the desk. "I assume you're here about our relationship. I still can't believe he's gone."

"We're sorry for your loss, Mr. Rutherford," Bishop said, his tone respectful but direct. "We understand this is a tough time, but we need to gather some information about Ryan's recent activities and any possible threats he might have faced." He'd gone for professional while I'd started with sarcasm.

Rutherford sighed deeply, rubbing his temples. "Ryan was complicated. The divorce proceedings hit him hard. He wasn't himself these past few months."

I leaned forward slightly. "Can you elaborate on that? What exactly do you mean by not himself?"

"Ryan was always a fighter, always the optimist," he explained, his gaze distant as he recalled the past. "But the divorce with Lara? It's drained him. It wasn't just the end of their marriage; it was the fighting back and forth about everything, the public spectacle, the media circus. Every detail of his private life was on display. It was brutal."

"Did he want the divorce?"

He shook his head. "He loved her. He was aware of her affairs, even blamed himself, saying his career got in the way of his marriage. He forgave her every time she cheated, but it got to him, and I guess he finally had enough. To be honest, I am not, nor was I ever a fan of Lara. She is manipulative and coldhearted. I always felt Ryan could do better."

"Were they having any problems other than the cheating?" I asked.

"Isn't that problem enough? Like I said, he blamed his career, which is the reason he retired two years ago. He wanted to focus on his marriage. His family. And that's what he did, but it didn't matter. It was too late."

"And you handled his end of the process?" I asked.

"Yes, ma'am."

"According to Lara, her husband gave her a pre-nup, but they didn't sign it."

"That's partially correct. Ryan signed it but Lara refused. In the end, against my suggestion, Ryan dropped it."

"Is she in the will?"

"Initially, yes. Thankfully, Ryan took my advice and removed her from it six months ago."

"How does that work with the divorce and his death in Georgia?" I asked.

"If the deceased left a will that explicitly excludes the surviving spouse, the terms of the will generally prevail. However, the surviving spouse may have the right to claim an elective share or year's support from the estate, which is designed to provide for the spouse's needs for a certain period."

"And if he left it to the kids?" Bishop asked. We knew the answers, but he needed to pass the test.

"Georgia law is complicated in this situation, but we created a trust and named a trustee to make sure she didn't get access to his entire estate."

"And the trustee is?" Bishop asked.

"Me."

Everyone could have guessed that.

"You said Ryan tried to focus on his family and his marriage, but it was too late," Bishop said. "What happened?"

"Jerome White happened," he said. "Have you talked to him?"

"We're working on getting his contact information," Bishop said.

He opened a drawer and removed a business card, then handed it to me. "Check him out. Lara tried to take everything Ryan had. It's my unofficial opinion she never loved him, and she and this Jerome guy want to run off with the money Ryan spent his life working for."

"Thanks for this," I said. "We'll contact him."

"Please do."

"Have you met him?" I asked.

His receptionist's voice blared from the phone on his desk. "Mr. Rutherford, you have a phone call. She says it's urgent."

"I'm in a meeting. Please take a message."

"Yes, sir."

He shrugged off what looked like slight annoyance. "I'm sorry. What was your question again?"

"Have you met Jerome White before?" I asked.

"Yes, yes. Multiple times. He escorted Lara here when she came to pressure me about the divorce. The guy is a worker. Pool maintenance, chauffeur, lover. A man of many talents."

"Like you," I said.

"I've gathered expertise in fields beneficial to my clients. It's what a good representative does."

"What kind of pressure did Lara attempt to inflict on you?" Bishop asked.

"She wanted the divorce wrapped up quickly."

"She came to you directly?" I asked. "Not through her attorney?"

He nodded. "Lara's always been reactive. She's trying to be something she's not, some form of popular celebrity status, I'm assuming, and when she feels like something's not working, she reacts."

"Did you offer any kind of resolution?" Bishop asked.

"She wanted everything. Their homes. Their vehicles. Most of the money. She gave me no option but to skip mediation and head to court."

"How did she respond to that?"

He pointed to the window behind him. "That's a new window."

I nodded. A bold move on her part. "Did you file charges?"

He shook his head. "Not worth it. Ryan paid for the new window." His expression darkened. "Describing the divorce as rough wouldn't cover it. Lara's lawyers have gone after him with everything they have. They've tried to paint him as an unfit father, a reckless spender, an unfaithful husband. It was a smear campaign, pure and simple."

I was aware that he had kids but wasn't sure how many he had. "How many kids does he have?"

"Two. He kept them out of the limelight because they're little and don't understand.

And did a good job of it.

"How old are his children?" I asked.

"His oldest, Harmony, is five, and Rylan, his son, three."

Harmony? They gave their daughter a stripper name? Poor kid would hate that eventually. "Does his wife have the kids?"

"I spoke to her after hearing the news. They're with the nanny at her own home in Roswell."

"How did Ryan handle the smear campaign?" Bishop asked, his pen poised over his notepad.

"He was devastated," Rutherford admitted, his voice thick with emotion. "He loves his kids more than anything. The idea that he might lose custody of them tore him apart. He fought back, but it took a toll on him. I hate to think it wasn't even close to over because I felt it would only get worse."

I felt a pang of sympathy, but not for Rutherford. Something told me he wasn't just telling us what he knew, but that he was hitting his client when he was already down.

"Did Ryan receive any threats or have any problems with fans or competitors recently?" Bishop asked, cutting to the chase.

He nodded slowly. "Yes, there were threats, but that wasn't unusual, and they weren't from competitors. He was well respected as an athlete. The threats were mostly from fans who were angry about his performance on the field, blaming him for losses, others who were mad he retired. But there were also a few from people who I'd say took pleasure in his personal troubles. I reported the more serious ones to the authorities, but nothing ever came of them. Ryan usually made sure of that."

I made a note of that. "Why?"

"That's just who he was. He didn't want anyone to struggle because of him."

"Were any of these threats serious enough to act on?" I asked.

"It's hard to say," Rutherford replied, a frown creasing his forehead. "Ryan tried to brush them off, but I could tell they bothered him. He was always looking over his shoulder these last few weeks."

"So, he'd received a threat recently?"

He retrieved a file from his desk, flipped it open, and swiveled it toward us. "This is a list of the people who've threatened Ryan over the years."

The spreadsheet was three pages long. "May I have a copy of that?"

"Of course. Most of them were anonymous, as you'll see."

His cell phone vibrated on the desk. He glanced at the screen then set the phone face down on his desk.

I scanned the list. "The recent ones are anonymous, but alarming." Threats of killing Ryan and Lara topped the last five threats and were all from the past few months. "You have no idea who made these?"

"Unfortunately, no. It's the way it works. Celebrities are threatened constantly."

"And these weren't reported?" Bishop asked.

"As I said, Ryan wasn't interested in involving the police."

Until he had with a note to me.

"Can you tell us more about his state of mind recently?" I asked, sensing there was more to uncover.

"He was erratic," Rutherford admitted. "One minute he'd be talking about the school, and how excited he was to help his community, and the next he'd be in a dark mood, convinced he had nothing left. He started internalizing even more, staying home alone, distancing himself from others. It was like he was on a self-destructive path. I assumed it was the divorce, but I'm not sure now."

Was he for real or did he want to put us off track?

Bishop glanced at me before speaking. "Do you know if he was seeing anyone new? Any new relationships that might have caused tension?"

Rutherford shook his head. "Not that I'm aware of. Ryan was private about his personal life because of the pending divorce. He'd spend time with family, me, and his horses, but that's about it. He didn't trust people anymore."

I decided to probe a bit deeper. "What about his professional life? Any business dealings that might have gone sour or problems with the school?"

"Problems with the school?" He shook his head. "Actually, some, yes. The normal things, construction delays, investors griping, the usual things. If there were more serious issues, he didn't tell me. He was very motivated and excited about it. As for other business dealings, we had some investments together," Rutherford said, leaning back in his chair. "But nothing out of the ordinary. Ryan was quite savvy with his money. He made sure his finances were in order, especially because of the divorce situation. He didn't want Lara to get more than she deserved."

His phone vibrated again, but he ignored it.

"Had any investors dropped out recently?"

"Just the one as far as I know. Ryan was supposed to come by today to update me on the school, so I can't say there weren't more. There had been some issues recently, and he'd promised to tell me about them." He exhaled. "I guess I'll have to look into that."

"Who's the investor that backed out?" I suspected it was Slider Johnson, but we needed to know for sure.

"Slider Johnson, but he wasn't in for much. Maybe 25K."

"And the reason?"

"Slider respected Ryan, but he also saw the school as an opportunity. My theory is he felt he'd generate more exposure for himself, and when that didn't happen, he wanted his money back."

"Was there contention between them?" Bishop asked.

He sighed. "That was rough. According to Ryan, Slider had approached him asking for his money back. He stated personal problems, but Ryan didn't tell me what they were, or if he even knew them. As I said, it was probably ego more than anything." He rubbed his chin.

"Did Ryan have any support system? Friends, family, anyone he could lean on?" I asked.

"His parents were supportive, but they moved to Florida last year," Rutherford said. "Celebrity makes it hard to have real relationships. Ryan never recognized when or if someone had inappropriate or ulterior motives, or if they truly cared for him."

"Including you," I said.

"I've proven my loyalty many times already. I wish I could have done more."

"Is there anyone else you feel might have had ulterior motives?" Bishop asked. "What about another business partner or former teammate?" Rinse. Wash. Repeat. Interviewing anyone required a consistent, repetitive set of questions to make sure they told everything.

"As I said before, no. Ryan was a good guy, but yeah, when you've got that kind of cash, and you're that well known, people hate you just because you're you. I could give you some names, as well as a few reasons outside of general envy, but I don't want it getting out that I provided it."

"Your secret's safe with us," Bishop said.

"I'll send it over," he said.

"Mr. Rutherford," I asked. "Can you tell us where you were last night between six p.m. and midnight?"

His mouth twitched. It was quick and subtle, but it happened. He fumbled with papers on his desk, his voice a steady drone that didn't match the slight tremor of his fingers. "I was on a flight back from a business conference in New York City," he said, laying out receipts, a crumpled conference badge, and several glossy photos of him with other attendees.

I leaned forward and squinted at the photos. "You flew back last night but got photos printed already?" My voice might have been casual, but my mind raced, trying to piece together the timeline that could place him miles away from the crime scene or right in the thick of it.

"I didn't print them. The conference photographer had a printer set in the corner," he explained, sliding a photo toward me as if the glossy paper could scrub clean any doubts of his innocence. "That's Stephen Shepherd. He's the most sought-after business manager in my field. I got to hear him talk."

"Can he or anyone else verify that?" I asked.

"I'm sure someone can," he said. "Here." He handed me a small file. "Here's the information about him and the conference."

Bishop chimed in from the corner, his tone flat. "And you landed back here at what time?"

"I got home around 8:30 p.m.," Rutherford replied, his eyes briefly flitting up to a framed award on his wall, a quick flash of nostalgia before he reeled it back, eyes snapping to ours.

I caught that quick glance, too quick. Was he trying to cling to any part of the room that wasn't us? Something that might anchor him away from the lies he was weaving?

"I came straight home. The conference is three days, and it can be brutal, but it's worth it," he continued, his hand absently smoothing down his tie.

"Mr. Rutherford," I said, "what size shoe do you wear?"

"An eleven. Why? Did you find footprints at his house?" he asked.

"We're just covering every base we can at the moment."

Bishop said, "We'd like copies of all pertinent files including emails, etc. of all communications with the victim. We can get a warrant, but I'd rather not go through that hassle."

"Why do you need those? Am I a suspect?"

"Everyone's a suspect right now," Bishop said.

"I'm not sure I can provide that. We have lawyer client privilege."

"But not all your work with Mr. Hicks was legal, correct?" Bishop asked.

He nodded. "It will take me some time."

"How long?"

"A few days or a week, I guess. It's a lot of things. I've been with him for a long time."

Bishop nodded. If necessary, we'd get a warrant. It was likely the easier way to go anyway.

My phone dinged with a text message. Seconds later, Bishop's did as well. I checked for the both of us. Nikki notified us to say the assistant coroner had completed Ryan's autopsy and officially labeled Ryan's death a murder, but she would call us with more details. She also said Lara Hicks prints weren't in the system. We didn't think they would be.

We thanked Rutherford for his time and reminded him to provide the list.

I didn't like the guy. His demeanor showed him as polished and in control. Too polished. On our way out, I exchanged a glance with Bishop. I knew he felt it too. Colin Rutherford was hiding something. But what?

Maybe I was wrong, but Rutherford's emotions didn't ring true to me. "He's smarmy," I said in the elevator after leaving his office.

"Smarmy?" Bishop asked. "My mom used to use that word."

"So did mine, but it's fitting."

He nodded. "Something doesn't sit right with me either."

"Right? He talked over himself back and forth about people respecting Hicks and people hating him."

"It could be both for any of them and at different times."

I agreed. "Still wishy-washy."

"Agreed. All the documentation on his desk was a little too convenient for me."

"He was expecting us, he all but said it when we got there."

"We'll have Bubba confirm everything, but he's on my list. Being at a conference is a great alibi for someone who's hired a killer."

"My assumption as well."

"Let's ask Bubba to pull reports of threats. See what he can dig up."

"I'll text him after we call Jerome White." I dialed the number on the business card. The call forwarded straight to voicemail, so I disconnected.

"Didn't want to leave a message?" Bishop asked.

"I'd rather catch him off guard if at all possible."

"We are good at that."

I called Bubba on speaker phone through Bishop's vehicle. After telling him Rutherford's information, he said, "I ran a check on Jerome White. No criminal record. No tickets. His business gets five stars on Yelp. Reviews make him sound like a miracle worker. One reviewer wrote that he's easy on the eyes."

"Who wrote it?" Bishop asked.

"Not Lara Hicks if that's why you're asking. I'll text you his home and business addresses."

"Can you text them to Levy and Michels, too? That way we've got our bases covered."

"Sure thing," he said. "Anything else."

"Not yet. Thanks for your help," I said.

"Just doing my job."

"Slider Johnson, though," Bishop said as we headed to the former MLB player's home. "I can't see him as the shooter. The guy's an a-hole, sure, but he was one of the best players in the league. No way he'd throw away his life like that."

I cleared my throat. "Said O.J.'s attorneys."

"That's different," he said.

"If the glove doesn't fit, you must acquit."

Bishop rolled his eyes as he turned left at the light and merged onto the highway. "I'm just saying, I don't see it."

"O.J. required his family to sign non-disclosure agreements to be with him on his death bed. I bet he cleared up the little glove issue then."

"Did he really do that?"

I shrugged. "I heard it somewhere, but I'm not sure it's true."

"Ah, so Abe Lincoln wrote about it on the internet."

"Probably," I said smiling. "We investigated a former White Sox player for robbing a bank once."

"Was that the Billy Jacobsen case?"

"Yep."

"Yeah, well, he was a scumbag, and he sucked at baseball."

"You sound a little too invested in this. Should you recuse yourself from this investigation, Detective?" I held back a laugh.

Bishop shot me a look. "Just calling it like I see it. Can't help it if I have a nose for these things."

"Uh-huh, and your nose is never wrong, right?"

He grunted. "Never."

I leaned back in the seat grinning. "Alright, Detective Nostradamus, let's see if your sixth sense pays off this time."

Bishop shook his head but couldn't help a small smile. "Just don't be too disappointed when I'm right again."

"Yeah, yeah. Let's just catch this guy." I sent Bubba a text to check for any complaints filed that involved Hicks.

Thirty minutes later, we rolled up in front of Slider Johnson's place. The house exuded wealth without being too obvious about it. Big, but not a mansion, with a meticulously maintained lawn and a driveway that curved around to the back. The hedges were precisely trimmed, and the flowers in the beds looked impeccably arranged, either by a professional or they were fake.

Bishop cut the engine and glanced over at me. "Ready?"

"Always," I said, pushing the door open and stepping out into the warm Atlanta afternoon.

The house's brick facade, a classic Southern style with white columns framing the entrance, looked stately but not ostentatious. I paid attention to the little details as we walked up the path to his door. The polished brass knocker, the freshly painted shutters, the immaculate welcome mat that probably never saw a speck of dirt.

It wasn't new, suggested old money and good taste, unexpected for someone with Johnson's rep. Had he bought something to represent an image? If so, in my opinion, it didn't fit with his baseball nickname or lifestyle. I'd Googled him on the way there. He liked to party, and it wasn't always just with women.

My guess was he'd picked a house where he could live comfortably and still fly under the radar.

Bishop reached out and rang the bell.

"Let me handle this," I said. "You can get your baseball card signed when I'm done."

He flipped me the bird.

"That's getting old. Might want to try something else."

He flipped me the bird with his other hand. "How's this?"

I laughed, but said, "Not feeling that either."

While waiting, I mentally cataloged his security cameras, which I suspected were active. Remaining quiet at that point, we listened to the muffled sounds resonating from the other side of the large, heavy door. When it finally swung open, Slider Johnson stood there looking like he'd stepped right off a page from GQ. Crisp white shirt, perfectly pressed slacks, and an expression that oozed entitlement.

"Detective Ryder, Hamby PD," I said, flashing my badge. "This is my partner, Rob Bishop. We'd like to ask you a few questions."

Slider's eyes darted to me, then to Bishop, then back to me. "Is this about Hicks?"

Bishop said, "Yes, sir."

"It won't take long," I said smoothly.

Slider stepped back, opening the door wider. "Come on in."

I glanced down at his feet. "Mr. Johnson, what size shoe do you wear?"

He looked at me. "Shoe size? Twelve. Why?"

"I like your shoes. I wondered if they made them for women too," I lied. He wasn't the right size for the print, but that didn't mean he hadn't worn the shoes, and the same went for Rutherford. Criminals used that move all the time to stump the cops.

The inside of the house was just as immaculate as the outside. Hardwood floors gleamed like they'd been buffed by an army of obsessive-compulsive elves. Sunlight streamed through huge windows, making the place look like an HGTV fever dream. The furniture, an artful blend of modern sleekness and classic comfort, had been arranged with a precision that proved an interior decorator did the work. Whoever set up the place would take one look at mine and immediately call for a Hazmat team.

We followed Slider through a hallway lined with framed photos—action shots of him on the field, candid moments with teammates, and a few of him with celebrities. The guy had lived a life, no doubt about it, but good enough to stop him from committing murder?

He led us into a spacious living room where he gestured to a couple of leather armchairs. "Have a seat. My decorator just bought the chairs. He's some HGTV guy from Atlanta. They're not my style, but he said they'd be a big hit because they're so comfortable."

Bishop and I sat as Slider took a seat across from us, leaning back in his chair with the easy confidence of someone who was used to being in control, oblivious, or interviewed.

The chair instantly made my sciatic nerve throb. His decorator exaggerated the look of the place along with the comfort of the chairs.

"We're told you are one of the investors in Ryan Hicks's new project," Bishop said.

"Yeah, definitely want to help the kids, you know. So, this is clearly about Ryan. Man," he said with a head shake. "It's unbelievable he's gone. How can I help?" he asked, his tone friendly enough, but there was an edge to it.

"How much did you invest?" Bishop asked.

"One and a half million," he said.

I glanced at Bishop. Rutherford had said $25,000. Why the discrepancy?

I leaned forward slightly. "We understand you and Mr. Hicks had some issues. We'd like you to tell us about them."

Slider's smile didn't falter, but there was a flicker of something in his eyes. "Issues? What kind of issues?"

"How about you tell us," I said, keeping my tone neutral.

Slider laughed, a short, sharp sound. "I liked Hicks. He was a little too high on himself, sure, but with that kind of record, who wouldn't be? Did we come to blows a few times? Yeah, but that's the game. Egos get bigger, stress gets worse. It's bound to blow up occasionally."

"Enough to kill him?" I asked.

He blanched. "Come on, you don't take me for a killer, do you?"

I must have had Cubs fan written across my forehead because he directed the question to Bishop.

"Mr. Johnson," I said, "Much like you to a baseball, a detective's ability to read and react is our most important skill, but we're reading people, not balls. And right now, my read on you says you're lying." I smiled. "Now, we can do this the easy way, or we can do it the hard way. You choose."

I glanced at my partner and noted his scowl. He'd read me the riot act later if for no other reason than he wanted free tickets to the next game. If he did, I'd remind him that accepting gifts from possible suspects was like accepting bribes. That would yank his chain even more.

"Okay," Slider said, holding up his hands in surrender. "You got me, but I didn't murder the guy. We had words, that's all."

"What happened?" Bishop asked.

"It's about the school. I think he's been stealing cash, and so I called him out on it. Let's just say it didn't go over well."

How many baseballs had that guy taken to the head? Did he realize he'd just thrown himself under the bus? I looked at him, and then at Bishop, and said, "Sounds like a good reason to kill someone, right, partner?" I adjusted my handcuffs on my belt to drop a little fear in the air. "Perhaps you ought to come to the station for a little chat?"

His eyes widened. "I didn't mean it like that. I swear." His eyes darkened. "Am I under arrest?"

Bishop was quick to respond. "No, but Slider, you got to admit that was the wrong thing to say."

"I know," he said, "I've never been good at interviews, not any kind, but I wasn't alone. You can ask my attorney. He was there."

"And what happened?"

"I wanted to see the books. The school was supposed to be done months ago."

"They haven't even broken ground," Bishop said. He must have felt my eyes on him. "I drove by there the other day. What?" He asked me. "It's hard not to notice with that big sign hanging in front of the land."

"And he showed you the books?" I asked.

"No. He said everything was online, and something happened that wouldn't allow him to access the information. He called Rutherford down, but he couldn't access it either."

Why hadn't Rutherford mentioned that?

"My attorney suggested we deal with the accountant directly. We've got an appointment with him later today." He looked toward the ceiling. "Probably will end up canceled because of all this."

All this? Was Hicks's murder an inconvenience to the guy?

"Who's your attorney?" Bishop asked.

"Steven Hall. We can call him right now. That way you'll know it's legit."

Bishop checked his phone, then connected to the attorney's office and pressed the speaker button. "This is Detective Rob Bishop with the Hamby P.D. May I speak to Mr. Hall? It's regarding an important situation with a client."

"One moment, please," the receptionist said.

A moment later a deep voice came on the line. "This is Steve Hall. What client are you calling about?"

"Mr. Hall, can you tell me which client you were with yesterday around ten a.m.?"

"That's confidential information."

"It's okay," Slider said.

"What is this regarding?"

"We're investigating the murder of Ryan Hicks."

"Slider, keep your mouth shut."

I glanced at the guy, but I wouldn't be the one to say, 'whoops, too late.'

"We know I didn't do it," Slider said. "And I want to help in any way I can."

The lawyer exhaled. Sounding annoyed, he said, "Mr. Johnson and I went to meet Mr. Hicks at his office located in the King building."

The King tower?

"And the reason?" Bishop asked.

"Slider?"

"Go ahead."

"Mr. Johnson has some concerns about mismanagement of funding for a project he invested in. We were supposed to discuss it with Mr. Hicks, and my client would determine whether to pull out of the project entirely."

"Didn't you already pull your cash?" I asked Slider.

"I told him I was going to, and that's why we set up the meeting."

"Is my client a suspect?"

"We're gathering information," Bishop said.

"Slider, I suggest you end this meeting."

"It's all good," Slider said.

Bishop finished the call quickly. "Thank you," he said to Slider. "And the accountant?"

His stare turned vacant. "David Cohen, I think."

"And what did you do afterward?" I asked.

"Steve and I had lunch after the argument. We talked about what I could do to get my money back, if anything. He told me I could file a lawsuit, and they'd hire a forensic tax guy to take a look at the books or something, you know, to see if there's anything shady going on."

"And that took until this morning?" I asked.

"No," he said with a nervous laugh. "After lunch I stopped at the batting cages to hit some balls." He smiled at Bishop. "Gotta keep in shape, you know, in case I decide to un-retire."

"You mean come out of retirement?" I asked knowing that's what he'd meant but annoyed by his poor grammar skills.

"Yeah, yeah, that's what I mean. Anyway, after that I had a date."

"And that lasted until?"

"About midnight or so. Give or take." He chuckled and looked at Bishop. "I wasn't really checking the clock, if you get what I mean."

I exhaled. "May we have the name and contact information for the date, please?"

"I don't have the date information."

I tipped my head back and groaned. "For the love of baseball, you brought a hooker back to your house?" I looked at Bishop. "How stupid is this guy?"

He waved his hands in front of his face. "Wait, wait, wait, wait, wait, wait.

She wasn't a hooker. She's an escort. I can get you the number of the woman that runs it, but I don't have my date's."

"Did you sleep with her?" I asked.

"Well, yeah, of course I slept with her."

"And you paid for her to see you?"

"Yeah, that's what escort services require."

Maybe it wasn't a ball to the head? Maybe it was a bat? I kind of felt sorry for him. "Then you just admitted to pandering. We could arrest you for that." I thought I'd enjoy it, but I didn't.

"Ryder," Bishop said. "A moment, please?"

"Oh, yeah," Slider said, "I'll go in the kitchen." He twisted his hands together. "Anyone want a beer?"

"We're on duty," I said flatly.

"Oh, right. My bad." He headed toward his kitchen.

"You asked the guy a question, and he's being honest. We're not here to bust him on a pandering charge. We're here to find a killer."

"The guy's one strike away from jail."

"I'm sure a Cubs player or two has slept with a prostitute as well."

"Doubtful, but a Sox player? Definitely."

4

I needed a shower just from walking into Elite Companions, the escort service Slider Johnson had used the night before. A young blond woman sitting at a desk smiled at us. Bishop turned his head to the side instead of looking at her implants. The girl could be his kid, and I know he pictured his daughter Emma sitting at that desk.

"Well, hello," she said. She'd gone for sultry or sexy, but it came out more tween-trying-too-hard. "Are you looking for a date for the both of you or just for one? It will help us put you with the right escort."

"Neither," I said, flashing my badge. "We're here to talk to Alessandra Mateo."

She blinked, and the smile disappeared. "I'm sorry, but no one by that name works here."

Her eyes shifted down and to the right as she lied. "Have a nice day."

I channeled my inner Savannah and her Southern charm. "Sweetheart, I just hate that I've made you nervous." I smiled at Bishop. "The women in the jail cells at Fulton County will just love passing around this Barbie doll tonight, won't they?" I looked back at her and noticed her face had paled. "That's a lot more than a threesome for you, honey." I pointed to the phone. "Now, go on and give her a call, will you, please?"

That was fun.

"One moment," she said. She jumped from her desk and rushed to the locked glass door on our right.

We followed behind. As she unlocked the door, Bishop put his hand on the handle to open it.

"You can't come back here," she said. "It's only for customers."

"We'll tell Mateo we forced our way through," I said.

Alessandra Mateo's office could have been the model for a masterclass in understated luxury. Wealth and sophistication exuded from the walls. Hardwood floors covered the room in a horizontal pattern and were probably sourced from some endangered forest in a remote part of the world where the locals still venerated trees. Dark, rich, and gleaming, I suspected they'd been polished with the tears of environmentalists.

The walls showcased abstract art that probably cost more than my car, but nothing too flashy. Just the right amount of color and shape to make you think, hmm, nice, without pondering their deeper meanings or wondering why a red square was juxtaposed against a blue circle. A low-key statement that said, "I have taste, but I'm not trying too hard."

Mateo sat at a massive desk made from some exotic wood that matched the floors and dominated one end of the room. She kept it clean—just a sleek laptop, a leather-bound notebook, and a pen that looked expensive enough to have a tracking device.

"Kristin," Mateo said. "I don't believe I have any appointments today."

Kristin's shoulders slumped lower than when we entered the door. "They're—"

Bishop flashed his badge. "Detective Rob Bishop." He gestured toward me. "This is my partner, Detective Ryder."

She motioned for Kristin to leave and close the door behind her.

If I didn't know the woman was a madame, I'd think she was the president of some Fortune 100 company. Black hair, pulled back into a ponytail, then twisted into a bun on the back of her head—I couldn't judge the bun.

It was my go-to work hairstyle. Savannah would have high-fived her makeup application skills. Sexy, but conservative, unlike mine, which, when I wore the stuff, left me looking like Barbie gone hooker.

"Please have a seat," she said. "Would you like something to drink?"

"No, but thank you," Bishop said. He smiled so big it was embarrassing. Was he smitten with the sex-seller?

"Ms. Mateo," I said, "It'll be easier for everyone if I just shoot straight with you. Your client Slider Johnson claims he was having sex with an escort he purchased from your company at the time of Ryan Hicks's murder. Can you verify that?"

She kept her face completely emotionless. "We are an escort service, Detective. My escorts do not have sexual relations with our clients."

I rolled my eyes. "We're not here to arrest you for prostituting women, but if you don't give us what we want, we'll make sure the Atlanta PD, zone two to be exact, has a chat with you and our suspect about your services." I leaned back in the chair and said, "You've got five seconds to decide."

She made eye contact with Bishop. He stone-face stared her down until she finally said, "He was with my escort, however it is against company policy for the escorts and clients to engage in such a manner. Unfortunately, I can't chaperone the dates, therefore, I can only rely on the word of my escorts." She opened a file drawer on the left side of her desk and removed a file, then opened it, and handed me a piece of paper. "This is the escort Mr. Johnson books on a weekly basis."

I glanced at the paper then up at her. "He books her on a weekly basis, and you don't think they're having sex?"

"That document is an agreement between Clarissa and my company. She knows if she has sexual relations with a client she will be terminated."

"How much does Johnson pay?" I asked.

Her lips straightened into a thin line. "Our clients pay by event and escort tier. There are four tiers. Clarissa is a level three tier, so her nightly rate is $15,000."

I almost choked on my tongue. "And he books her once a week?"

"He's a very wealthy man."

"He's also," I looked at Bishop, "forty, tops?"

"Forty-two," Bishop said. He understood Atlanta baseball as well as he did football.

I looked Mateo in the eye. "And you didn't think they might be having sex?"

"I trust my escorts, Detective. I'm going to call Clarissa in to terminate her, so, if you'd like to wait, you may do so in the lobby."

I checked the paper again and committed her name to memory.

"We're investigating a murder, ma'am," Bishop said. "It would be much appreciated if you would provide us with her address and phone number instead, and it would also be helpful if you didn't let her go until after we talk to her."

She checked the calendar on her desk. "Her next client is tomorrow evening. I'll need to terminate her by four pm."

"We'll talk to her before then," he said. He stood. "Thank you for your time, ma'am." He gave her a head nod as I stood.

When his back was to me, I pointed my first two fingers to my eyes and then to hers. She blanched, so I knew she got the drift.

Bishop called Clarissa Masters on the way back to the department.

"Ryan Hicks is dead? When did that happen?" she asked.

"Sometime last night."

"That's awful, but I'm not sure how it concerns me."

Sure, she was. Even a fifth grader could make that connection.

"We understand you were with Slider Johnson last night. Can you tell us when you left his place?"

"How do you know I was—have you talked to Slider? He's not supposed to say any—oh wait. Did you talk to my boss?" If I were there, I would have seen the lightbulb go on over her head. "She gave you my phone number, didn't she?"

"Yes, ma'am," Bishop said.

"Oh, my God. That's it. She's going to fire me." Panic rose in her voice. "I need to call her. She doesn't understand."

"Ma'am," Bishop said. "We need to know what time you left Mr. John-son's home last night."

She cleared her throat, but it didn't eliminate the stress in her voice. "Eleven-thirty. I was there until eleven-thirty."

"Is that when the date was scheduled to end?"

She eased up a bit and half-laughed. "No. That was when he fell asleep. Let's just say the entire night was quick."

I bit my bottom lip to stop myself from laughing.

"You left him sleeping in his home, then?" Bishop asked.

"Yes. He'd been aggravated when I arrived."

"With you? Bishop asked.

"No, of course not. It's my job to make him emotionally happy and stress-free, not upset him."

Emotional support wasn't the only kind of happiness she offered.

"Did he say what was wrong?"

"Slider is a talker, and he trusts me. We've been connected for some time now. He had the impression that someone was deceiving him, as he had described. I tried to relax him, and eventually I did, but it took a while."

I couldn't believe I didn't bust a gut from laughing.

"Did he give you any names?"

"Not that I can recall, but he did say it was a former teammate." She gasped. "Do you think it was Ryan Hicks? Do you think he murdered him?"

"We're just gathering information, ma'am," Bishop said.

She was silent for a moment, then said, "He said he'd take care of it personally if he had to, but I can't say what that meant."

"Can you elaborate on that?" Bishop asked.

"I'm sorry, but I really need to call my boss."

"We may call you again," Bishop said.

"That's fine," she said. She added, "If Slider Johnson is a murderer and you arrest him, please let him know I faked it every damn time." She ended the call.

"I'm not telling him that," Bishop said.

"I'd be happy to. It's within the possible timeframe," I said. "His time with her. If he rushed."

"It'd take him at least thirty minutes with a clear interstate to get to Hicks's place. Still doesn't give enough time for Hicks to get home from your place, do whatever he needed to do, then end up in bed."

He had a point. "Slider doesn't strike me as the kind of guy that wakes up after a night of fun anyway," I said.

He laughed. "I'm not going there."

"But we need to remember, Hicks was in sweats. He might not have been going to sleep."

"Someone could have made him go there."

"It's possible."

The unmistakable aroma of Chick-Fil-A permeated the office building like a secret mission gone public. It hit me square in the gut. "I'm starving," I admitted, tracing the scent back to its source with the dedication of a bloodhound.

"That smells amazing," Bishop echoed, his voice an expression of my own craving.

We followed our noses to the investigation room, where the source of the olfactory temptation lay unveiled: bags of Chick-Fil-A spread across the table just begging for our tastebuds to savor them. "Whoever brought this is officially my hero," I announced, snagging a bag and fishing out a sandwich. I plopped down in a chair, eager to devour my find.

"You got a message," Bubba interjected, his tone casual. "From Colin Rutherford. Said he would be delayed in getting that list for you. He said he had something for you though, so I gave him your email."

"Thanks," I muttered, already halfway through my sandwich. I borrowed one of the laptops strewn about, logged into my email, and found Colin's message. "He sent the full list of investors." I downloaded the file he sent, the printer whirring to life as it began spitting out the list of names and information. "Slider Johnson, Lynette Burns, Heraldo Herrera, Mason Reinhardt, and Bryson Hayworth." I glanced at Bishop. "Why didn't we get this when we were at his office? Is our new friend withholding information?"

"That or he did some research and wants to help."

"Maybe, but I don't want to give him the benefit of the doubt. I don't trust him."

Michels and Levy arrived. Michels saw the bags and snatched one instantly. "I'm freaking starving."

"I did some digging and came up with a list as well," Bubba said. He slid a piece of paper across the table. "You're welcome," Bubba said.

"Oh," I said. "Thank you. You're my hero."

He smirked. "That's what all the girls tell me."

Levy yanked a sandwich from the paper bag and flopped down across from me. Her eyes sharp, like she was ready to interrogate the sandwich.

"Find out anything?" I asked, my mouth stuffed with a chunk of chicken sandwich that was putting up a decent fight.

"Yeah. Mason Reinhardt is a tool," Levy grunted, unwrapping her sandwich with more force than necessary. "Clammed up faster than you can finish talking with your mouth full, but Michels finally got him talking."

"Touché," I said. "In reference to your slam on my manners and Michels's hard work."

"He shut up because you hit him with the subtlety of a baseball bat," Michels chimed in from the corner as he unwrapped his own sandwich.

Levy shot Michels a look that could curdle milk. "He didn't even blink when I mentioned Ryan Hicks's murder. The main investor in the charter school he just gave over three million bucks to. Doesn't that strike you as odd?"

"Three million bucks is a lot of cash. Pulling that out could kill a project," Bishop said. "What was his reason?"

"Delays," Levy said. "The project started two years ago, and construction should have been completed. Reinhardt wanted answers, but all Hicks could give was supply chain issues and problems with the builder."

"Did he ask to see the financials?"

Michels nodded. "Hicks sent a general statement to everyone, but he claimed he couldn't provide access to the financials due to some technical issue with the accounting firm."

"Slider Johnson said he couldn't see them because of an access issue," Bishop said.

"He's not our guy," Michels countered, not looking up from his paperwork. "We cleared him already."

"How?" Bishop interjected. He bit into a waffle fry. The crunch echoed slightly in the quiet room. He pushed the box of fries toward the center of the table and Michels immediately nabbed them.

"His new wife vouched for him. Said he was on a flight back from Vegas," Michels explained. "With her."

"Yeah, but that doesn't mean he was really on that flight," I pointed out, chasing a stray piece of lettuce with my finger. "Spouses cover for their partners all the time."

"He was," Bubba said, looking up from his laptop with a nod. "They called me, and I checked the airline records myself."

Bishop shrugged, swallowing another fry. "Still could've paid someone. Think about it—someone walks in, shoots the guy in his sleep, walks out. Classic hitman style."

"Sounds like every Liam Neeson movie made," Michels said.

"If the glove fits," Bishop said with a smile.

"Any suspects could have paid someone to kill Hicks," I said. "But until we have evidence leading us in that direction, let's just sit on it."

Levy held up her Styrofoam cup. "I'll drink to that." She added, "Reinhardt said he was one of the original backers, and that the other four initially in the project backed out a few weeks ago."

"How 'bout you start at the beginning of your little chat with the manager?" Michels asked.

"Yes, sir," I said jokingly.

"Our sit-down with Mr. High-flier was interesting to say the least," Bishop said. "He was all set up with receipts, badges, and even photos from a business conference in New York City—which he claims to have flown back from just in time to *not* murder our victim," I interjected, a bit too sharply. I passed around copies of Rutherford's receipts and the photo of him with Stephen Shepherd I'd had his assistant make for us. "Notice the boarding pass. Tight timeline, but it's doable with a plan and decent traffic back from the airport."

"That's never a sure thing," Levy said.

Michels piped up. "Could be he's just really organized?" His smile betrayed his attempt at seriousness.

I snorted. "The guy's desk was a stage, for sure. Everything placed just right to sing the perfect alibi. Too perfect."

Bishop took a bite of his sandwich, speaking between chews. "He mentioned the conference was important—big names, big talks. He saw some guy named Stephen Shepherd, ever hear of him? Supposed to be some business guru."

"He's the most popular sports athlete manager in the country," Michels said. "Think *Jerry Maguire* but bigger."

"Got it. So, apparently hearing this guy speak was a good reason to not kill someone," I added dryly. The team chuckled, but the laughter didn't last.

"He jumped to show the photos," Bishop said. "Like he was waiting to pull them out of a magician's hat."

"Hold on," Levy said, "he got the photos printed already?"

"Claims the photographer printed them at the conference."

"Because that's what you do at a business conference—get instant prints like it's a tourist trap," Michels said.

"I've been to a few where they take pics, and the photographer prints them there and sells them. Like when you go to an escape room, how they give you a pic before you leave, " Levy said.

I surveyed our team. "We need to verify his story. Check the conference schedule, speak to this Shepherd guy if he's real, and see if anyone can place Rutherford there at the times he claims."

We filled him in on the rest of the details of our meeting with Rutherford, as well as what he'd left out.

"He did say Hicks had received threats." Bishop reminded me, still focused on his half-eaten sandwich.

"Right, the threats," I sighed. "According to Rutherford, Hicks received threats from fans or God only knows who. Said he reported them, most were anonymous, and those that weren't, Hicks didn't want to pursue." I set the list on the table.

Bubba grabbed it and made copies on the printer, then handed them to the team. He checked the list he'd put together. "Yeah, a few of these are on the list from incident calls at Hicks's home, but not many."

"Rutherford also spun a tale about Ryan's state of mind," I continued. "Said he was erratic, paranoid, almost self-destructive. If true, could be someone took advantage of his vulnerability. Or it's possible Rutherford's painting a picture, trying to steer us toward a suicide angle or an obsessed fan."

"A guy can't shoot himself in the back of the head," Levy said.

"Right, but the public isn't aware of where he was shot, just that he was," I replied.

"So, we've got a potentially vulnerable, emotionally unstable victim and a suspect with a convenient alibi who just happens to have every receipt ever issued in the history of commerce," Bishop summarized, not without irony.

The team mulled over it, our mental gears turning as we considered angles and motives.

"I'll check Rutherford's flight information now." Bubba pushed his empty Chick-fil-A box aside, crumbs scattering across the scarred tabletop of the interrogation room. "Which reminds me," he interrupted, swiping a greasy thumb over his tablet. "Like I said before, there are a few matches on that list. Found a few records, all pointing to the same guy—some Daniel Watkins. Mostly trespassing, but he got tagged with a peeping tom charge once. Got dropped, though. They all did."

I leaned forward, my chair creaking under the shift. "Let me guess. Hicks didn't want to press charges?"

"Nailed it," Bubba replied, eyes still glued to the screen.

Bishop had stood, and leaning against the wall, asked, "Got an address?"

Bubba cracked a smile, raising an eyebrow. "You didn't really ask me that, did you?"

Bishop pursed his lips as the annoyance flickered across his face as if someone had scolded him.

"Hold on," Bubba said. "I'm putting in a request for Rutherford's flight information."

"Thank you," Bishop said.

After tapping away on the keyboard, he said, "I've got more. Did a little digging while you all were scarfing down chicken sandwiches. Hicks was in a fancy rehab in California—place swarms with movie stars. My guess is an opioid addiction."

"When was this?" I asked.

"He went in twice, about a year and a half ago, and then six months ago."

Bishop rubbed his jaw, thinking. "Probably from that shoulder injury a few years back. Took him out of the game for most of the season."

Michels chimed in from his corner. "That's right. We didn't make it out the door that season, either. Without him, the team was trash."

"Not surprisingly," I added, "neither his ex-wife nor his business manager mentioned it."

Levy, sitting opposite, shrugged. "Probably something they think should stay private. In Pennsylvania, we had a former NFL player who'd been injured, got hooked on opioids, then overdosed. His family tried to keep it under wraps to protect his legacy, but the press blew it wide open."

"I'm sure that's what it is. You think he told his investors? Slider Johnson never mentioned it."

"It would be ethical to disclose," Bishop said. "They sunk millions into that charter school. Addiction adds a layer of risk to their decision."

"Which is probably why he didn't tell them," Levy pointed out. "Ethical or not."

"How was Slider?" Michels asked Bishop.

"Kind of a doofus, but less than I'd expected," I said.

"He's not that bad," Bishop said.

"He pays for sex," I reminded him.

Levy nearly spit out the food in her mouth. "What?"

"He admitted to being with an escort that night, and when I asked him if he slept with her he admitted it like it wasn't a big deal."

Levy rolled her eyes. "You should have arrested him for that."

I narrowed my eyes at Bishop. "He didn't want to touch it."

"Let's be real," Michels said. "If you're a celebrity, it's probably easier to pay for sex than deal with the emotions of some chick chasing after you or another celebrity. I mean, she probably tests for STDs a lot more."

"You're disgusting," Levy said.

"Just telling it like it is."

"Anyway," Bishop said, "he hadn't received his investment back and believes Hicks was messing with the cash. They met but Hicks claimed he couldn't access the accounts."

"He was up to something," Levy said. "Could be one of his investors found out, and couldn't get their cash back, and killed him."

"That's my guess," Michels said. "Like buying drugs?" He glanced at Bishop. "I hate to think it's that, but it's a possibility."

"Correct," Bishop said.

"Let's try the wife again. Their divorce proceedings weren't going well. She might want to throw Hicks as far under the bus as possible, and drugs would be a good place to start."

"The media would eat that up," Michels said.

"Unfortunately, they will," I said.

Levy leaned in, her voice low. "Why don't Rachel and I go? It'll go better with two women. Make it more relatable for her. If she's got an attorney, we'll get him or her there as well."

"You assume I can relate to women," I quipped, only half-joking.

"We'll take the rabid fan," Michels said. "Daniel Watkins."

"No," I said. "He sounds fun. I've got dibs." I smirked at Bishop. "You okay with holding off on him for now?"

"We'll hit the silent investors then."

"Wait a minute," Bubba said. "Nikki told me to call her before you left. She might have something." He dialed her extension and let her know we were leaving, and she arrived just minutes later.

"Hey, everyone," Nikki began. She placed her papers on the projector tray and flicked the machine to life. The first slide popped up, an image of the gun and a bullet casing, magnified to show details most eyes never see.

"I've completed the initial analysis of the weapon," she said, pointing to a series of highlighted areas on the image. "First up, the weapon used was a Ruger LCP Max, obviously a nine-millimeter."

"That can be a hard pull for a woman," I said. "Especially if she hasn't shot much."

"Or is just weak," Levy added.

"We can't be sure who it was just yet," Nikki said. "No fingerprints other than one belonging to our victim, which, in my professional opinion, looks purposeful. Otherwise, it's clean, which suggests our shooter wore gloves."

Bishop's brows knit together in concentration. "Any traces from the gloves themselves?"

Nikki nodded, flipping to the next slide—a microscopic image showing tiny fibers and particles. "Yes, we found latex particles and fibers on the grip and trigger. They're microscopic, consistent with what you'd expect from a latex glove, especially if it's low quality or deteriorating."

Michels chimed in. "Can we trace the glove type or brand from those particles?"

"Tricky," Nikki admitted, her gaze flicking to her notes. "These particles are generic; they don't carry unique markers that would pinpoint a specific brand. However, the presence itself supports the theory of a premeditated act, using gloves to avoid leaving prints."

Levy, who had been scribbling notes furiously, looked up. "What about smudges or impressions? Anything that could show us the pattern of the glove?"

"On that," Nikki clicked to another image, one showing faint smudges on the gun's metal. "There are smudges consistent with the texture of latex. These aren't clear enough to give us a print, but they show the surface of the gloves wasn't smooth. This could suggest a textured grip pattern on the gloves."

Her next slide showed a detailed analysis report. "I did a chemical residue analysis. There are trace chemicals left behind from the latex. This isn't a home run, but it's a solid glove theory and helps establish the context of the incident—deliberate, prepared for a jury."

She had a point. I found myself leaning closer, intrigued by how much I could learn from what wasn't there. "What about biological material?"

"That's where it gets a bit more interesting," Nikki replied, her voice hinting to excitement. "I did find trace amounts of biological material— skin cells on the exterior of the trigger. It's not much, but it's possibly from when the shooter put on or removed the gloves. I've sent samples for DNA analysis, but it'll be a while before we get anything back."

"That's great," I said. "So, we're looking at someone who tried to cover their tracks but might not have been as careful as they thought."

"Exactly," Nikki affirmed. "Or it could belong to Hicks. I've got more work to do, but we've got something to go on."

Bishop said, "Nikki, great work. Let's make sure we're cross-referencing all known associates of Ryan Hicks with our DNA databases. It's a long shot, but maybe our shooter got sloppy."

Nikki looked to Bubba as she collected her papers, her part mostly done. "Bubba and I have my interns on that as we speak. Are you ready for the bad news?"

"Give it to us," Levy said.

"We haven't received any follow up on the shoe print, and the sole is a standard ADIDAS print. We can continue to pursue, but I'm not sure it's worth it."

I scanned the room. "Everyone okay with holding off on the print for now?"

We all agreed.

"I'll keep you all posted on any new developments from the lab," Nikki said.

We changed our plan, divvying the interviews up differently. Bishop and Michels were off playing footsie with Daniel Watkins while Levy and I took the short straw—making that house call to Lara Hicks holed up in her condo. Downtown Alpharetta was packed with millennials chasing the next craft beer and a caffeine kick strong enough to propel them into the next week. I insisted on a pit stop at one of those high-octane coffee shops; I needed a buffer before I played the repentant fool for Bishop. Apologies weren't my thing, especially when the blame rested on someone else.

Levy flicked a glance at her watch, her expression all business. "We've got fifteen minutes to burn before you have to face the music with her."

"I got this," I said. "You can relax."

"I hope so. She's doing this as a favor to Jimmy, so dial up the charm." She eyed me as I knocked back an iced coffee. The place was cute but not my style. It gave off a vintage vibe but had tripped over into hipster territory instead.

"Roger that, boss," I shot back, all grins.

We dumped our cups and strolled to her building, weaving through a crowd all about the latest iPhone model and upcoming urban condos. Lara lived on the sixth floor of a mixed-use building, smack in the heart of it all and not far from the Alpharetta and Hamby city line, and close to Ryan Hicks's shiny new charter school location.

"Handy," I remarked.

"Think he was keeping her close on purpose?" Levy speculated, arching an eyebrow.

"Doubtful," I said. "I don't think Lara Hicks likes anyone making decisions for her."

Just then, a woman nearly bulldozed me, nose glued to her phone. The thought crossed my mind to just stand my ground, to make a point, but why bother? She'd just dive right back into her digital world once I was out of the way.

"You sure you're good with all this?" Levy pressed, bringing me back.

I shrugged. "I don't think Bishop was wrong to hit her hard, but yeah, I see the need to confess his sins."

"That sounds encouraging."

"We haven't ruled her out, and we shouldn't any time soon."

"Even if White confirms they were together?"

"Maybe," I said. "Maybe not."

"Do you have it in for this woman or something?"

"Of course not. I just don't trust her. Look at the stats—women are stepping up in the crime charts, have been for the last forty years. Spousal homicides? Nearly a third are committed by women. It's not a leap to suspect her."

"Got it." She halted and squared up to me with that no-nonsense look. "I can handle this solo if you're going to clown."

"Nah, I'll eat a slice of Bishop's humble pie. She'll love me when I'm done."

"Let's hope," Levy sighed, pushing open the lobby door.

Lara Hicks answered wearing yoga pants and a workout bra. She was at least a double D, probably from a good doctor, not genetics. Just the thought of carrying that weight without enough support made my back ache. Was she trying to show off? Possibly, but it didn't impress me. Bishop and Michels would have tripped over themselves, slipped on their drool and hit their heads hard enough to require stitches, but Levy and me? We had it covered.

"Oh, she's here, too?" Hicks said. She held the door open and sighed.

Looking right at me, she said, "I'm only doing this because I want you to find my husband's murderer."

"That makes two of us," I said.

We stepped into the main area of the condo, and it struck me—the place was a shrine to minimalism, every piece of furniture and decor meticulously chosen to exude understated luxury. The walls, a pristine canvas of soft whites, featured just a couple of abstract paintings, splashes of color that disrupted the monochrome without disturbing the peace.

A sleek, charcoal gray sofa, its lines sharp and crisp, faced a glass coffee table that seemed to float above the polished concrete floor. Two minimalistic chairs flanked the sofa, their frames of brushed steel and their cushions a whisper of dove gray. There was no clutter, no stacks of magazines or remotes, just a single vase of stark white lilies that emitted a faint, crisp scent.

It resembled a model home, like no one lived there. Uninviting, yet something a wealthy woman would adore, and definitely not a place for kids.

"Have a seat," she said. "I just moved in last week. I'd been staying at a hotel since the separation, but it was time to put down some roots."

"Understood," Levy said. "We understand your children are with a nanny?"

She nodded. "Yes, at her house. My place is temporary, and I don't think they feel at home here just yet." She sniffled. "They're too young to understand any of this."

"Mrs. Hicks, thank you for agreeing to speak with us again," Levy said, keeping her tone professional yet empathetic. She pulled out her notebook. "We just have a few more questions."

"Did you contact an attorney?" I asked.

"No," Hicks said, sitting down on the couch across from us. "I realize I wanted one before, but I've decided to talk without one at this time. I'd like it on the record that I didn't kill my husband, and I will provide the contact information for the person I was with last night. Is that what you're here for?" She talked to me, not Levy.

"That is appreciated," I said, "and I would like to apologize for my partner coming down a little hard on you earlier."

She waved it off, though not entirely casually. "I understand now, for the most part. It's always the spouse, right? I see why the police could think it was me, but I can promise you it wasn't. Now, what else can I help you with?"

"We've learned there were multiple investors in your husband's school project who either pulled out a few weeks ago or were trying to pull out at the time of his death. Were you aware of this?"

Lara hesitated, then shook her head slightly. "I haven't been involved in the school project. Our relationship was already over when he decided to take on that project."

Her annoyed tone surprised me. "You don't seem thrilled with the project. Why?"

"Oh, it's not that I'm not happy he made the decision. It's just that we had already decided to divorce, and then out of nowhere he announces this big money suck school. The money was still technically ours. He should have come to me first."

With a husband's combined income from the MLB and his endorsement deals, I doubted she earned the millions of dollars in their bank accounts.

"Did he ever express any concerns about the project? Any issues with the investors or financial troubles, perhaps?" Levy asked, watching her closely.

"Not that he told me," Lara replied. "He was always positive about the school. Said it was going to be his legacy, though, if I'm being honest, we didn't talk much. Most communication has been through our attorneys."

"I thought you two were still best friends?"

She blinked. "Initially, yes, but as of late things were becoming a bit strained due to some disagreements regarding the divorce. I wasn't being dishonest with you then, I just wanted to protect Ryan's legacy. We came together for the sake of the kids and shared the same statements with the media to make everything easier on us."

Levy scribbled down her answer, then looked up, her gaze sharp. "Are you aware of any financial issues Ryan had?"

She laughed. "Ryan? Financial issues? He made sixty-five million last year. I can't fathom what kind of financial issues he would have."

"You'd be surprised," I said.

"Maybe, but money wasn't something we discussed while together, so I wouldn't expect him to talk to me about it during our divorce proceedings. I'd be happy to give you my attorney's name and request he share the details of our divorce."

"We'd appreciate that," I said.

"Just a moment." She walked into the kitchen and removed a pen and pad of paper from a drawer, scribbled on it, and handed it to me.

"About a year and a half ago," Levy said, "Ryan first checked into a high-end rehab facility. Were there any specific incidents that prompted this?"

Lara flinched. It was subtle, but unmistakable. She smoothed a strand of hair behind her ear, a nervous gesture. "Can this remain confidential?"

"Of course," Levy said.

"He chose to go because he had a problem with opioids. He became hooked on them after his shoulder injury."

"Did rehab work?" I asked.

"Yes," she said. "For a while, but he relapsed and admitted himself again about six months ago."

"Did you know he'd been using again?" Levy pressed, her tone still gentle but insistent.

Lara paused, her eyes darting between us before settling on the coffee table. "I suspected he might have been, but I wasn't sure. Again, that wasn't something we talked about. It was a very touchy subject for me. I don't say this publicly, or to anyone really, but for me, our marriage ended because of his addiction. I wouldn't expect him to share about it with me."

"Was anyone else aware of it?" I asked, trying to keep the conversation as open and non-judgmental as possible.

"I'm not sure who knew. Colin, his business manager obviously, but I only know that because I'd called him for help when Ryan came home high one night. I thought he was dying. I'd never seen someone high like that before." She exhaled, and added in a voice barely above a whisper, "Again, with respect for my deceased husband and our children, I'd prefer this be kept private. He was insanely proud of his sports career. He didn't want anything tarnishing that, and I'd like to keep it that way."

Levy nodded, making a note. "Understood. We just need to understand all the factors surrounding his death."

I chose my words carefully. "When did you find him like that? Before or after his first time in rehab?"

"Before," she said.

"Did he have regular meetings with anyone that might have seemed out of the ordinary?" Levy asked.

"I wish I could help you," she said, "but it's been a year with very little communication. You'll have to talk with my divorce attorney, and I suggest you talk to Colin. He's been more of a partner to Ryan than I ever could be."

Interesting statement. "One more thing," I said. "You understand we have to rule out everyone though, correct?"

She nodded. "Of course, which is why I'm telling you everything now."

"Thank you, Lara. That's very helpful," I said, giving her a reassuring smile. "You said you'd be willing to give us the name of the person you were with. May we have it?"

"Jerome White."

"The guy in the photo?" I asked for verification.

Her chest fell. "Yes, but it didn't start until after Ryan and I separated. Honest."

"He owns the pool service company, correct?" Levy asked.

"Yes." She gave Levy his contact information. "Aquatic Life."

"Thank you," Levy said.

"Just one more thing. Did you notice anything unusual in the days leading up to his death? Did you see him briefly or talk to him and notice changes in his mood or behavior?"

She sighed, her eyes clouding in thought. "I'd come by the house to get some of my things last week. He was different. More withdrawn. More secretive. I thought it was just because I was there, but now, I'm not sure." A tear slid down her cheek. "I guess I should have asked. Would he still be alive now if I had?" Her voice trailed off, and she looked away, clearly struggling with the weight of her grief and the reality of her loss.

"We'll look into everything you've mentioned," I reassured her, standing up to signal the end of our questioning. "And we'll handle it with as much discretion as possible. Your cooperation means a lot."

Levy and I thanked her again and made our way out of the condo.

"Think she's holding back?" Levy asked as we buckled in.

"Maybe. But she gave us enough to go on for now," I replied, starting the engine. "I don't understand why Rutherford wasn't upfront about the addiction issue. He had to assume we'd talk to the wife, and she'd tell us."

"Maybe he wanted to protect Hicks's reputation?"

"What's more important, finding his killer or being real about Hicks's problems?"

"I guess it depends on who you ask," she said.

5

I called Bishop on the way back to the office. "Anything?" I asked.

"Daniel Watkins wasn't home. Neighbors don't know where he works, but they confirmed he's still driving a 2012 Toyota. We tried Heraldo Herrera, but he wasn't home. His assistant had a lot to say. We'll fill you in later."

"You going back to the department?"

"No. Thought we'd give Bryson Hayworth a shot. That okay?"

"Sure. Want us to take the Burns woman?"

"That would be great. We'll give Herrera another shot if we've got time."

"Sounds good."

He texted Levy the information, and we headed to an office across from the Avalon, a large mixed-use community in Alpharetta, to interview Lynette Burns.

Traffic had choked up Old Milton Parkway worse than a hungover blues singer on a Monday morning. The stream of cars crawled along, bumper to bumper, with mine wedged between a shiny BMW and a beat-up Ford that had seen better days. The Avalon's glittering shops threw their neon invitations far into the street, luring in shoppers with the promise of high fashion at high prices and fancy coffees no matter the weather or time. That meant turn lanes overflowed into regular traffic lanes, which annoyed the heck out of me.

The Georgia sun showed no mercy, its glare giving me a headache. I rubbed my temples at a stoplight just a block from the entrance to Burns's medical building.

"You okay?" Levy asked.

"Just a headache from the glare."

"Want me to take lead?"

"Go for it," I said. "But expect interruption."

"Always do with you."

The medical office was tucked away on the fifth floor of one of those glass-and-steel towers that dominated the area. I parked in a guest spot near the entrance.

"That was luck," Levy said. "Any time I go to the doctor I have to park a mile away."

"Right? I'm not sure it's a good sign or an omen."

Inside, the place boasted all sharp angles and gleaming surfaces, and the sterile smell of disinfectant hit the moment the doors slid open.

"Elevator's to the right," Levy said.

The sign had directed us to the second floor for Burns Plastic Surgery Specialists.

Alpharetta had become the hot spot for plastic surgeons, and from the looks of the place, Burns topped the list.

"May I help you?" the receptionist asked.

Levy showed her badge. "We need to speak with Dr. Burns, please."

"Do you have an appointment?"

She showed her badge again. "We're not here for a surgery consult. We're here regarding an investigation."

The girl's eyes widened. "Oh. She can't see anyone without an appointment."

I didn't think I was better than anyone, but a murder investigation trumped a facelift any day. "Would you mind telling the doctor that Detectives Levy and Ryder are here to discuss Ryan Hicks, please?"

She stood. "Yes, Detective, but I can't promise she'll see you. She's very busy."

"As are we," Levy said.

No more than two minutes later, we sat in the doctor's office in front of her desk.

Lynette Burns must have exchanged her services for her own transformation. Her makeover resembled nothing like the photo on her wall and had to have totaled in the millions, even with a hefty discount for the fillers and surgical work, not to mention the hospital and doctor fees. Levy flipped open her notebook as we settled in.

"Dr. Burns, thank you for meeting with us. We're examining Ryan Hicks's activities leading up to his death. We understand you were an investor in his charter school project?"

"Yes, that's correct," Dr. Burns replied, her voice calm and measured. "I am one of the investors."

"We were informed that you pulled out your investment prior to Mr. Hicks's death. Could you elaborate on that?" Levy asked, pen poised.

Dr. Burns adjusted her glasses, her expression firm. "I didn't completely pull out. I reduced my investment by half. I'd committed to half up front and half when construction began. When the project hadn't progressed as planned, and Ryan's updates were unsatisfactory, I retracted my second investment."

"May I ask how much you invested?"

"It is my understanding each main investor, and I believe there are four, maybe five of us, were required to put in three million. I gave $1.5 million to start. I can't say for sure that requirement was enforced with everyone, though I'd expect it was."

Not with Slider Johnson. I didn't think he had that kind of money. He'd probably spent most of it on Clarissa.

"In what way were Mr. Hicks's reports unsatisfactory?" I chimed in, curious about her perspective.

"Are you aware of the delays in the project?" she asked.

"Yes," we said in unison.

"That was a problem for me. He was very vague about the project's status. Whenever I pressed for details, he'd brush off my concerns, simply insisting things were just 'a bit behind.' No substantial reasons given. It was all very dismissive, and that's not how I work."

Levy nodded, jotting down notes. "How would you describe his state of mind during these interactions?"

"Initially, things were professional, as one would expect. He was a smart businessman, and I respected him. Lately, however, he'd become volatile," she said without hesitation. "Something in him changed. He seemed increasingly paranoid and unstable as time passed. His temperament during our meetings was especially concerning."

"How so?" Levy asked.

"It felt like he was not just in over his head but drowning."

"Did he allude to anything happening in his life?" Levy asked. "His divorce, maybe?"

"We were all aware of the divorce. Given his celebrity, it would have been hard not to, but other than that, we didn't talk about personal situations."

"Were you aware of his addiction issues?" Levy asked.

"Ryan never discussed it with me, but that could explain his sudden disappearances."

"Disappearances?" Levy asked.

"About six months into the project and also six months ago. He was gone for a month each time. Colin, his manager, claimed he was away on business."

"Did he tell any of the others?"

"Not that I'm aware of, but I don't communicate with them outside of group emails from Ryan."

So much for doing the ethical thing and informing his investors about his problem.

"When did you decide to reduce your funding?" I asked, watching her closely.

"Last week. Monday."

"And how did Ryan react?"

"He was angry. He accused me of not trusting him, of sabotaging the project. He was quite off balance during that last conversation. It raised red flags for me, certainly."

Levy glanced at me before continuing. "Did you have any direct contact with him after that?"

"No," Dr. Burns replied. "I made it clear that unless the project saw real progress and I received better communication, my remaining investment was at risk too."

"Did you expect him to return it?"

"Of course. If not, I'd sue him for it."

I saw Levy processing her words, weighing them against what we'd already learned. "Dr. Burns, where were you on the night Ryan Hicks was murdered?"

Her posture stiffened slightly, though her voice remained steady. "I was at home. My husband and his business associate were with me until one a.m. I remember distinctly because I was quite upset—it was later than I'd wanted to be up, given I had surgery scheduled early the next morning."

"Can anyone else verify this?" Levy asked, her tone still friendly but precise.

"Yes, both my husband and his associate." She jotted their contact information on a notepad and handed the paper to Levy.

She stuffed it into her notebook and gave Burns a polite nod. "Thank you for your cooperation, Dr. Burns. We appreciate your insights into Mr. Hicks's state of mind and the challenges with the school project."

As we stood to leave, Dr. Burns handed us her card. "If you need anything else, please don't hesitate to contact me. Ryan and I had our differences, but he was a good man, and that project will benefit the community. I hope you find whoever did this to him."

Outside, Levy asked, "What do you think?"

"She's sharp. If what she says about Hicks is true, it could explain a lot about his last few weeks. We need to verify her alibi and determine if anyone else shared similar sentiments about his behavior.

"Yeah," she agreed as we walked back to the car.

She called the men from the paper from the car.

Bishop and I met in the pit. We said hello to a few of the officers, smiling as they each offered to help with the Hicks investigation.

"Appreciate it," Bishop said. "Rest assured, we will reach out if we require anything."

"You're so nice to them," I kidded as we walked away. "If they only knew what a true crank you are."

"I'm not a crank." He shrugged. "All the time."

I laughed.

He handed me a file. "Investor Heraldo Herrera. Arrested for assault in 2018, but the charges were dropped."

I glanced at the mug shot inside. "Interesting."

We walked to the investigation room to meet with the rest of the team. "When did he pull out of the deal?"

He held the door open for me. "Same time as Hayworth, last week. According to Herrera's assistant, Herrera was the largest investor to date."

"Why is this guy familiar? Did he play with Hicks?"

"For two years. Was traded to Minneapolis five years ago but got dropped after the first."

"I think I remember that." I sat across from Levy and Michels, acknowledging them with a nod then handing Levy the file. "And he was the largest investor? How much?"

"First his assistant said two million, but it looks like it was closer to three."

"At once?" I asked. I glanced at Levy who looked confused. "Herrera."

She nodded. "Got it."

"You mean did he invest the entire amount at once?" Bishop asked.

"Yes," I said.

"Why?"

"Burns said she had to drop a million and a half to opt in but promised an additional $1.5 when the project started. When the project wasn't progressing, she had a chat with Hicks and nixed the rest of her investment."

"Ouch," Michels said. "A million and a half? That had to hurt. Just curious," Michels asked. "What caused Herrera's arrest?"

"Drunk guy in a bar gave him crap for his lack of skills," Bishop said.

Michels replied, "Day-um. That's bold."

Bishop said, "Looks like he can swing his fist better than a bat. Broke the guy's cheekbone."

"Maxillary," Levy said. "Basically, the bone around the sinus cavity."

Michels cringed. "That hurts like hell."

"According to Garcia," I glanced at Levy. "It does."

She blushed.

"What about Hayworth?" I asked. "What's his reason for pulling his investment?"

"Same reason as the others," Michels said. "Said Hicks wasn't moving fast enough. Didn't like having his money sitting in someone else's bank account."

"How much was he in for?" I asked.

"Million and a half, but he didn't get it back yet. Worried now he won't."

"Did Herrera get his back?" Levy asked.

"Nope. His assistant said Hicks told them they were having problems with the bank and accessing their money."

Levy and I shared a glance.

"That's similar to what Burns said," I added.

"Any alibis?" Levy asked.

Michels tapped his pencil on the table. "Herrera's assistant confirmed a dinner he'd attended and paid for that night. Time stamp on the receipt says he paid at midnight."

"What restaurant is open until midnight?" Levy asked.

"One that a former MLB player brings twelve people to at nine."

"Spent over seven thousand bucks," Bishop said. "I'd stay open for that too."

"What about Hayworth?" I asked.

"Hayworth got out of the hospital at four p.m. the day of the murder. Gall Bladder surgery. His wife and daughter were with him all night." He chuckled. "According to the fifteen-year-old daughter, he whined until past midnight."

"That's funny," Levy said. "Dr. Burns was at home entertaining a business associate of her husband under duress. I called the guy and her husband on the way home. She checks out."

My cell phone dinged with a message from Steve Copeland, a builder in town who'd been intimately connected to a murder a while back. He'd been a suspect at first, but ultimately, an ally. I left it for later without looking at it.

Jimmy hurried in and left the door open. He chugged a Diet Coke, then sat at the head of the table. "We've got a new," he looked straight at me, "temporary public relations liaison." He pivoted toward the door. "Susan, bring her in."

A woman entered with a commanding presence that filled the doorway. Sturdy and solid, I figured she could handle herself in a tussle if it ever came to that. Her brown, smartly styled hair was nothing flashy, coordinating perfectly with her conservative blue dress. The best part? She gazed at us with an expression that demanded to be taken seriously the moment we locked eyes. A reporter would run and hide if on the receiving end of that look.

"Good afternoon," she said with a deep, authoritative voice. "I'm Liz Sanders. I'm looking forward to keeping the media off your backs so you can find Mr. Hicks's killer."

So far, I liked her.

We each introduced ourselves.

"Okay, now that that's taken care of, let's get an update," Jimmy said. He directed Liz to a chair beside Levy.

Bishop and Michels spoke first, detailing their interviews with Bryson Hayworth and Heraldo Herrera's assistant.

Jimmy eyed me when they finished. "I got a call from Lara Hicks. She said she appreciated your apology, and she's willing to do whatever's necessary to help. She's flying her kids to her parents' place in Kansas City."

"That's right," Levy said. "She's got kids. You would have no clue from her condo."

Sanders aggressively wrote down everything.

"Right?" I asked. "Not at all kid friendly."

"The point is," Jimmy said, "she'll be around tomorrow after five." He stood to leave "We're short on time for this one, folks. The governor called. He wants it handled and tucked away in a closed case box by the end of the week."

"What?" Levy asked. "We're just getting started."

"It's an election year. He doesn't want this sitting in his lap like a cold rag." He shook his head. "Let's just get moving."

"The governor's watching us." Levy shook her head. "Great. No pressure."

"Call it motivation," I said. "Unless you don't like the guy."

She laughed. "Yeah, if I didn't, I might take my sweet time, but I really don't have an opinion either way."

"Right there with you," Michels said.

A printer near Bubba hummed to life. He leaned over, grabbed the documents, and passed them around the room. "I put together a list of suspects based on our conversation and what we have already. I thought it would be easier to review it this way." He smiled at Sanders. "Jump in if you have any questions."

"I will," she said.

I scanned the pages. "Did you just do this?"

"Just finished it, yes," Bubba started. "It's my version of mind mapping." He smiled. "Just neat and orderly."

"Interesting way to say it," Bishop said.

"Bubba," Jimmy said, "this is great. Take lead then on the review. Ms. Sanders and I need the information."

Bubba blushed. "Me? Oh, yeah. Sure. First, we have Lara Hicks," he announced. He pushed his glasses up his nose. "Estranged wife of Ryan Hicks. She claims she was otherwise engaged," he wiggled his eyebrows, "at the time of Ryan's murder, though she hasn't provided specific details."

"Yes," I said. "She has. She was with Jerome White. He owns the company that services their pool."

"That's not all he services," Michels said.

"Ha, ha," Levy replied. "Like that wasn't everyone's immediate thought, Mr. Creative."

"Initially cooperative," Bubba continued, "she then requested a lawyer when pressed, but later was more vocal. She provided details about Mr. Hicks's drug addiction. Motive-wise, we're looking at personal grievances from a contentious divorce and possible financial gain from Mr. Hicks's estate."

"I don't know," Michels said. "Sounds like a victim of circumstance to me."

"Is that a joke?" Levy asked.

"More like sarcasm," he said.

There was a short pause as Bubba ensured we were all following before he continued.

"According to her recent interview, she and Hicks didn't talk much, and she knew nothing about any financial crisis within the project."

The receptionist beeped into the room from the loudspeaker. "The coroner is on line one."

I hit speaker. "Detective Ryder."

"Detective, this is Mandy Simpson. I have a preliminary report for Mr. Hicks."

"I'm with the team. Go ahead."

"Mr. Hicks had fentanyl in his system, however, it is not what killed him. The cause of death is determined to be a gunshot to the back of the head, resulting in immediate death. The presence of fentanyl in the system is noted as a contributing factor that would have led to death through respiratory depression had the gunshot not been fatal."

"Thank you," I said.

"You're welcome." She ended the call.

"Drugs," Michels said. "Can't believe it. I mean, I can, but wow. Fentanyl kills immediately, so I'm not sure I understand how it wasn't the main cause of death.

"Not our call," I said. "We're not doctors."

Bubba continued. "Next is Slider Johnson, Ryan's former teammate and business associate. Slider's alibi is that he was with an escort from Elite Companions until 10:30 p.m. the night of the murder. His attitude has been somewhat evasive, but he cooperates under pressure. According to Bishop and Ryder, it's possible he could have left his home after the escort, drove to Hicks's home, shot him, then returned home. I spoke with the patrol officers who walked door to door on Hicks's street. No security videos show any vehicles on the street until the first cruiser arrived."

"When did you find that out?" Bishop asked.

"About an hour ago. The chief said he'd put guys out interviewing and asked me to follow up."

"Good job," Jimmy said.

"It's possible he could have parked elsewhere," I said. "Maybe we need to make that trip at the same time?"

"It wouldn't hold up in court," Jimmy said. "Too many variables to consider, ones that could add time to either drive."

"It looks like the motive here appears to be financial disputes over the school project, where Slider felt Ryan might have been mishandling funds." Bubba looked at me and Bishop. "He's meeting with the accountant. Are you going to talk to him as well?"

"It's on the list," Bishop said.

"Okay. I'll make sure to add that to the group notes."

"We'll have to talk with him again," I said. "So far, he's the closest thing we've got to a solid suspect."

"But it ain't much," Michels said.

Bubba moved on to the next suspect. "Then we've got Colin Rutherford, Ryan's business manager, lawyer, and agent. Colin claims he was returning from a business conference in New York City during the murder. I was able to confirm his flight information, as well as his attendance at the conference. He seems cooperative but also could be evasive about the specifics. His motives might include financial entanglements and grievances over managing Ryan's assets, intensified by Ryan's personal issues and their impact on their business ventures."

Switching to the next page, he continued. "Clarissa Masters, an escort from Elite Companions, associated with Slider Johnson during the murder."

"She's not a suspect," I said.

"I know, but she's someone connected to one."

He had a point. "Got it."

"As we discussed a minute ago, she confirms being with Slider until 10:30 p.m. that night. Initially, she was reluctant to share details but eventually confirmed her whereabouts.

"Bryson Hayworth and Lynette Burns are next, both linked through business dealings involving the school. Both invested heavily. Each are professional, willing to talk, but financial gain or resolving conflicts could be potential motives."

"Except their alibis check out," Bishop said.

"I was just going there," Bubba added.

"Don't mind him," I said. I winked. "Bishop wishes he had your mind."

Levy raised her hand. "Ditto."

"Me, too," Michels said as he raised his hand as well.

"Aw, thanks everyone," Bubba said, blushing again. "Heraldo Herrera wasn't available to talk, but his assistant was. She mentioned him being unhappy with how slowly Ryan was moving with the investments, uncomfortable with his money sitting in Ryan's accounts. Also possible financial motive, but he was at a dinner with twelve others in Atlanta until midnight."

"We also have Daniel Watkins, an obsessed fan with previous arrests for watching Hicks. Ryan dropped the charges, but the obsession might be a significant motive."

"Alibi?" Jimmy asked.

"We haven't made contact," Bishop said. "We'll try again."

He set the papers down, eyes scanning the room. "That's the rundown so far. Any thoughts on other angles we need to push or additional suspects we might be overlooking?"

Levy chewed on her pen, thinking, while Michels nodded slowly, absorbing the information. Bishop, as usual, looked skeptical, already formulating his next moves.

"We have to connect with the people we haven't yet," Bishop said. "Watkins, White, and the accountant."

"I'd like to go back to Rutherford and ask why he didn't mention Hicks's drug problem," I said.

"Good plan," Bishop said. He eyed Michels. "How about you two take Daniel Watkins again? We'll hit up Rutherford again and have a talk with the accountant."

"That works," Levy said.

"Meet back here after?" Michels asked.

"Always," I said.

"I'm staying here," Bubba said. "Nikki and I are going to go over some of the crime scene stuff. What else can I do?"

"Run background checks on the investors," I said. "The whole deal. Dig deep on all of them. If they picked their nose in public, I want to know about it."

"Got it." Bubba cringed. "That's nasty."

6

"Drugs," Bishop said in his vehicle.

"Let's hold off on judgment until we find out more," I said.

"I'm not judging him. I'm just shocked."

"It's possible he was drugged so he couldn't stop his murder."

He nodded. "He had an injury. He wanted to play again. What if the pain wasn't going away?"

"Could be," I said. "We'll figure it out."

"We will." He pulled up to the Dunkin' drive-thru window.

"Bubba's not long for our world. Some bigger department or agency is going to grab him like the DEA did with Ashley."

"You sound bitter about that still," Bishop said, handing me my large black coffee.

I sipped it right away, desperate for the caffeine boost.

"Obviously, I'm not anymore. Nikki's amazing, which means we'll lose her, too."

He laughed. "Ever thought about giving positivity a shot?" He turned left at the light to head back to the interstate.

"I'm positive."

He laughed. "You don't really think that do you?"

"Give me some credit. I was a wreck when I first came to town." I smiled. "Look at me now."

"Why do you think I asked in the first place?"

"You're not going to let me win this argument, are you?" I asked.

"Nope, though God does work miracles. One day, you'll see a path to happiness."

"I'm a living miracle already," I said.

His eyes shifted to me and back to the road. "I thought you didn't believe in God."

"It's not that I didn't believe. I just couldn't understand how God could take Tommy from me like that."

"He has his reasons."

"So, I'm told."

"Do you understand them now?" he asked.

"I'm not sure I'll ever understand, but I don't blame God, either. Look at my life. I've got a great job in a fantastic department, incredible friends who are like family to me, and Kyle. I'd be an idiot to think I did that all myself." I cleared my throat. "See? Positive."

"Give it a few hours. The old Rachel will return."

He was probably right, so I changed the subject. "Everything okay with Cathy?"

He turned onto Freemanville Road. "Why do you ask?"

"That's not an answer." I sipped my coffee.

"It's fine. I've just had to make a few decisions about our future."

"Good decisions?"

He smiled. "I guess we'll have to wait and see, won't we?"

"You're a pain in my butt," I said.

"As are you."

I had an idea of the decisions he'd made, but I didn't want to pressure him into talking if he wasn't ready. "Can we stop by Ben Cooper's place first?"

"Of course."

～

Bennett Cooper towered over most folks, his frame carved from a lifetime of wrangling livestock and mending fences. He didn't quite dwarf Bishop, who'd let himself go a bit of late, but Cooper could probably bench press him without breaking a sweat.

Years of sun had etched deep lines around his sharp blue eyes, giving him a look that didn't miss much. His eyes crinkled as we walked over.

I cleared my throat.

"He even makes me sweat," Bishop said.

"I'm not sweating," I lied. "He's just a nice guy."

"Right," he said, laughing.

Cooper always rocked the same cowboy hat, boots, and Texas-sized silver belt buckle. Normally, he'd pair them with a leather vest and some button-down, but that day, he'd slipped into a plain white tee that hugged him tight. Any woman with decent eyesight might've needed a moment to steady herself at the sight of him. Still, I didn't want Bishop acknowledging that.

"Howdy, Ryder," he said. He tipped his hat to Bishop and me. "I was expecting you. Come on in and have a seat."

We followed him to his office and sat in front of his desk.

"Find out what happened to Ryan yet?" he asked.

"We're working on it," I said. "We met with Lara Hicks and a few others."

"His manager, Colin something-or-another? That guy's a piece of work, that's for sure."

"Why do you say that?" Bishop asked.

"You mean aside from the fact that he stole money from Ryan?"

That caught our attention. "How do you know this?" I asked.

"Ryan told me himself. Said he was going to fire him."

"When was this?" Bishop asked.

"Few days before he was killed." He aimed his eyes at me. "You were here that day. Came in just as we finished talking about it."

"I remember," I said. "He did seem a little jumpy that day. I didn't think much about it then, but that makes sense now."

"Did he say how much Rutherford had stolen?" Bishop asked.

He shook his head. "He didn't know yet. He said he'd been having some problems with the bank and accessing his accounts. Claimed to have proof though."

"That's motive," Bishop said.

"I'm not a cop, but it sounds like one to me," Cooper said.

"Right," I said. I looked to Cooper again. "Other than that, did you notice Ryan acting different?"

"You talking about the pain killer addiction?" His expression softened. "He'd worked hard to clean up his act, and he had. I don't think he touched the stuff since he returned from rehab."

"He's been to rehab twice," I said. "Did you know?"

"I did. The first one was a few months, but this last one, just a month. He'd called me to let me know he'd be gone and asked me to give the horses a little extra attention. Called again the day he got back and came by to see them." He leaned forward. "I should have mentioned all this earlier, but I didn't want his name dragged through the mud." He raised his hands. "Not that I think you're going to do that."

"I understand," I said. "I guess I didn't think you two were that close, but maybe I'm wrong?"

He smiled. "We were friends. He liked that I kept my mouth shut and told me that. Also said he appreciated that I treated him like a person instead of a celebrity." He smiled at me. "Said he liked that about you. too, but he thought you were crazy for thinking the Cubs could make it to the World Series again in the next hundred years."

I laughed. "He told me that, too, the Cubs part."

"Had he ever mentioned any trouble or threats or problems with anyone?"

"He's mentioned a few fans getting in his space. Didn't seem like he cared too much. He was always happy to talk with them."

"Does Daniel Watkins ring a bell?" I asked.

He pursed his lips then said, "I don't think so."

"What about the construction of the school?" I asked. "It was supposed to start months ago, but it hasn't yet. Did he discuss that with you?"

"He said it was all good. Just some trouble with permits and the like. Oh," he added. "He switched construction companies just a few days before his death."

"Did he say who he went with?"

"Copeland Construction."

I turned toward Bishop. "Steve Copeland texted me earlier." I smiled at Cooper. "Did he say why he switched?"

"Like you said, construction was supposed to have already started. He was frustrated it hadn't." He cocked his head slightly to the side. "You know about the wife?"

"Depends on what you mean," Bishop said.

"Ryan said she's been sleeping with the pool boy. Has been for a while now, I guess. He told me that's why he filed for divorce."

"He filed?" I asked.

"That's what he told me."

I'd have to have Bubba check. We'd heard a few different stories on that.

"Has Lara Hicks been by here much?" I asked.

"She called about an hour ago. Said she wants me to look for a buyer for the horses. I told her I'd need a copy of his will before I traveled down that road."

"So, she'll have to pay for them for now?" Bishop asked.

"I told her I'd handle things through Rutherford, but I'm obviously not planning on doing that. I'll take care of them until I hear about the will. It's the least I can do for Ryan." He glanced at his hands and said, "I've been to Ryan's place, both before and after his wife moved out. That woman strikes me as someone who only cares about herself, with her kids a distant second."

We were on the same page. "Thanks for the information," I said. "We may be back."

"Sure thing. You stopping to see your horses?"

"Kyle's coming by in a bit. If I see them, I'll want to stay."

"Can't say I don't know that feeling." He stood. "Keep me in the loop on this, will you? Like I said, Ryan was a friend."

"Will do."

"Oh," he said. "One more thing. I've got a spare key to Ryan's place. Would you like it?"

"That would be great."

I checked the message from Copeland as we hurried to the car.

Call me about Ryan Hicks.

"He wants to talk about Hicks."

"Call him. See if we can drop by."

With Bishop behind the wheel and me riding shotgun, I punched the speaker button to get Steve Copeland on the line. His voice was a battle cry against the heavy metal band of a construction site playing in the background. Back-up alarms, the clanking of metal, and the distant shouting of foremen lost in the rumble of engines all drowned out his voice.

"Steve? You're breaking up," I yelled into the phone. I clicked off speaker and pressed my phone to my ear, but it didn't help.

His voice came through again, laced with annoyance. "I can't—hold on —" A scream of power saws tearing through something metal cut him off. "Rachel, just text me, okay?" he shouted back, his voice popping and fizzling.

I hammered out a message: *Where are you?*

His reply zipped back fast: *New city center, Cumming. Big construction on a five-story mixed-use. You'll see it.*

Bishop turned right on the next street, steering us toward Cumming. The emerging structure of the new building soon dominated the skyline with cranes pirouetting with massive steel beams and workers scattered across the high-climbing scaffolding. The ground shook with the heartbeat of a pile driver and echoed through my ribs.

We parked in a cloud of dust, the windshield graying faster than the wipers could clear it. Bishop killed the engine, and we stepped into the concrete perfume of progress. Body odor filled the air, getting worse as we walked toward his crew.

"That's nasty," Bishop said. "How can we smell that through all the construction materials?"

I coughed and pointed to a group of sweaty, dirty men only a few feet away. "I don't remember smelling BO at his other site." My heart sank at the memory of the lives lost from the explosion that day.

"I think you had other things on your mind," he said. Then, brightening the mood, he added, "Looks like Copeland's messing with the big toys today." He nodded toward a crane lifting a massive wall panel toward the gaping fourth floor.

"Yeah," I agreed, watching a forklift zigzag through the organized mayhem, "Let's just hope he's got as much information as this place has steel beams." We crunched across the gravel toward the foreman's trailer, ready to wade into whatever mess awaited us. I stepped cautiously, keeping a watch on our surroundings.

"It's not going to happen again," Bishop said. He referred to the previous bombing.

"You can't guarantee it."

"No, I can't, but the odds are slim."

"I'll give you that, but that won't stop me from being hyper-alert."

"Whatever works for you."

Steve Copeland greeted Bishop with a hearty handshake and me with a smile and a nod.

"Thanks for coming by. Seems we're always getting together when something bad happens, huh?"

"Makes me wonder if you're the common denominator in all this," I said, smiling. A while back I would have meant that, but not anymore. Copeland was a decent enough guy. He'd come through when we needed him, so I trusted him to the degree I trusted most people, enough to verify only about half of what he says, but not all.

He laughed. "Thanks for that. We need some laughter given the situation."

"We understand Hicks hired you on to build his charter school a few days before he died," Bishop said. "Can you tell us about that?"

He walked us into the trailer where we could hear probably one percent better than outside.

"Yes. That's why I contacted you. I wanted to make sure you were aware of our agreement. I've known Ryan since he played for Hamby High. Our business sponsored the team for several years. Ryan was a good kid and a good man." He grabbed a bottled water from the small fridge in the corner. "Would you like one?"

"No, thanks," I said.

"I'm good," Bishop said.

He unscrewed the cap, took a drink, then continued. "He called me a few months back and said the construction company he'd hired was giving him the runaround. He asked if I could take on the project. I told him I'd be happy to, but it would be a few months."

"When were you scheduled to start?" Bishop asked.

"This week. We met and signed the paperwork a few days before he died."

"The other company's sign is still up," Bishop said. "Have they been informed?"

"I would assume so, but I'd suggest talking to Colin Rutherford about that. He was supposed to handle it."

"We're heading there in a bit," Bishop said. "When did you talk to Ryan last?"

"Three days ago, so the day before he died." He shook his head. "I can't believe he's gone."

"How did he seem to you?" I asked.

"He seemed okay, though not his normal cheerful self. Maybe stressed about the project, but he said he was excited to get things moving again."

"We've been told he's been acting different, paranoid at times," Bishop said.

Copeland pursed his lips. "Paranoid?" He shook his head. "I didn't notice that. Like I said, he's been stressed, but anyone with that big of a project would be. He's been doing well since he got back from rehab."

"You know about that?" I asked, surprised. Hicks's best kept secret wasn't so well kept after all.

He nodded. "Like I said, I've known him since his days at Hamby High. Ryan didn't trust a lot of people, but he trusted me. He confided in me because we're friends and because he wanted to make sure I understood how serious he was about making the project a success."

"Did he mention anything that was bothering him lately?" Bishop asked. "Maybe something with his divorce or a business associate?"

"He said he had some issues to work through, one being a funding problem."

"Such as lack of?" Bishop asked.

"More like lack of access. Something going on with his accounts. That's where he showed some stress. Typically, I take money up front, a percent of the total cost of a build, to get started. Without access to his funds, he couldn't provide that."

"What did he say had happened?" I asked.

"He didn't elaborate on it, but he said he'd be making some big changes over the next week or so, and he'd have the money to me then."

"Did he mention Rutherford?"

"With respect to the funding? He did not. I assumed the project would be on hold given the circumstances, but I put a call in to him anyway. Haven't heard back."

"What's your opinion of Rutherford?" I asked.

"Don't trust him."

"Any particular reason why?"

"Just that something seems off about him." He eyed Bishop and then me. "Do you think he has something to do with this?"

"We're looking into everyone," Bishop said.

"Then you're looking at his wife, I assume?"

"Why do you ask?" I asked.

"I've spent a lot of time with Lara and Ryan. Not one of those times did she act like she loved him. Put a camera in front of them, and sure, she was the doting wife. Outside of that, she acted like he and the kids didn't exist. That nanny she hired spent more time raising Ryan's children than she did."

"Nanny?" I asked.

"Ryan fired her when Lara moved out. He expected Lara to rehire her, but she's been keeping the kids in day care before and after school. That's why Ryan lost it when she said she wanted full custody. The woman doesn't know how to be a mother. A while back, Ryan said she was messing around with their money. When he called her out on it, she threatened to take the kids away and never let him see them, and apparently, threatened to kill him."

"You could have started off with that, Copeland," I said.

"I'd forgotten about it until now." He exhaled. "She married him for the money and fame. I'm not sure she ever loved him, and she doesn't love those kids."

"She said she was taking them to her parents' place in Kansas City," I said.

"Interesting."

"Why?" Bishop asked.

"Because Ryan said they were already there when I talked to him last."

I looked at Bishop. "Maybe her cooperation with me and Levy was an act?"

"I wouldn't doubt that," Copeland said. "She's been trying to break into acting since college. She auditioned for a spot on that *Baseball Wives* show in Atlanta, but the other women said they wouldn't be on it if she was."

"Wow," Bishop said, almost laughing. "That says a lot."

"I'm telling you, she's a piece of work."

I mentioned the previous case we worked on. "Bury-a-body-on-top-of-another-one piece of work?"

"Dear God, I hope not."

"Thanks for the information," I said. "If you hear from Rutherford or Lara Hicks, give me a call."

"Will do."

7

Hicks's accountant's office looked like it had been ransacked. Walking in, I half-expected the same pristine order that marked his lobby and the outer offices, but instead, I encountered chaos. Piles of file folders were heaped like barricades across his desk and a large table, threatening to send my Type A personality into cardiac shock. For me, messiness was a special kind of hell.

Cohen seemed unfazed by it. "Have a seat," he offered, clearing a chair by scooping up an armful of folders and dumping them onto another growing mound by the window. "Please excuse the mess. Bought out a small accounting firm recently. Old school types—everything's in hard copy. We're digitizing, but what you're seeing are the stragglers."

His glasses slid perilously down his nose as he spoke. He pushed them back up with a finger, his eyes magnifying behind the lenses. The poor guy probably couldn't see past his nose without them. The glasses, along with his short-sleeved button-down, retro striped tie, and high-waisted trousers, completed a look that screamed accountant rather than trendsetter. He fit the stereotype to a T. In another life, Savannah could have flipped his style on its head and paraded him down a runway. But for us, David Cohen was just a victim's accountant in a room in desperate need of a file purge.

Finally sitting, he said, "I'm assuming you're here about Ryan Hicks's death?"

"We are," I said.

"I'm not sure what I can tell you," he said. "I just took him on as a client a few weeks ago. I'm still going through his accounts and records, though I do have some concerns."

"Do you have access to his bank accounts live?" I asked.

"Yes, ma'am."

"Did Mr. Hicks provide that access?"

"Yes." It sounded more like a question than an answer. "How could I access the accounts without his log in?"

"He claimed to be having trouble accessing his accounts," Bishop said.

"Mr. Hicks believed someone with access to his accounts was stealing money. I suggested he stay out of them and to tell anyone asking that he couldn't access the information due to a technical issue."

"Why?" I asked.

"We changed his log ins completely. Anyone trying to access would be suspicious. We agreed it was important to keep our business arrangement private."

"Are you a forensic accountant?" I asked.

"Yes, ma'am."

"Have you found anything?" I asked.

"I've found inconsistencies, yes, but I'm still in the early stages."

"Inconsistencies that would prove someone played with his money?" Bishop asked.

"Based on what I've seen so far, I believe someone within his organization either acted on his behalf with the money or manipulated it to their benefit."

"And did you tell him that?"

"Of course. My job is to find discrepancies in the accounts and determine if that money is traceable. If someone's logged into his account as him, I wouldn't know without checking IP addresses."

"How much are we talking?" Bishop asked. "With the inconsistencies?"

"Upwards of seven million."

Bishop and I made eye contact. Seven million was around the same amount as the initial investments.

"Seven million?" I repeated. "That's a lot of money to disappear from an account."

"Multiple accounts," he said. "I'm not finished going through them all either. I wouldn't be surprised if I find more discrepancies."

"Can you explain how you've found the ones you have already?" Bishop asked.

"Hold on," he said. "I have a binder for his account." He twisted his chair and grabbed a binder from the shelf behind him. Then turning around, he leaned back in his chair, fingers drumming on the binder. "The first thing that jumped out was the unusual transactions," he explained, opening the binder and tapping a page filled with spreadsheets. "My staff and I noticed abrupt and large sums being transferred out of his accounts —amounts that didn't align with his typical business operations." He flipped the binder our direction. "We've got copies of the invoices, but they don't tell us much."

I scribbled a note. "Could these have been personal expenses?"

"It's possible, but improbable." Cohen shrugged. "The frequency and the amounts suggest otherwise. They were too systematic."

"What do you mean?" Bishop asked.

"They could be anything. Personal debt. Gambling debt. Blackmail payments. Maybe he's transferring them to a shell company. I can't say for sure just yet, but there is a pattern, and that will probably lead to something."

Bishop leaned forward. "Any invoices from the company?"

"Companies," Cohen said, flipping to another tab in his binder. "Several invoices came from entities with minimal to no digital footprint. It's as if these companies popped up overnight, billed substantial amounts, and then vanished. No definitive business history, no verifiable activities."

"Smoke and mirrors," Bishop muttered.

"Exactly," Cohen nodded. He pulled out a few examples and laid them across the desk. Each invoice was for a round number, a red flag. "We're seeing a lot of payments that are suspiciously even—fifty thousand, one hundred thousand. Not what you'd expect for legitimate varied business expenses."

"Any of them from Aquatic Life?" I asked.

"I don't recall that name, but as I've said, we're only in the early stages of our investigation."

I tapped my notepad, thinking. "So, it looks like someone laundered money through these transactions?"

"Possibly," Cohen confirmed. "I can't say for certain yet. We've tracked a series of small payments, too. It looks like an attempt to fly under the radar —numerous small amounts to the same entity, likely to avoid any single large transaction that might raise eyebrows. Could be Mr. Hicks's own shell company, though that would be surprising considering he'd come to me with these concerns."

Bishop raised an eyebrow. "How small are we talking?"'

"Mostly under the threshold for mandatory reporting. Several thousand dollars each. They add up. The pattern doesn't fit with normal expenditures for his type of business."

I glanced at Bishop, then back at Cohen. "And all these payments, were they cash?"

Cohen nodded as he flipped to another section. "Yes, a lot of these transactions were in cash. Far more than you'd expect for a business of this nature. It's a classic red flag for money laundering—cash is much harder to trace, but like I said before, it could be anything. I won't know until we've finished our deep dive, and as I've said, we only just started."

"Who has access to his accounts?" I asked.

"Anyone can deposit money if they have a deposit slip, just as anyone can withdraw money with a card."

"I understand. I'm asking who else can access the accounts in the same manner Mr. Hicks could, with their own log in."

"Of course," he said. "There are multiple accounts. One is his personal business account listed under Ryan Hicks LLC. That account feeds into his two other personal accounts, one I assume, based on the amount of money deposited, is his main personal account. Until recently, his wife could access that account, as well as his manager, Colin Rutherford. Six months ago, Mr. Hicks opened an account for just he and his wife, though Mr.

Rutherford still had access. It appears Mr. Rutherford accessed Mr. Hicks's personal account, withdrawing fifty thousand dollars monthly and depositing it into the Hicks's shared account."

"Hicks didn't want his wife having access to all his money," Bishop said.

"One can assume that, yes. Mr. Rutherford transfers the money from Mr. Hicks's main personal account at the beginning of the month, and Mrs. Hicks usually spends it all by the last day. Sometimes sooner."

"Are these the accounts you've mentioned with the inconsistencies?" I asked, though I assumed they weren't.

"No, ma'am. Those are the school accounts, but as I said, I can't provide too many details on our investigation at this time."

"Does anyone else have access to the school accounts?" Bishop asked.

"Yes. Colin Rutherford."

Colin Rutherford looked guiltier by the second. "Thank you," I said. I treaded carefully with my next question. "Have you seen anything that would lead you to think Mr. Hicks was using money for say, an addiction?"

"The personal account without Lara Hicks's name on it consistently had money transferred to another with the same bank, just not one belonging to Mr. Hicks."

"Who did it belong to?" Bishop asked.

"I'm currently not privy to that information, and if I was, I wouldn't be able to provide it to you without the agreement of the bank and account holder."

"Understood," he said. "Can you say how often and how much?"

"Five thousand once a month."

"That's not a lot. I doubt it's for a woman," I whispered.

"I thought the same," Cohen replied.

I knew he'd say no, but I had to ask, "May we have copies of his financial records?"

"Absolutely," he said with a smile. "If you provide a warrant. My client might be deceased, but I still have a responsibility to maintain his privacy."

I didn't mention he'd blown that. "We'll get the warrant," I said.

"Colin Rutherford's got his name written all over this," Bishop muttered under his breath, glancing sidelong at me.

I nodded slowly, still gnawing on Cohen's report about the holes he'd dug up in Hicks's story. It was a big lead, what he'd told us about Rutherford's connection to the accounts. Big enough to make things unravel fast if yanked on hard enough.

"If Hicks thought Rutherford was stealing from him, why didn't he get him off the accounts sooner?"

"That's one of the million-dollar questions. Maybe he wasn't ready. Wanted to give him the benefit of the doubt or something? He did hire Cohen last week, so could he have been trying to make sure?"

"I guess," I said. "Didn't look like he trusted that many people, so who would he have brought into the fold so soon? Who could he hire to replace Colin and his multiple professional personalities?"

"Right. That would take time."

That all-too-familiar itch started dancing up my spine as we walked to our vehicle. The one that alerted me to something in my surroundings. "Something's off here," I said, more to myself than to Bishop.

Just then, as our boots hit the first row of cars, a peripheral flash of motion snagged my attention. A shadow, swift and purposeful, skirted the far edge of the building, melding with the shadows.

"Hold up," I snapped, my fingers clamping down on Bishop's forearm with urgent pressure. My nod was sharp, directing his gaze. "We got company."

Bishop responded immediately, his veteran eyes narrowed into slits and the lines around them deepened. "Where?" His voice, a low growl, barely audible over the roar of traffic.

"There—around the corner. I saw a shadow slip away." The words had barely left my lips before I sprang into motion, muscles tensing as I sprinted toward the shadow I'd seen. "Could use some help here, partner," I hollered to Bishop.

"Rachel, wait!" Bishop's voice sounded like a distant echo against the pounding of my heart and the blood rushing loud in my ears as I charged forward.

8

I rounded the building's edge in a burst of speed, eyes scanning, catching a glimpse of the figure—a man about six feet tall, shrouded in a black hoodie, his features obscured by a low-drawn baseball cap, and wearing sunglasses. He'd seen me and taken off, moving with the fluidity of a shadow, slipping around another bend with ghost-like precision.

"Bishop, he's looping around back! Six-footer, sunglasses, black hoodie, jeans, and a cap!" My shout ricocheted off the walls, my voice straining against the din of traffic a short distance away.

Adrenaline surged as I chased the echo of my own steps, the man always just out of reach. By the time I skidded around the back of the building, he had vanished, swallowed by the area's gaping maw. I staggered to a stop, chest heaving, my breaths sharp and ragged.

"Damn it," I hissed, the word a venomous whisper in the cool air. Anger simmered just below the surface, frustration coiling tightly within. I bent forward and placed my hands on my knees, focusing on catching my breath while internally cussing myself out for forgoing real exercise for months.

Moments later, Bishop's steadier footsteps rounded the corner. His presence always a calm anchor in the storm. He acted as though he'd just gone for a walk, when I knew he'd run around that side of the building. His gaze methodically swept the area. "See his face?"

I shook my head, the movement jerky with irritation. "He saw me coming." The confession gritted out between clenched teeth.

Without a word, Bishop pulled out his cell, his fingers swift over the keys as he dialed dispatch, his voice a steady command as he issued a BOLO.

I surveyed the scene again, desperate for any clue, any slip that might give our ghost away. But there was nothing.

Bishop ended the call. His eyes met mine as a silent communication passed between us. "He's probably ditched the hoodie by now."

I nodded, finally regaining my breath. "If he's watching us, he's keeping tabs on Levy and Michels too."

His hand stroked his stubble. "Might make him easier to catch then."

"I don't think he's our shooter," I muttered.

He chuckled, a low, rumbling sound. "You really believe that?"

I wiped sweat from my brow, the run's heat clinging to my skin. "It's too obvious."

"Maybe that's exactly his game," Bishop mused, his eyes narrowing as he peered into the distance. "Taunt us and get us off our game."

I tapped my weapon on my belt. "Like that's going to happen."

"It's getting late," he said. "Let's call Rutherford's office and see if he's still there."

I dialed his office, but his receptionist said he'd left over an hour before. "We'll hit him up tomorrow. Let's head back to the station and update Jimmy on what we found out."

"You know," Michels said after we'd provided our updates for the night. "It's you. Nothing like this happened here until you came around," he added as he and Levy headed to the department's back entrance.

A part of me thought he was right. The other part knew he was, she just didn't care. "Just keep an eye out," I said.

"Tall guy dressed in a black hoodie with sunglasses and jeans." He smirked. "Shouldn't be a problem."

Levy punched him in the arm. "Stop razzing her." She looked at me. "What about weight?"

"Thin, so maybe 170? Honestly, he was gone so fast, I didn't have a chance to see much. I'm not even sure he's white, though I think he is."

"At least there's that," she said.

"Is it just me, or is it strange Watkins is MIA again?" I asked her.

"It's strange," she said. "But we'll find him."

We parted ways at the hallway leading to the back door.

"See you in a few hours," Michels said. He held the door open for Levy, who walked out waving her hand in the air.

We'd gone back and forth all day and Jimmy had forced us all to clock out and sleep.

I stopped in his office before hitting the road. "You heading out soon?"

"I'm working on a statement for tomorrow's press conference."

"There's a press conference tomorrow?"

"There is now," he said. "Just got the call from the mayor's assistant."

"What about Sanders? Why isn't she handling it?"

"She'll be there to answer questions after the mayor and I finish."

"You're not mentioning the bank account information, are you?" I didn't think he was, but I asked just in case.

"I'm not mentioning any possible motives or any potential suspects for that matter."

"Ah, the standard, 'we're doing everything in our power, following leads,' spiel."

That got me a partial smile. "I thought about suggesting eliminating mayoral positions, but I don't think the mayor would appreciate that."

I laughed. "Probably not. I could heckle when he talks if that'll help."

"I appreciate the offer, but I'll pass."

"If you change your mind," I said, smiling. "I'm out of here. I'm calling Savannah on the way, so remember that when you get home."

"Thanks for the alert."

Outside the station, I strode to my Jeep, the one I'd bought after a serial killer obliterated my previous Jeep. It was the second vehicle I'd purchased because I'd returned the first one. It didn't feel right to me. The new Jeep wasn't as broken in as the first, which had belonged to Tommy, but it suited me, and I knew he would have loved that I bought a stick over an automatic. Driving a standard in Georgia was a vacation compared to driving one in Chicago.

Tommy never dressed up his Jeep, preferring to go against the cult of Jeep owners who plastered stickers all over their vehicles. I felt the same but still placed one special sticker on the back window of my new vehicle. I smiled as I ran my fingers across it, an American flag with the blue stripe and Tommy's initials printed on it. "Miss you, babe," I whispered.

I froze as the scene of Tommy's murder played in my head again. We'd gone to dinner, and since parking in Chicago stunk, Tommy left me waiting outside the restaurant while he ran to the car. I'd worn a pair of heels that night, something I rarely did, and he didn't want me walking in them any more than I had to.

I should have gone with him, but I didn't. When too much time had passed, I sucked it up and headed to the parking garage to find him standing with a gun against his head. I paused for just a second, long enough for the shooter to pull the trigger. Tommy dropped. I drew my weapon a second too late to save my husband, but I sent his killer straight to hell where he belonged.

I leaned against the vehicle and sucked in a breath. I thought of that night often. Even though I loved Kyle, and I knew logically Tommy's death wasn't my fault, thinking about it still knocked the wind out of me. I shook it off as best I could and checked the area but saw no one lurking in the shadows. Disappointment washed over me. I hated ending the night on a loss. We'd catch the watcher. We just needed time.

I flicked on my Bluetooth and dialed Savannah. The tires hummed against the asphalt, creating a steady backdrop to our late-night confab. "Hey. I didn't wake the babies, did I?"

Savannah's voice crackled through the speakers, sugary and smooth as always. "Are you kidding? They've been knocked out for hours. I'm here sipping a glass of wine and catching up on today's episode of *General Hospital* just waiting until my husband gets home."

I snorted, my headlights cutting through the pockets of darkness ahead of me. "He's working on a statement for a press conference tomorrow. I don't know how you watch that stuff. It's the same storylines on repeat."

"I know, but I can't help myself. My granny watched it every day, and I've been keeping that tradition alive for as long as I can remember. You headed home now?"

"Finally, yes."

Her tone took on a more serious note. "I hope you find the killer quick. It's been all over the news. Apparently, people have gathered at the school site, and it's become a makeshift memorial."

"Really? We were by near there earlier and didn't see anything, but I didn't pay a lot of attention."

"They showed it on the national news earlier. I'm not downplaying Princess Diana's death, but from the looks of the crowd, she's got some serious memorial competition coming."

"It made national news? Great. No one said a thing to me or Bishop."

"Jimmy's got people on it. That new public relations ball-buster for starters. I met her today," she said. "I think he's kept all y'all out of the loop so you wouldn't get distracted."

"Ball-buster." I laughed. "That's perfect. You weren't supposed to tell me about the national news, were you?"

"As if you wouldn't have seen it anyway."

"Good point."

"Jimmy said Lara Hicks pitched a fit this morning but turned out to be halfway decent after you apologized later."

"I'm not sure I'd put it that way."

"I still don't like her. My momma would say she's about as clear as mud on a rainy day."

I laughed because it was true. "Have you had any interactions with her outside of today?"

"A few. She was at the governor's ball last year before she and Ryan split. She wore this hot pink mermaid dress, two sizes too small, and honey, I swear to you she was showing her religion."

I laughed again. "At the governor's ball? Tacky."

"So tacky, but some women want to be the best of the best, and they use what they've got to get there. God gave her a good starter package, and the rest she acquired professionally. Lord knows she needs it because she's got the personality of a drowned rat."

"Why do you say that?" I asked, navigating a curve.

"Because every time she opens her mouth, the devil comes out. I'm surprised she hasn't grown horns."

"You got all this from watching her at the governor's ball?"

"Rach, God knows I've tried and failed to make you a normal woman a thousand times, but normal women gossip. And the talk about Lara Hicks, especially since her split from Ryan, is juicier than a watermelon at a summer picnic."

"You and your southernisms. They crack me up."

"When they fit, I can't help but use them."

"I wonder if people think she killed her husband?"

"I'm sure they do. I'll snoop around, see what I can find out, and let you know."

"Sav, you don't have to—"

"I know I don't, but it's fun. Just don't tell Jimmy. He'll pitch a fit."

That he would.

I swung onto my street, the skin on the back of my neck prickling as I caught sight of my garage door gaping open—a bad sign in my quiet community. Kyle, meticulous to a fault, never left that door open, especially not after the sinister shadows that had lurked around our place last spring.

"Hey, I gotta cut this short. I'll call you tomorrow, okay?" I said, my voice tight, clipped.

"Sure thing," she replied. The line went dead.

I detected danger, the kind I knew all too well. I guided the Jeep into the driveway, my senses on high alert, my heart already racing. My eyes darted to the security cameras, my heart plummeting as I saw them—dangling by mere threads, violated. "Damn it," I hissed, fear and anger churning in my gut. My gaze locked on a piece of paper, stark against the dark wood of the door. "Please tell me that's not another celebrity death note," I muttered under my breath, the words barely a whisper.

I reached over, gripping the cold handle of my gun on the passenger seat.

9

With deliberate, cautious movements, I scanned the surroundings. Kyle's vehicle sat inside the immaculate garage—his obsessive tidiness leaving no space for unwanted guests unless they were tucked inside his vehicle or lurking around the side of our townhome.

I sent a voice text to Kyle, my voice a breathless shadow, ensuring silence for ears possibly eavesdropping nearby. *Garage door's open. There's a note. Checking your vehicle and the perimeter. Stay sharp.* Another quick text followed. *Cameras are sabotaged. I'm on it. Just be ready.*

I slid out of the Jeep, the door closing with a soft click that echoed ominously in the quiet night. I swept my eyes through Kyle's vehicle but found nothing. Every shadow was a potential threat. My pulse hammered as I pivoted, my back against Kyle's vehicle for the best view of all angles. That's when the soft scuff of a shoe on pavement spun me around, gun aimed in one fluid motion.

"All clear out back," Kyle announced, emerging from the darkness, hands raised in mock surrender.

"For God's sake, Kyle!" I snapped, the adrenaline surging then ebbing away as I lowered the gun. My hand trembled as I moved to the door and grabbed the note, my eyes darting to the ink-black corners of the garage. The message was clear and chilling: *Stay away or next time it won't be just a note.*

"Get inside," Kyle ordered, his voice a low growl. But I shook my head, the decision firm in my mind.

"You take the left, sweep the far end. I'm going right, and I'll check the street." Our steps were silent, calculated as we split, each step a beat in the tense silence.

Moments later, after an eternity stretched into minutes, we converged, signaling the all-clear with a nod.

"Great," I muttered. "What's the point of security cameras if they're so easily destroyed?" The meticulousness of it all sent a shiver down my spine. Whoever did it wanted to send a clear message, and they had.

I backed into the house, waited for Kyle to follow, then locked the door behind us.

"I checked the interior already," he said. "I promise you, Rach, I didn't leave the garage door open."

"I didn't think you did. I don't get how they opened it without the code?"

"Bubba can probably tell you that."

"I'll talk to him tomorrow."

"No." His jaw tightened. "I'm calling Jimmy. We need to catch whoever did this before it escalates."

Jimmy said he'd be right over and suggested I contact Bubba about the garage door. I sent him a text.

As we waited for Jimmy to arrive, Kyle said, "You look like hell."

"What every woman wants to hear after chasing an invisible note-leaver. Thanks."

He pulled me into a kiss. "A beautiful hell."

Within minutes, our driveway was filled with flashing blue and red lights.

Standing outside our townhouse, I said to Kyle, "Our neighbors are going to hate us even more."

"Until they need us," he said.

"Good point."

Jimmy arrived first with two squads on his tail. He approached me, his face grim. "Always making trouble, aren't you, Ryder?"

Officers spread out, combing through the yard and the garage, flashlights cutting through the darkness.

I handed him the note. "This is the note I found taped to my door when I got home. Like Kyle said, the garage door was wide open, and all the security cameras have been ripped out."

His jaw tightened as he read the note. "Stay away or next time it won't be just a note." He shook his head. "You think it has to do with Hicks?"

"You don't?"

"You've pissed off a lot of people in this town. We need to consider all the options."

"It's a note," I said, only a little annoyed because he was right. I had pissed off a lot of people in town. "Seems a little too coincidental don't you think?"

"I'll have a team on it. If it doesn't lead anywhere, we'll try another angle."

"Okay," I said, though I would have preferred investigating it myself.

"We need to figure out how they got in," Kyle said.

"Probably a universal remote," I said. After thinking on it a bit more, I added, "Or they were here when you came home before and hacked our remote."

Jimmy nodded. "We'll look into it. For now, let's focus on securing the area and making sure you're safe."

The officers continued their search, scouring the yard and checking the perimeter of the house. They found nothing—no signs of forced entry, no suspicious footprints, nothing that could point us to the intruder. I knew they wouldn't.

One of the officers approached Jimmy and me, shaking his head. "No luck, Chief. Whoever did this knew what they were doing. They left no trace."

Jimmy sighed. "Alright, give it one more sweep, but I doubt we'll find anything tonight."

Turning to me, he said, "I'll have a squad car do regular patrols in the neighborhood, and I'll make sure our guys are extra vigilant."

I nodded, knowing the problem wouldn't go away until we found who killed Ryan Hicks. "Thanks, Jimmy. I appreciate it."

"I'll keep a watch on things," Kyle said.

I smiled, grabbed his biceps, and squeezed. "He'll kick ass with his bare hands if he has to."

Jimmy glanced between Kyle and me and laughed. His face turned serious as he said, "Stay alert. We'll catch this guy soon enough."

"Have you eaten?" Kyle asked.

"I seem to remember Chick-Fil-A, but that could have been last year for all I know."

"I made skillet lasagna. I can heat some up for you if you'd like?"

My mouth watered. Kyle's skillet lasagna was better than most Italian grandmothers regular stuff. I would have been kicked out of Chicago if I'd said that there. "I'd love some, but I need a shower."

"Take one, I'll get it ready."

I popped up onto my tiptoes and kissed him. "You're the best."

"That's what all the women say."

I laughed. "You're DEA. Most women you deal with are prostitutes."

"That doesn't mean they don't know a catch when they see one."

"They've got a quota to make." I jogged up the stairs two at a time. "Oh," I said when I hit the top. "Did you feed Louie?"

"A catch like me? I fed him twice."

I chuckled. It felt good to talk about something other than the investigation and threatening note. I understood Kyle well enough to know he wanted to discuss it but wouldn't unless I brought it up first. Which I had no intention of doing.

It took me fifteen minutes to scrub the day from my body and feel somewhat normal again. I threw on a pair of gray sweats and Tommy's Chicago Cubs sweatshirt. It engulfed me, but it felt like home.

Kyle flashed a grin as I strolled into the kitchen. "Look at you, all dolled up like some kind of film noir femme fatale after a day of chasing down killers. I'm sure Tommy loved you in that sweatshirt as much as I do." He glanced at the ceiling. "Thanks, man."

He respected my life with Tommy and never felt threatened by it. How could he? What we had was as much a miracle as my time with my husband. He handed me a plate heaped with his killer skillet lasagna, and I made my way over to the leather couch.

"Your cooking could start wars, you know," I said as I dug in. "Every Italian mama in Chicago would want you dead for this masterpiece."

He chuckled. "That's a compliment, right?"

"Absolutely," I said between bites. "Just keep one eye open when you sleep. So, what happened in your world today?"

"Ran into Daryl Rasmussen. Always a pleasure."

I raised an eyebrow. "Isn't that the goon you collared last year?"

"Twice," Kyle said, taking a pull from his beer. "We exchanged a few pleasantries."

"It's a real treat bumping into old conquests, isn't it?"

"The guy's a regular with us now," he said with a wry smile. "I'd bet he knows half the DEA by their first names."

I tore through that pasta heaven without taking a break. Scraping up the last of the lasagna and wishing there was more, I asked, "Was he thrilled to see his favorite DEA agent?"

"He's always a ray of sunshine." Kyle grinned. "Offered to rearrange my anatomy."

I set down my plate on my trunk coffee table and leaned back. "Let him try. He'll get a two-for-one deal with me."

"I thought it best not to mention you. Doesn't look good when a guy in my position is seen unleashing his better half on the bad guys."

"We'd keep it our little secret," I said, stretching my legs across his lap. "Let it be a surprise."

He smiled. "So, I know you don't want to talk about the note."

"You know me so well."

"Normally I wouldn't ask, but it's a big case. Can we at least touch on that?"

"Wow, I'm shocked you're asking. I thought you'd leave it."

"MLB player? A man's got to do what a man's got to do."

"What do you want to know?" I asked.

"Any good news?"

"Poor Jimmy. Coming here was the last thing he needed." I yawned.

"He's got a press conference tomorrow, and we're up the creek. The mayor's going to have a fit when he finds out we're still drawing blanks."

"I'm sure he's aware."

"Probably, but it still sucks for Jimmy, which then means it sucks for us."

"You guys aren't making any headway at all?"

"Yes and no. We're chasing ghosts," I said, shaking my head. "Every clue leads to another mystery. It's like trying to track a buck that keeps sprouting new antlers faster than we can follow."

He chuckled. "What a comparison."

"I just got off the phone with Savannah. She was on one of her southernism rants about Lara Hicks."

"I've been there for one of those rants. Poor Lara." He eyed my empty plate. "Want seconds?"

I exhaled. "I do, but I'll save it for tomorrow. I don't want to end up with heartburn."

"Got it. Tell me about the investigation."

Kyle had often collaborated with the department, either in an advisory capacity or as a Drug Enforcement Agency representative. Technically, I wasn't supposed to disclose details on open investigations, but his DEA experience could be invaluable, so I regarded him as a professional resource.

I ran my hand through my wet hair, then twisted it into a clip on the top of my head using one I'd attached to my sweatshirt earlier. "Did you know Hicks was an addict?"

Kyle nodded. "I've heard it through the grapevine. I think they kept it from the media. Either that, or the media liked him enough to keep it out of the headlines."

"I can't see the media missing an opportunity to ruin someone's reputation."

"Good point," he said.

"Does his addiction have something to do with his murder?"

"I'm not sure. His drug of choice was opioids, but we've yet to hear or prove that led to heroin."

"It's possible," he said, "Did you get a look at his bank accounts?"

"Sort of. I've got to request a warrant for them tomorrow."

"Any unusual cash withdrawals?"

"Those and a bunch of other things. He'd switched to a forensic accountant recently. According to him, Hicks thought someone was stealing money."

"Then I doubt he was paying a dealer."

"He has a private account with consistent deposits from another one of his accounts and withdrawals to someone at the same bank, but the accountant claimed to not know who."

"How much were the transactions?"

"Five thousand a month."

"It's possible he's putting it into a shell account for a dealer. It's rare, but it happens. In today's market, that would get him about three hundred grams of the higher quality stuff, which I'd assume he'd want given the risk of fentanyl in the lower quality drugs."

"How long would that last him?" I asked.

"You know how it works. The more someone uses, the higher their tolerance. He could need several hundred milligrams per hit if he's got a high tolerance. Less if he doesn't."

"So, let's say he's paying three hundred a gram, and he's dropping five thousand at a time, that's—" I did the math in my head, "that's roughly around sixteen and a half grams."

"Right, and each gram has a thousand milligrams, which means three-hundred-thousand grams of the higher quality stuff."

"That's a lot of uses," I said.

"For a month? Maybe, maybe not. It depends on if the user is doing it alone, and how often, but still, in my world, that's a red flag for drugs, but that doesn't mean that's what it is."

"Right. The kicker is his business manager has access to most of his accounts."

"Even the one with the regular transfers?" he asked.

I nodded. "I'd call that a red flag."

10

The conference room at City Hall steamed like a sauna. "It's too hot in here," I said as I wedged myself between Bishop and Levy.

"Consider it one step closer to your goal weight," Bishop said.

I nudged him in the arm with my elbow. "Some of us aren't as vain as others."

Levy raised her hand in front of her face. "I am."

I shook my head. The only weight she would lose was muscle. The woman didn't have an ounce of fat on her. I eyed the gaggle of reporters from various local outlets, and a few I recognized from national shows as well.

Sweat dripped down everyone's foreheads. I wiped mine away with my fingers but stopped complaining. Like the interrogation room technique, Jimmy had likely asked to kick up the heat when it was his turn to speak. Politicians used the same trick to clear the room quickly. Our mayor loved to hear himself talk, as had every mayor since I'd joined the department, so it would have been a cold day in hell for him to up the temp.

The reporters fanned themselves with whatever was at hand—mostly notepads and the occasional cell phone. It was crowded, sweaty, standing room only.

"You missed the mayor," Bishop whispered. "We're just waiting for Jimmy."

"Intentionally," I replied. "I didn't want to heckle him."

"Have you ever liked a politician?" Bishop asked.

"Yes."

"Really? Who?"

"She's lying," Levy said.

Michels nudged his way over. "I smell like other people's BO."

"It's you," Levy said. "Trust me."

"I'm not lying," I said. "I was my eighth-grade class president. I happen to like myself."

Bishop rolled his eyes, then said, "Jimmy told us what happened last night. Everything okay?"

"Other than my annoyance at it all and the need for new security cameras? We're good."

"We need to be careful."

Before I could respond, Bubba had pushed his way through the crowd. "I contacted your security company last night. They pulled videos from about an hour before you got home. They show a man walking down your street and cutting off to the opposite side around the corner of an end unit, but nothing near you. I think he shot them out first, then ripped them from their base just in case."

"When we catch this guy, he's buying me new cameras."

"I think they got into the garage with a universal remote."

"Great," I said. "Whoever did this knew what they were doing. They left no evidence on the scene, so however they got in won't point to anyone either."

"You sure?" Bishop asked.

I nodded. "For now."

Jimmy strode up to the podium, his face a mask of solemn duty. The room plunged into a sudden hush, every eye locked on him as he prepared to address the crowd about the murder of the state's golden boy turned baseball legend. The silence was almost reverent, as if the whole room held its breath. The silence would end as soon as he opened his mouth. Reporters weren't the best at being patient.

"Good morning," he began, his voice steady and commanding despite the stifling heat. "As you are all aware, we are gathered here today under tragic circumstances. The Hamby Police Department is currently investigating the murder of Ryan Hicks, a respected member of our community and a national sports hero."

The flash of cameras punctuated his words as reporters jockeyed for a better angle. He waited for the flashes to subside before continuing.

"Unfortunately, I don't have much to add to what our mayor's already said. As of now, we are pursuing multiple leads, however, given the nature of the investigation and out of respect for the family, we are not able to disclose any further details at this time."

That was like throwing chum into shark-infested waters and he quite possibly would have a pink slip waiting on his desk. He didn't care. He did what was necessary to close an investigation and catch a killer, politics be damned, and I respected that.

The reporters surged forward like a wave of collective sharks ready to bite. They shouted questions at Jimmy. Sanders stepped up beside him.

"Chief Abernathy, can you confirm if there are any suspects?" one reporter from a local TV station called out, his microphone poised like a weapon.

"Is it true that the murder weapon was found at the scene?" another voice added, rising above the din.

Jimmy handled each question with practiced ease, respectful yet firm. "I understand your concerns and the community's need for answers. However, I must stress the importance of the integrity of our investigation. Speculating or releasing unconfirmed details could compromise our efforts to bring the perpetrator to justice."

His answers were the verbal equivalent of a well-oiled door—smooth, polished, revealing nothing.

The heat in the room ratcheted up a notch with every non-answer. I wiped a bead of sweat from my brow, feeling both admiration and frustration. Admiration for Jimmy's ability to stand his ground, and frustration because, like everyone else, I wanted an ice bath.

"Chief, how is the department handling the pressure of such a high-profile case?" a voice rang out, softer, almost respectful.

Jimmy's expression softened marginally. "We are fully committed to solving this case. Our officers are working around the clock, and we will not rest until justice is served."

It was the closest thing to an emotional reveal he'd give them, and that revelation resonated through the room, though not in a positive way. They wanted more. They wanted substance. They wanted the inside details, things they'd never get.

"This guy's a politician," a reporter nearby whispered.

I snorted, and Bishop elbowed me in the arm.

"What?" I whispered. "It was funny."

The reporter eyed me suspiciously. I smiled at him and winked. He just shook his head and turned away.

Another reporter asked, "What about the wife? Is she a suspect?"

That guy wasn't getting the fact that Jimmy wasn't going to give them anything.

I watched as his patience waned. "Do you have children?" he asked the reporter.

"Yes, sir."

"How many?"

"Two."

"Married or divorced?"

"Married, sir."

"Then consider how you'd feel in this situation."

That shut the guy up immediately.

"Thank you for your time," Jimmy said. He walked away from the podium.

Liz Sanders took his place. She steeled her eyes into the crowd, her face blank of expression. "As Chief Abernathy stated, the investigation is ongoing, and it would be inappropriate to comment on specifics at this time. We ask for the public's patience and cooperation in this highly sensitive matter."

The room wasn't having it. Questions kept coming, each more probing than the last. 'Was there any sign of forced entry?' 'Has the family been given police protection?'

I scanned the room noting the hungry looks on the reporters' faces.

Every one of them was on edge, desperate to snag something juicy. From the seasoned veterans to the green-as-grass interns, they all shared that look of rabid curiosity mixed with the adrenaline rush of covering a high-profile case.

Sanders fielded a few additional questions and responded with the same line she'd used before. I liked her. I leaned my head toward Bishop's. "She's got some serious cajónes."

"She's scarier than you."

I laughed.

Sanders left the stage. A clear shot to the back exit of the large conference room had her out in seconds, offering nods and tight-lipped smiles but no more information on the way.

After she left, reporters clustered together swapping theories and jotting down final notes. I listened to the conversations filling the room.

"That was completely useless," a reporter for the Hamby Herald said.

I recognized his face but couldn't place his name, nor did I care.

"The mayor was too busy looking at himself in the camera and that chief and the useless liaison," he continued, "they won't toss any bait. How can we report on something without any information?"

"We make it up," the other reporter said.

I eyed Bishop who shook his head slightly. He wanted me to keep my mouth shut, which I did even though I wanted to tell the reporter where he could stick it.

"Let's get out of here before you end up behind bars for assault," Bishop said and hurried me out of the room. Levy, Bubba, and Michels followed.

Back in the investigation room, Levy said, "I heard about last night. You okay?"

"All good," I said, signaling that what had happened, happened, and I just wanted to move on.

"Do you think it's related to the investigation?"

"The note told me to stay out of it. What else could it mean?"

"Makes sense."

I stood in front of the side table, staring at the coffee options. "They're going to write some BS about the investigation and throw us all under the bus." I poured myself a cup of coffee from the pot since the Keurig died after a mild fire the week before. I made a mental note to ask HR for another one, though I suspected that was already in process.

"You can't let what they write get to you," Bishop said. "We're here to do a job, not appease the media."

Levy said, "If we let them, then they win."

"No," Bishop. Poured himself a cup of coffee. "We win when we find Hicks's murderer."

"That'll only last a few minutes in the media, but the damage they could do beforehand will last forever," I said.

The worry on his face told me he knew I was right. I sat down then and stretched my arm to the center of the table to drag the landline toward me.

"Who are you going to call?" Bishop asked.

Bubba said, "Ghostbusters?" He laughed, but the rest of us just gave him a blank stare.

"Bad timing?"

"Bad joke," Michels said.

"As if you haven't told those multiple times," Levy said. "My father tells better jokes than you."

"I have better timing than your dad and Bubba," he said. "Ask my wife."

"Gross," Levy said, laughing.

I dialed Judge Nowak's personal cell phone and put the call on speaker. Nowak and I shared a love of the Chicago Cubs, and really, all things Chicago. Because of that, we'd connected on a different level than I had with any of the other judges in the state. I had to admit though, the ones I'd thought were part of the good old boy network and would never respect me had proved to do just the opposite.

"Detective Ryder," he said without asking.

"How'd you know it was me?"

"You're the only person from Hamby PD with my personal number."

"Oh, well, I consider that an honor, Judge."

"Shame what's happened to that baseball player, isn't it?"

"Yes, sir, and that's why I'm calling. I need a warrant for his bank records, and all accounting associated with them."

"You got something that might lead to his killer?"

"We've got suspicious activity and an octopus growing tentacles on the daily, a few of them leading to financial activities."

"Understood. Any suspects currently? That's not required for the warrant. Just a baseball fan asking."

I filled him in on our concerns about Colin Rutherford.

"You planning to interview him again today?"

"Yes, sir."

"Okay. I'll have that for you by lunch. If you need one for the manager, let me know. Anything else I can help you with?"

"Not at the moment, but if something comes up, I'll give you a call."

"I know you will," he said, and hung up the phone.

"Did you have relationships like that with judges in Chicago?" Bubba asked.

"A few, but there were so many corrupt ones, they weren't always very helpful."

"I bet you scared them all." He smiled. "You scared me the entire first year we worked together."

"She still scares me," Michels said.

"Try being her partner," Bishop said.

Levy flicked her chin toward me. "I'm not afraid of you."

"That's because you're just as scary," Michels said.

"We're nothing compared to your wife," I said. "She survived a serial killer. That woman is bad ass."

"Truth," Levy said.

Ashley had survived a serial killer, one whose torment hit Ted Bundy's level. To be grateful she survived was an understatement.

Jimmy stormed in. From the look on his face, we all knew it would be an even longer day than we'd expected. Michels sunk low in his chair, likely trying to protect himself from the daggers shooting from the chief's eyes.

Like the patriarch of a family, he sat at the head of the table. His shoulders visibly loosened as he got as comfortable as possible in a crappy metal chair. "I hate news conferences."

I smiled and applauded quietly. The rest joined in, our claps a slow, rhythmic beat. "You handled it well," I said. "And I like Sanders. She's tough."

"She is." He smirked. "It's all about sounding serious and looking mean."

"You both nailed that," Michels said.

"Practice for when Scarlet starts dating," Bishop said.

"I don't need a mean look for that," Jimmy said. "She's not dating until she's forty." He chuckled. "Where are we today?"

"Still chasing ghosts, but a little closer," I said.

"Don't send her to any of those thinking classes again," Michels said. "She made us mind map the investigation. It was torture."

Jimmy eyed me.

I shrugged.

Levy's cell phone dinged. She glanced at the screen then turned her phone upside down on the table.

"Rutherford is ahead in the game," Bishop said. "He's got access to Hicks's accounts. He failed to mention Hicks's drug addiction, and it's a little too convenient that Hicks has an office in the King tower as well."

"We got a warrant for Hicks's financials," I added. "Should be here by lunch, but knowing Nowak, it'll be earlier."

He nodded. "Who's doing what today?"

"Daniel Watkins is still MIA," Levy said. "We've been by his place twice."

"He's the fan?" Jimmy asked.

Levy nodded. "He's the peeper with multiple calls on him."

"I checked his record," Bubba said. "Nothing unusual."

"Can you check his social media accounts?" Levy asked.

"Sure." He tapped away on his keyboard then massaged his mouse pad. "There are a ton of Daniel Watkins on Facebook. It's going to take some time to go through them. I can compare his driver's license photo to the profile photos, which will speed it up, but I'm going to need at least an hour." He looked up from the computer and said, "Oh, I checked the county court for the divorce petition." He handed each of us the petition. "He filed."

"Interesting," Bishop said.

"We'll take Jerome White," Levy said. She looked at Bishop. "Unless you want him?"

"We're going back to Rutherford's."

"I think we'll be there a while," I added. I grabbed the phone and called Nowak again.

He answered on the second ring. "Forget something?"

"Yes. We need access to Hicks's office and his home."

"For?"

"Emails, financials, his will. Anything that has to do with the school project, his wife, the investors, fans, cell phones, all the things."

"So, the kitchen sink?"

"You got it, Judge."

"I was just issuing the first request, so I'll do this one now as well."

"Thank you. I'll let you know if we need anything else."

"If you're going to need additional warrants, get them fast. I'm leaving in a week for Italy."

"Got it," I said. "Thanks."

"Okay," Jimmy said. "Levy, Michels, you talk to the pool boy. Bishop and Ryder will take Rutherford. Bubba's got the fan." His eyebrows furrowed. "What's his name?"

"Daniel Watkins," Bubba said.

"When you're done, I want you on Hicks's house," Jimmy said.

"If we can, we'll check the office first," I said. "Though I'm not sure Rutherford will let us without the warrant."

"Let's see how much time there is," Bishop said. "Levy and Michels could finish before us."

"I'll try to get the warrant," Jimmy said. "But it'll be hard to convince a judge without a strong connection to the crime."

"Appreciate it," Bishop said.

"We'll run by Watkins's house again," Levy said. "We need to consider this guy as a viable suspect. Being MIA since the shooting looks bad for him."

"Agreed," Jimmy said. "Michels, get a BOLO out before you leave."

"Yes, sir."

11

Bishop whined about the sludge from the coffee pot and pulled into the Dunkin' once again. While waiting in line before reaching the order station, an employee appeared at Bishop's window, two large to-go cups in her hands. He opened the window.

"Hey, detectives," Hailey said. We all knew each other by name. "I saw you pull in, so I made your regulars. Hope that's okay."

"Thanks," Bishop said. "Let me get you my card."

I dug into my wallet and pulled out two tens. "I got it." I handed him the cash.

"No. This one's on us," she said. "The owner's here. He said you probably need this because of the big investigation."

He handed her the money. "Then keep this for yourself," he said. "And tell the owner thank you."

"My pleasure," she said. She smiled. "Thanks for the tip."

He pulled out of the drive-thru line with his shoulders looking a little more relaxed. "Question for you."

"Okay," I said after sipping my much-appreciated free caffeine hit.

"If Kyle were to propose —"

I had just taken another sip and spit it all over his glove compartment.

"Hey, I just had this car cleaned." He laughed. "There are napkins inside the compartment."

"Is Kyle proposing?" I stared at him, unable to focus on cleaning up my mess.

"I don't know. This is hypothetical."

I exhaled then opened the compartment. While grabbing a few napkins, I said, "You might want to lead with that next time."

"Noted."

I tossed the wet napkins on the floor by my feet, leaving them to stuff into my cup when I finished. "Go on."

"If Kyle were to propose to you, since you've been married already, would you want an engagement ring?"

My eyes widened. "I knew it! You're asking Cathy to marry you!"

"Hypothetical scenario, remember?"

"Whatever, but yes. Of course I'd want an engagement ring. Being previously married has nothing to do with a rock on my finger. That's a sign of commitment. You'd better not ask her empty-handed."

"Hypothetically ask her."

"Whatever."

He took the same route to Rutherford's office as he had before. "What's our strategy with Rutherford?"

"Hold on, you're not changing the subject yet. We've got at least thirty minutes to figure that out. Do you need help looking at rings?" I couldn't have wiped the smile off my face if I'd tried. "I love Cathy. She's your better half."

"Thanks, partner." He exhaled but couldn't hide the smile that came after. "This needs to stay between us."

I rubbed my hands together. "I'll try."

"No trying." He glanced at me then back at the road. "I'm serious."

I dropped my hands. "Okay. Yes. I can keep it between us. When are we going shopping for rings?"

"I'm going after we find a killer. If you can handle it, yes, I'd like you to tag along."

"Hell yeah, I can handle it."

Nothing like a splash of good news to lighten the load of a murder investigation.

"Can we talk about Rutherford now?"

"I think we go with the slow burn. Start out with some additional questions that lead into what we know."

"You think you can do that without jumping the gun?"

I blew out a breath. "Ye of little faith."

He laughed.

"If Hicks believed Rutherford was stealing from him, wouldn't he remove him as trustee of his money?"

"I would."

I dialed Bubba.

He answered quickly. "I think I've got the right Daniel Watkins. It was easier than I thought."

"That's great," I said. "I have another favor. Can you check and see if there's any recent record of Hicks changing his trustee on his trust?"

"Is it irrevocable?"

"I'm not sure. Would that matter?"

"Yes. It would require a hearing. If not, then nothing is required unless there is land involved, they usually record that with the county recorder. Want me to check?"

"I'm pretty sure there's land involved."

His fingers clanked on his keyboard. "Hold on. I'll check the county court first."

"You can call me back," I said.

"No, it's okay. It's not—got it. Yes. Ryan Hicks changed his trustee four days ago."

"Who is it now?"

"Ben Cooper." He paused. "Hey, isn't that the guy with the horses?"

Bishop and I made eye contact.

"It is," I said. "Thanks for this. Oh, who's the attorney of record?"

"Denise Nixon. Want her number?"

"Please."

"I'll text it over. Anything else?"

"Not yet. Thanks for the help."

"Any time."

I contacted Cooper on the way to see Rutherford.

"He asked me if I'd be willing to take on that task, and of course, I obliged," he said. "Though I didn't think it would come to pass. I bet the voice-mail I received from a Denise Nixon has something to do with this."

"She's the attorney on record for the filing.

"I'll give her a call back now then. Appreciate you letting me know."

"Let me know what she has to say."

"Sure thing, Rachel."

Rutherford appeared excited to see us when he met us in the lobby. "Have you found Ryan's killer?"

"We're still investigating," Bishop said. "We've got a few more questions for you."

"Sure," he said. "Come on back."

As we walked past three other doors, I casually asked, "Is one of these Ryan's office?"

He kept going, pointing to the one ahead. "He doesn't have an official one, but he used this one for meetings."

In his office he offered us drinks, but we declined. "So, what questions do you have for me?" His phone vibrated on his desk. Without checking it, he closed it in a drawer. "My apologies. My clients tend to be a bit high maintenance."

"Can you verify who filed for the divorce?" Bishop asked.

"Yes, it was Ryan. I had my assistant make a copy of the petition for you." He handed Bishop a file on his desk. "There is other information in there as well."

His receptionist carefully opened his office door. "Mr. Rutherford. I'm sorry to bother you, but Lara Hicks is on the line."

His upper lip twitched slightly. "Please tell her I'm in a meeting."

"I did, sir, but this is her third call today. She says it's urgent, and that you haven't returned her calls."

"What line?" he asked.

"Two."

"Thank you." He picked up the line as she left the room. "Mrs. Hicks, as I said before, I will only speak to your attorney. If you have something to say, please do so through him." He set the receiver back on its base. "My apologies again."

"Does she call you often?" I asked.

"When she wants money, yes."

"Does Mr. Hicks share a bank account with his wife?" Knowing the answer made it even more important to ask the question.

"He opened one in both their names. I transfer money into it every month. It's part of the separation terms."

"And you have access to all his accounts, correct?"

He nodded. "I managed his money as well as his life."

"Including the school project?" I asked.

"Except that. It was his project. He wanted skin in the game, if you will."

"But you still had access to it?" I asked.

"Of course. If necessary, I handled things for him when he couldn't."

"Like when he went to rehab?" Bishop asked.

Rutherford cleared his throat and said a shaky, "Yes."

Bishop nodded. "About that. How come you didn't tell us?"

"I wanted to maintain his privacy. I made him that promise."

"Mr. Rutherford," I said, "Ryan Hicks was murdered. That kind of information is crucial to our investigation. We lost time having to hear about it elsewhere." That wasn't exactly the case, but he didn't need to know that.

"I apologize. In retrospect, I see my mistake."

"Can you tell us about his addiction?" I asked.

Rutherford's face went blank. "I'm not sure I understand."

"As you said, you managed his life. Was he high often? Did he deplete any bank accounts or have any run-ins with his dealer?"

He held up a hand. "Ryan's addiction wasn't like the people you see on the news. In fact, I wouldn't have called him an addict, but it wasn't my call."

"What would you call him then?" I asked. I scanned the items on his desk. A pen and pencil set in an opened case. Several notepads. His coffee cup, half full, a laptop, multiple files, and a crystal paperweight with a photo of him and Hicks inside.

"He didn't spend his time focused on drugs. He continued to function, but he felt his reliance on painkillers had become problematic. Opioid addiction is all over the news, and I believe he wanted to make sure he didn't fall into the trap others had."

"Did you ever tell him that?" I asked.

"He never asked."

"Were you here when Slider Johnson and his attorney met with Ryan?" Bishop asked.

He waited a moment before answering. "I stepped into the meeting briefly, yes."

"According to Mr. Johnson, there was an issue with accessing Mr. Hicks's accounts."

"Yes, it appeared that way, but I realized Ryan was attempting with an old password. He'd asked me to change them last month."

"And you did the same?"

"I'm sorry?"

Bishop cocked his head to the side. "Attempted to access with an old password. Mr. Johnson said you tried to gain access as well and couldn't."

He blinked. "Oh, yes. Since I'm rarely in those accounts, I'd completely forgotten about it. After Slider and his attorney left, I realized the mistake after the meeting ended."

"Got it," Bishop replied. "And you cleared that up with Mr. Hicks?"

"Yes. Of course. Accessing the accounts was no longer an issue."

"Except Mr. Hicks told the other investors it was," I said.

He furrowed his brow. "I wasn't aware of that, and I can't offer any reasons he might have done it."

"It's also come to our attention that Mr. Johnson's contribution to the fund was one and a half million, not twenty-five thousand."

"As I said, I'm not actively involved in the project, so I don't have all the details."

"That's strange," I said, "given you and Mr. Hicks were so close."

"I believe I told you before that Ryan wanted to handle it himself. I think it was a distraction from the divorce." He cleared his throat again.

"Were you able to put together that list of people you thought might have something against Mr. Hicks?" Bishop asked.

"About that," he said. "After thinking it through, I couldn't come up with anyone outside of a few players who weren't thrilled when he retired, but that was so long ago now, I didn't think it was necessary to provide."

What was he hiding?

"We'd like the list anyway," Bishop said.

I had my pen and notepad ready, as did Bishop, so I asked him for the names, and jotted them down. Two, both former MLB players, had moved to other countries, one lived on a ranch in Montana last I'd heard, and the other died in an auto accident last year. Either he'd lied before and planned this to cover his lie, or he was lying about the names right to our faces. Either way, we'd have Bubba check them out and see what sewage he could uncover.

"Did you have any disagreements with Mr. Hicks?" Bishop asked.

"As I said, we were friends and business partners. I am his advisor in many aspects of his life. Did we have arguments? Of course, but they were rare and always quickly resolved." He stared at Bishop and then me. "Do you think I killed him?"

"We're just asking questions," I said.

He smiled, a sleek, yet annoyed smile. "Very well. I appreciate your efforts to find Ryan's killer, but I do have other clients and must take care of them as well." He stood. "Please keep me updated."

"Mr. Rutherford," I asked. "We'd like a list of businesses you shared with Mr. Hicks."

I watched his Adam's apple move up and down. "It's only two. Both are real estate investment companies. We own HR LLC and RH LLC. The first flips homes and the second owns three commercial buildings. Management is done by a small staff. We haven't actively pursued any new purchases in over a year."

"And who manages the companies?"

He opened the center drawer of his desk and handed me two business cards. "I'll authorize them to give you whatever you need."

I waited back as he walked around the desk and opened the door.

～

We were barely clear of the King Tower's shadow when Bishop slammed the gas, fusing onto 400 with a grit that matched my mood. Our interview with Rutherford had coated my thoughts with a slick residue, like oil over water, everything clear but somehow tainted. I knew he was involved, maybe even responsible, for the murder, but connecting him felt daunting. I watched Atlanta's skyline shrink in my side-view mirror, a jagged line against a blazing sun as I assembled my thoughts. "You believe him?" I asked, my voice barely carrying over the hum of the Charger's engine.

Bishop's grip on the steering wheel tightened, his knuckles whitening. "About as much as I believe in Santa," he grumbled. His speed flirted aggressively with the legal limit as he weaved in and out of traffic.

"That much?" I said jokingly.

"He's connected. I'm not sure he's the one who pulled the trigger, but he played a part in Hicks's murder. We'll know more if Jimmy can get the warrant."

"I agree." Traffic thinned as we left the city's pulse behind. I stared out the window. "What if he tried to access the accounts and couldn't, and he found out he'd been removed as Hicks's trustee? That's serious motive."

"The warrant should be ready. We'll bring it to Cohen's office and get what we need. If Rutherford's been dipping into Hicks's funds or setting himself up for a big payout upon Hicks's death, it'll show up in the records."

"How bout we get Bubba and two officers to deliver the warrant to Cohen. He can assist in getting what we need. Hopefully, it won't be much."

"He'll give copies or computers, but he won't be happy," Bishop said.

"That's not our problem. We'll take Michels and Levy to the house and go through everything there. I'll have Levy contact Rutherford's office and finagle information on his plans for the afternoon. I'd rather go there with the warrant without him around. He'll show up, but we need the element of surprise."

"Okay," Bishop confirmed, his tone brooking no argument. His gaze flicked to the rearview mirror, then back to the road. A muscle ticked in his cheek. He was chewing over the possibilities as much as I was. "Communication records might be more telling. If he's threatened Hicks or even hinted at something about the changes in Hicks's trust, the school, or anything, it could be enough to bring him in for more questioning." His hand shifted, the signal to change lanes clicking in a steady beat.

"That'll be covered in our warrant for Hicks's place."

"Let's get Nikki back to the house with us and have her look for anything associated with Rutherford around Hicks's personal files, his home office, laptops, etc. DNA, fingerprints, fibers," he listed. "Hell, even a partial print on that note left at your place could tie him to this." He exited 400 on Windward Parkway and headed toward the road to the department. "His body language was off, Ryder. Too controlled. Like he's practiced in the mirror."

I nodded, remembering the way Rutherford's eyes had dodged mine, the slight tremor in his fingers as he opened his desk drawer. "People don't get that polished unless they've got cracks to fill."

We met Levy and Michels in the pit, walking out of Jimmy's office.

"How'd it go with Jerome White?" Bishop asked.

"Come on in," Jimmy said. "We'll go over that again and your talk with Rutherford."

We stood inside Jimmy's office. Liz Sanders sat in front of his desk. "Would you like me to leave?" she asked Jimmy.

"No. You need to hear this as well. Just keep what's important private."

"Yes, sir."

"I'll do a quick rehash of our talk with White," Levy said. "They were having an affair. It started about six months prior to Ryan Hicks filing for divorce, but the affair ended two months ago."

"But she said she was with him at the time of the murder," Bishop said.

"He verified that," Levy said. "She came to him begging him to take her back."

"But he didn't?" Bishop asked.

Michels chimed in. "Nope. Said she'd made all these promises about their future and what she'd get from Hicks from the start, but he was never in it for any of that. He thought they had something, but he realized he was a pawn in her game, and he wanted out."

"Who initially ended it?" I asked.

"Him," Levy said. "She didn't take it well."

"He had a lot to say about her and Hicks though. During those six months she brought him to the house often. He heard a lot of their conversations," Michels added. "He's willing to come in and put it all on record."

"Good. When's that happening?" I asked.

"As soon as possible. Just say the word."

"Let's move on that. What about Rutherford?" Jimmy asked.

"We can't confirm whether he's involved or not, but we're heading that direction," Bishop said. "Bubba confirmed Hicks removed him as his trustee."

Michels whistled. "That sounds like motive right there."

"Right," I said. "He's also received multiple calls and possibly text messages from Lara Hicks, some while we've been present. He claims it's her wanting money, but I'm not so sure."

"We've got the warrants," Jimmy said. "We can go through Hicks's place and pull everything related to Rutherford. I'll get Bubba on phone records."

"We'd like to have Bubba take two sleeves to Cohen's office and get copies of everything," Bishop said. "He can make sure we're getting it all."

"The four of us will go to the house and do a full sweep. Nikki needs to come and check documents, computers, desk drawers, whatever she can find, for Rutherford's prints."

"Do we have his prints on file?" Jimmy asked.

"I'm not sure," I said.

He nodded. "It's a good idea to check. I'll call Nikki," he said. "Let her know."

"Actually," I said, "I've got a few questions for her. I'll let her know."

"All right," he said. "Let's get a move on this. The mayor's climbing deeper up my ass for an arrest."

"Sounds enjoyable," Bishop said.

"Not even a little."

I hurried to the lab.

"Hey," Nikki said. "I've pulled prints from your note, but so far, there's no match in the system."

"I didn't think there would be," I said. "Speaking of prints. We've got a warrant for Hicks's home and office. We need you to come with us and check for prints in his home office."

"Am I looking for someone specific?"

"Colin Rutherford."

"Is he in IAFIS?" she asked.

The Federal Bureau of Investigation managed IAFIS, the integrated automated fingerprint identification system, a national criminal history system that allows for the electronic storage, exchange, and comparison of fingerprints. "I was hoping you could get one of your interns to check."

She smiled. "I'll get Taylor on it. When are we leaving?"

"As soon as you're ready."

"Give me five."

12

Given that Hicks was a national celebrity, Jimmy arranged for a professional to repair the door and lock immediately after the coroner removed Hicks's body. Normally, this responsibility would fall on the family, but delaying posed risks of theft, squatters, and media backlash. Thankfully, they hadn't changed the lock. We arrived at the house in two separate cars, with Nikki in the tech van. Bishop killed the engine, and we all paused for a moment, absorbing the gravity of the task ahead. "We'll find something," he said.

"We have to. We need something to break this thing open," I said.

I climbed out of Bishop's cruiser and headed toward Michels and Levy in front of us.

"I'm still amazed at this place," Michels muttered as he closed his vehicle's door. "It's a fortress."

I said, "Let's hope his files aren't as well-guarded as a fortress," and headed to the door.

The others followed.

Nikki and Carl trailed behind us with their kits ready. "Start with the office," I directed. "That's ground zero for anything related to his financials and communications. We'll search the rest of the house first. When you're done, let us know."

Bishop directed the rest of us. "Split up. We'll cover more ground quickly. Shout if you find anything out of the ordinary. I'll start with the bedroom again. I doubt I'll find anything since we already swept it, but it's worth a shot. Then I'll hit the kids' rooms."

Michels and I stormed into the kitchen. He attacked the junk drawer first, rifling through old receipts, dead batteries, and takeout menus. He probed the back of the drawer for a false bottom but uncovered nothing. Undeterred, he ripped open cabinets, scrutinizing each one for hidden compartments, dissecting spice containers, and flipping over the hanging pots and pans, inspecting each lid and bottom meticulously. I climbed on the counter where I could see the top of the cabinets, encountering only dust and a few dead bugs. "You got this?" I asked.

"Got it," he said.

I walked into the main living space to help Levy. "Find anything?"

"What's to find in this space?" she asked. "I checked inside the fireplace. Just starting on the bookshelves." While she inspected the built-ins, thumbing through hardcovers and paperbacks, feeling for loose pages or hidden notes, I pulled up the floor rugs in there and the front foyer, tapping the floor for any hollow pieces.

Levy crouched in front of the cabinets at the bottom of the built-ins, extracting stacks of magazines and unveiling carved boxes that contained an assortment of coasters and remotes. She flipped each remote, inspecting battery compartments. Sometimes people taped spare keys or notes inside them, though I wasn't sure why. Everyone replaced remote batteries, so anything hidden would be easy to find.

I looked back towards the kitchen, hearing the clink of Michels handling glassware as he examined wine glasses and searched under the sink. "Anything?" I called out.

"Just a really expensive taste in wine and a leaky faucet," he replied, his voice echoing slightly.

I moved to the drapes, running my hands along the curtain rods and pausing to examine the heavy fabric for anything sewn into the hems. Meanwhile, Levy lifted cushions and felt between the couch sections again.

Her hand emerged with a small, crumpled piece of paper. She unfolded it, revealing a hastily written note with an address and a time. No names, just that. "Got something," she announced, her eyes locking with mine.

She handed me the paper. "Call it in. See if we can get something on it."

She contacted dispatch and gave them the address.

"I'll be upstairs," I said.

"I'll check the media room and the rest of the main floor," Michels said.

"I'll help," Levy said after disconnecting her call. She smiled at me. "It's a hotel in Alpharetta off Union Hill."

"Let's put a pin in that until we finish," I said. "I'm heading upstairs to help Bishop."

The kids' bedrooms looked practically unlived in. The beds were arranged neatly, with nothing out of place at first glance. I yanked open drawers, peered under beds, and scoured closets in each room. Clothes hung in meticulous order, shoes paired neatly below. In one walk-in closet, behind a row of winter coats, I spotted a small, fireproof safe resting on the floor. No key in sight. I shouted to Bishop.

"Can you pick this?" I asked.

"Fire safes are hard to break, you know that," he dangled a set of keys. "But I found these in a dopp kit in one of the kids' bathrooms."

"Interesting place for a set of keys," I said.

None fit. "We'll have to bring this one back with us," Bishop decided, marking it down in his notebook.

I was searching through a guest bedroom when Michels called out, a hint of excitement in his voice. "Found a stash of envelopes!"

We all hurried to the room, Levy taking the stairs two steps at a time.

He'd found them neatly tied with a shoestring stashed at the back of a drawer in the chest beneath a false bottom—a classic hiding spot. None were sealed or addressed to anyone.

He opened the first one and read it out loud. "In the quiet hours, I think of us. There's a certain thrill in keeping our secret, isn't there? Each stolen moment feels like a victory against a world that isn't ready for us yet. But here, in these lines, it's just you and me—no need to hide." He cleared his throat and grimaced. "Who writes this crap?"

"That's a good question," Bishop asked. "We'll go through them at the department."

"I need another evidence bag," he said.

"I've got two," Levy said. "Look at this." She held up a prescription bottle with Ryan's name on it. Inside, a small bag of white powder. "I found this in a man's jacket in the closet downstairs." She sealed the bottle in an evidence bag.

We finished upstairs and headed back downstairs to the office, hoping Nikki would allow us to do our thing while she and Carl did theirs.

The office sprawled with imposing bookshelves lining the walls. A massive oak desk commanded the center of the room, flanked by a fireplace on the left side. A desktop computer and a laptop occupied the desk alongside perfectly arranged stacks of documents.

Nikki said, "Obviously, we've got fingerprints on everything. Carl's been documenting where each item was found before we pack it up."

"Good job," Bishop said. "Can we go through anything now?"

"We haven't touched the stuff on the shelves, so be careful."

"Yes, ma'am," he said. He and Michels headed straight for the shelves, sifting through the books and awards with methodical precision, examining the titles and pulling each book to check behind it. "People hide keys, envelopes, sometimes cash behind these things."

"We found folders labeled by year and category in the locked part of the desk," Nikki said. "Taxes, property deeds, investment portfolios. Put the letters together. I'll have Carl go through them back at the department and summarize them on a spread sheet. That way, you won't have to go through them yourselves."

"Thanks," I said, then got back to the desk. I pulled out a folder marked 'Insurance.' "Jackpot," I said, flipping it open to find several policies. "Life insurance and look at this," I showed Levy the file. "Hicks recently changed the beneficiary for a five-million-dollar policy." I flipped through the papers stapled to it. "The previous policy is attached. Rutherford was the beneficiary, and the new one is Ben Cooper."

"What the hell happened with those two?" she asked.

"It's looking more and more like Hicks had reason to believe his theory about Rutherford stealing from him was true."

"There's another policy in a different folder," Nikki said. "The wife was the original beneficiary, but it was changed to Cooper too."

"Keep digging," Bishop said. "There's got to be more."

The breakthrough came when Carl called out from underneath the desk. He held up a small, brass key with an intricate design. "What do you think this is for?"

"Any idea where the safe is?" Levy asked.

"I bet it's for the lockbox in the son's bedroom," I said.

"Let's give it a shot," Bishop said.

"Don't open it here," I cautioned. "Let's maintain chain of custody. Everything gets opened back at the station under proper protocols."

Nikki and Carl moved through the room, dusting for prints on the safe, the desk, the computers, even the doorknobs. "We'll take the computers and hard drives," she said, making a checklist. "Michels, can you and Bishop handle the desktop?"

Together, they unplugged the cables, ensuring we documented everything before disturbing it. Carl photographed our actions, preserving the state of the room as we worked.

"Everything from this room needs to be cataloged and bagged," Nikki instructed. "We've done so with what we've found so far, but let's make sure we get it all."

Four hours and six growling stomachs later, we'd finished loading Nikki's van and headed back to the department.

"Nikki will run the prints against the system and see who we can match within the scope of the investigation," Bishop said.

"Which is limited to who? Lara Hicks?" I asked.

"Pretty much."

"Doesn't leave us much of a chance of catching the killer from prints."

He glanced my direction. "Did you think it would?"

"No, but it would be nice to have a golden ticket like that. Case closed."

He laughed. "Has that ever happened to you?"

"No. You?" I said.

"Nope."

∾

Susan laid out a spread of Mexican food on the investigation room table. Like the Chick-Fil-A, Bishop and I smelled it from the hallway and had nearly knocked each other down to get to it.

She walked out as we walked in. "Food's inside."

"You're a Godsend," I said.

She smiled. "So I'm told."

Nikki appeared in the door, moaned, then filled a plate with food. "I'll start analyzing the prints now. Carl's unloading the things from the house and logging it into evidence. What do you want him to bring here?"

"All the files," I said.

"I'll take the computers," Bubba said. He stuffed a chip into his mouth. "Please."

"Sure thing."

Levy and Michels arrived.

"What took you so long?" I asked.

She raised an eyebrow. "Do you want the details of our potty breaks?"

"We'll pass," Bishop said just as Michels opened his mouth to say something no one ever needed to hear.

"Bubba," I said, "can you give us an update on Cohen's search?"

"The guy's place is a train wreck, but he showed us where everything was, and I made copies of what I thought might matter. It's account information, and I'll be honest, I don't understand half of it. Jimmy said to get him to agree to update us if he found something we should know, and he agreed."

"Where's the stuff you brought back?" Bishop asked.

"Nikki's got it. One of her interns is supposed to be cataloging it."

"Thanks," he said. He looked at me. "Can we pin that until we find something that points us in that direction?"

"You mean until Cohen finds something that points us in that direction?"

He smiled.

"Good idea. When we need concrete proof about Rutherford, we'll have to dig into that hurricane of an office."

"I feel for you," Bubba said.

We took a fifteen-minute break to eat and talk about anything except the investigation. Running hard on a case rarely allowed for downtime, but sometimes, it was what we needed most. Unfortunately, that downtime didn't last.

Susan walked back into the room.

"You're still here?" Bishop asked.

"I was just leaving when I took a call for the chief. Alpharetta PD is on line one. It's important."

"Thanks," I said as she walked out.

Levy, closest to the phone, grabbed it and put it on speaker. "This is Detective Lauren Levy. I'm with four other detectives, and you're on speaker. How can we help you?"

"This is Sargent Bellwood with the Alpharetta PD. We received a call from Marsha Lance regarding her daughter, Lara Hicks."

We all stopped eating.

"Mrs. Lance has been trying to contact her daughter for twenty-four hours and has received no response. We executed a wellness check and found the door to her residence broken open."

"A robbery?" Levy asked.

"Based on the condition of the residence we believe we're dealing with a possible abduction."

"Sargent Bellwood, this is Detective Rob Bishop. What points you that direction?"

"Mrs. Hicks's cell phone and purse are still in the residence. There are signs of a struggle, and it appears someone was injured, but we don't believe it to be severe. We're currently gathering evidence, but given the scope of your current investigation into Ryan Hicks's murder, with your agreement, we plan to hand this over to you."

"We'll be right there," Bishop said.

"Thank you," Bellwood said and disconnected the call.

Michels dropped a string of cuss words fit for a Chicago Italian. "I'm starving." He grabbed a street taco and shoved half of it into his mouth.

"Grab your plates and let's get on this," Bishop said.

"She contacted Rutherford multiple times," I clipped my equipment belt around my waist. "When we were there earlier today, he told her he'd only talk to her through her attorney. I'll check if he's heard from her again."

"I'll call White and see if he's heard from her," Levy said.

13

We arrived at Lara Hicks's condo to find a crowd clogging the road while police tried to disperse them. An officer pointed Bishop to a line of police cruisers parked in front of the building. The Alpharetta PD restricted entrance to the building, allowing only those with proof of residence inside.

"Hamby PD," Bishop said to an officer at the door. "We've got four and a tech van with two."

"Welcome to the chaos, Detective." He allowed us through.

He wasn't kidding about the chaos. Lara's previously immaculate condo looked like a cyclone had torn through it. Officer Trevor Miller, a stocky man with a grizzled beard and biceps bigger than my thighs introduced himself. "I'll be overseeing the handover."

Bishop introduced us then asked, "We've been briefed, but do you have anything to add?"

"Yes, sir," he nodded his voice rough. He handed him a paper in a clear evidence bag. "This was on the bed in the master bedroom."

Bishop read the note out loud. "Five million for the wife."

"Kidnapping." Michels muttered a cuss word. "Ain't this icing on the cake?"

"We'll continue our analysis of the scene and provide what we find to your tech team. If we can do anything else, feel free to ask. When you're ready, I'll clear my other men out, and hopefully that will eliminate the crowd downstairs, but I can't promise that."

"Got it," Bishop said. "Has anyone spoken with the neighbors?"

"We've got two men going door to door. I'll get an update from them. Would you like them to continue?"

"Yes, please," he said. He asked the rest of us what we thought about sending the others home.

We decided to keep officers on the neighbors and at the entrances checking for proof of residence.

Levy knelt by the front door, inspecting the contents of Lara's purse strewn across the floor. Lipstick, a wallet, keys, all spilled out and abandoned. "I don't know the woman," she said, "but she's got expensive taste in makeup."

Nikki and Carl walked in. "Whoa," Carl said. "This place is totally fire."

I didn't bother asking what that meant.

Nikki directed him to photograph everything and anything.

Something didn't make sense. "Why would someone kidnap the estranged wife of a dead man for money? Who do they think they can negotiate with?"

"I doubt they thought that far ahead," Bishop said.

"Or it's a scam," Michels said. "Make it look like a kidnapping but it's not."

"Purpose?" Levy asked.

"Maybe she has something the killer wants?" he asked. "Or she's set this scene up to look like an abduction."

"Rutherford said she's been asking for money." I looked at Michels. "Which he can no longer access."

"Does he know that?" he asked.

"If he does, he's not telling us."

"Which means he doesn't think we know about him being removed as trustee and that Ryan thought he was stealing from him."

"He's either covering himself, or he doesn't know," Bishop said.

"Did you talk to him on the way here?" Michels asked.

"Left him a voicemail to call us," I said. "What about Jerome White?"

"Same," he said. "What if they're in on it together? What's the one thing neither have access to?"

"Money," I said.

"Right. They stage this setup, asking for cash. Rutherford's got to know he can't access the funds. It's public information," Michels said. "He's running low on cash or loses access to his credit cards, whatever. He freaks out and sets up this scam with Hicks thinking the trustee will get the money to them."

"Cooper," Bishop and I said in unison.

I caught sight of Lara's cell phone sitting on the coffee table, its screen dark and oddly serene amid the disarray. I motioned for Nikki to look and pointed to the phone. "Make sure we get that to Bubba ASAP." I stepped into the hallway and dialed Cooper.

"Evenin', Rachel," he said politely. "I hope you're calling with good news."

"Not really," I said. "Sorry about that. Has anyone contacted you?"

"About?"

"Someone took Lara Hicks and is asking for five million."

"And I'm the money guy now."

"Right."

"I don't negotiate with kidnappers," he said.

"Neither do we, but if the kidnappers know it's you, and I believe they do, expect a call. I'm sending a team to your place ASAP."

"Do you think this is real?" he asked.

"Not sure, but we have to treat it like it is."

He exhaled. "Send 'em on over. If I get a call before then, I'll let you know."

I rubbed my forehead after killing the call.

Michels opened the door and asked, "Anything?"

"I'm sending a team to Cooper's ranch now in case he gets a call. Can you and Levy babysit?"

"Yes, I'll let her know."

Most police departments employed trained negotiators skilled in crisis and hostage situations. These officers excelled at handling high-pressure scenarios, including communicating effectively with kidnappers. Our growing city and recent spike in crime necessitated such expertise. Jimmy presented the need to the board, and after pressuring them with statistics and crime scene photos, they approved the development of the Hamby PD Negotiation Team. I contacted Jimmy, updated him, and he made the call. Less than thirty minutes later, he called back and confirmed their arrival at Cooper's home.

Bishop and I left the condo as the scene analysis concluded, but instead of heading to Cooper's, dispatch provided Rutherford's home address. After calling him two more times, we drove over.

Rutherford's home didn't match Hicks's in size but surpassed it in pretentiousness.

Bishop surveyed the two story, modern design home from the circular drive. "Completely what I'd expect from the guy. It screams 'look at how rich I am.'"

"You think? All I hear is 'I've got a small trouser snake.'"

"Nice, Ryder."

I laughed. Bishop had a problem with slang terms for the male organ. Michels once asked AI for a list of slang words, and "trouser snake" was my favorite. Bishop insisted he was from a generation that didn't talk about male organs, but I challenged his bluff, citing a string of movies from his past where they'd mentioned it multiple times.

The house was dark, but we knocked on the door and announced ourselves anyway. After three attempts, Bishop tested the handle, but it was locked. "Let's inspect the perimeter, see what we find."

The front windows revealed no activity or dim lights anywhere in our line of vision. The first floor's left side had no windows, and no light shone from the second-floor windows. We advanced to the backyard.

Bishop shone his flashlight at the dark space. "Not bad," he said.

"His deck is bigger than my house," I said.

Designed for parties, the back yard housed a pool, hot tub, large two-story deck, kitchen, modern fireplace, large screen TV on the bottom, covered deck, and God only knew how many places to relax.

Bishop and I checked the large windows on both floors.

"He's not home," he said. "We'll get patrol to keep an eye on the place in case he returns."

We expected to pull an all-nighter at Cooper's place, and on the way there, called our partners to let them know.

"Anything DEA can do?" Kyle asked.

"Tell us who sold to Hicks," I said jokingly.

"I might be able to find that out," he said. "Our CI's might know something."

I hadn't expected that. "That would be great. Thank you."

"I'll come by in the morning if that works for you."

"Hopefully, we'll be home before then, but don't wait up."

"We need to be there, like, ten minutes ago," I murmured, my gaze fixed on the suburban landscape morphing into a blur past the window. Anxiety wasn't just buzzing in my veins—it was screaming, each beat of my heart a sharp, insistent drum. "I want to be there when the call comes through. It has to be tonight."

"Don't bank on it." Bishop's voice cut through the growing tension, his grip on the steering wheel white-knuckled, his jaw a hard line against the dimming light. Suddenly, he swerved, taking a sharp left out of nowhere. "We've got a tail," he hissed, his usual calm laced with a steel edge of anger.

Without a second's pause, he jerked the wheel left again, tires screeching a harsh protest against the asphalt as we plunged into a labyrinth of backstreets.

I flipped down the visor and checked the mirror, catching sight of the black sedan. It lurked a cautious distance away but close enough to keep us in its sight. The sedan faltered, then, like a predator sensing the moment to strike, it accelerated. "It's closing the gap."

"Damn it," Bishop cursed under his breath, his control over the car somehow both reckless and precise. "Hold on." His foot slammed down on the accelerator, our surroundings becoming a blur of shadow and streetlight.

"Dispatch, this is Detective Ryder," I said into the radio, forcing my voice to remain steady despite the jolts. "We have a tail—black sedan, license unconfirmed. We're heading toward Cooper's and need immediate backup."

"Copy, Detective Ryder. I've got your location. Assistance en route. Keep the line open," the dispatcher responded crisply.

The sedan hounded us, shadowing our every twist and turn with unnerving precision. Bishop took another sharp turn, and I braced against the dashboard, my other hand gripping the radio with white-knuckled intensity. The quiet suburban night seemed an alien backdrop to our desperate flight. Bishop's next maneuver was even more drastic; he veered right onto Birmingham Highway, attacking the plethora of curves at a speed that made my stomach churn.

Our vehicle skidded off the road slightly as Bishop took one curve faster than normal. The sedan's headlights, a glaring menace, bore down on us. As we hit a straight stretch, the distant wail of sirens offered a thread of hope.

The driver of the sedan must have heard them too, for they made a bold move, swinging out wide and accelerating with a clear intention to overtake.

"They're trying to box us in!" I shouted, instinctively bracing as the sedan pulled alongside. For a heart-stopping moment, I caught a glimpse of the driver's cold, determined profile through the tinted window.

As the car surged past us, Bishop's response was immediate; he floored the gas, the engine roaring in defiance. The tail became the head.

I yelled, "Gun it!"

The chase peaked in tension, a crescendo of fear and adrenaline when suddenly, the sedan veered down a side road, its brake lights flaring red before it disappeared.

The radio crackled to life again, "Patrol's on the tail on Maple Avenue," dispatch informed us. "Continue to Cooper's. Stay sharp."

"Ten-four," I acknowledged, trying to steady my breathing. Bishop eased off the accelerator slightly, his focus still intense as we continued our drive to Cooper's.

∼

Poor Cooper. Cruisers illuminated his ranch making it feel like daylight.

"I hate how people gather at this stuff. It's as if they revel in other people's misery."

"I'm not sure it's always that. Sometimes it's just curiosity, but this is a big deal because it's connected to an MLB player," Bishop said.

"How do they know that?" I asked. "It's not at his house. It's not at her condo. For all they know it could be a basic breaking and entering."

He laughed. "With this kind of police coverage?"

"I know." I exited Bishop's cruiser. "And criminals will take advantage of that. We'll probably see an uptick in break-ins tonight. Both home and vehicle."

"I don't doubt that."

Jimmy arrived in his personal vehicle and not-so-politely ordered everyone back to work. The lot cleared quickly. He walked over to us. "Patrol can't find the guy that followed you, but we've got a BOLO." He nodded to me. "You okay?"

I gently touched my face. Did I not look okay? "I'm all good," I said, hopefully erasing whatever he might have seen. I hated showing weakness and, more so, fear, but sometimes micro expressions slide onto my face without me realizing it.

Inside, electric tension charged Ben Cooper's first floor. Our negotiation response team, four men who'd transferred to the department from different states, had set up a temporary command post, their equipment strewn across the dining room table. The equipment, all new and a budget buster, hummed and beeped. Bubba sat at the far end of the table, his fingers flying over the keyboard as he configured the tracing software and connected the various pieces of equipment needed to monitor the call. He looked up briefly, his usually jovial expression replaced with one of intense concentration.

Cooper sat in an armchair, white-knuckling the armrests, then stood when he saw us.

"How's it going?" I asked.

"This isn't what I signed on for when I agreed to be the trustee. I thought I'd get a manager for the money and just scribble my signature on a bunch of paperwork, and not for at least another thirty years or so."

"Understood," I said.

"They've got the latest and greatest equipment," Bishop said. "Hopefully, this will all be handled with one call."

Jimmy appeared beside me. "SWAT is ready to go. Once we get a trace on the call, we'll get them out there. All you have to do is keep them on the line."

Cooper nodded. "Got any suggestions on how to do that?"

I walked over to the team and asked Jim Scott, the lead, "Who's briefing Cooper on answering the call?"

"I am," he said. "Just finished set up." He walked with me back to Cooper and said, "Mr. Cooper, your main goal in this is to keep the caller on the line. If the signal is good, our equipment should determine the location in roughly ten to twenty seconds, but that's not always the case. Once we have it, you'll need to continue the conversation to give SWAT time to get to the location."

"How am I supposed to do that?"

"Engage the caller in conversation. Ask open-ended questions and ask them to repeat themselves. You're going to be writing it down, not for us, but to give the appearance of your emotions tied into this. Even though it's not video, they'll know if you're faking it, so you have to be as authentic as possible. Ask for proof that Mrs. Hicks is still alive. Ask them how they want the money, and anything related to the instructions they provide. They'll tell you no cops, so agree to that. Let them know it's going to take some time to get the money, especially since you've just been appointed trustee." He paused then added, "Any questions?"

Cooper shook his head. "I think I've got it."

I moved closer to him. "You've got this. Just take deep breaths and remember to do what Scott explained."

"It's not going to be a problem to appear authentic. My gut is twisted into a knot already."

Bishop squeezed his shoulder. "We know that feeling well."

Scott stood by the dining table, reviewing notes and coordinating with the other team members. His calm demeanor helped to steady the room, but I knew inside he was just as anxious as the rest of us. Cooper sat at the table in front of his phone, staring at it, probably willing it to ring like the rest of us.

Bishop paced the room. I checked on Bubba, curious to see the software in action.

"This is the coolest thing I've done," he said.

I smiled at his excitement. We were in the middle of a tense situation, and the guy was giddy to do his job.

The minutes crawled by, each second stretching into an eternity. I glanced at the clock on the wall, willing the call to come soon. The waiting was the hardest part. We had no idea if Lara Hicks was still alive or if they would return her safely.

Suddenly, the phone shrieked, cutting through the tense silence. Cooper flinched, but Scott was quick to act, snatching up the phone and putting it on speaker.

"Hello?" Cooper said, his voice calm and professional.

"Good evening, sir," a woman's voice said cheerfully. "My name is Stephanie and I'm calling from Prince—"

Scott killed the call then shook his head. "Telemarketer."

Cooper let out a shaky breath. Levy and Michels had been outside but walked over.

"SWAT'S holding steady at two separate locations," Levy said. "It would help if we had a clue where they're holding Hicks."

"They'll get there quickly."

"They've got two drones ready and waiting as well," Michels said. "That way, if he moves, they'll be able to follow him."

If he doesn't shoot them down, I thought.

We went back to waiting, the tension in the room ratcheting up another notch.

A few more minutes passed, feeling like hours, and then the phone rang again, that time flashing *blocked number*.

14

Cooper looked to Scott, who nodded. He tapped answer. He took a deep breath and said, "This is Ben Cooper."

"Mr. Cooper, you have something I want," the voice said. "You will follow my instructions exactly, or Lara dies. Do you understand?"

The kidnapper used a cheap voice changer app, but it worked well enough that we couldn't determine the gender.

Bubba gave me a thumbs-up, indicating the trace was active. I watched as the seconds ticked by on the screen, willing Cooper to work to keep the kidnapper talking.

"Yes, I understand, but I need to know if Lara is okay."

"She won't be if you don't do as I say."

"I understand, but please," Cooper said, "just let me talk to her for a second." He paused then, his tone more demanding and confident, said, "If you can't show me she's alive, we're done."

Labored breathing came through the speaker, followed by the muffled rustling of movement, as if the kidnapper shifted the phone around. Faint, indistinct background noises emerged—the distant hum of machinery and the echoing sounds of a large, empty space.

Everyone in the room remained silent, listening to the sounds coming through the phone, hoping to make a connection to the location.

Bubba quietly tapped on the laptop.

I strained to listen, my heart pounding in my chest. I made out the muffled sound of footsteps and a door creaking open, followed by a slight echo that suggested the kidnapper moved through a larger area.

"Talk," the kidnapper commanded, but not to Cooper. Harshness and cruelty laced the tone, sending chills down my spine.

A rustle followed and then a soft whimper came through the phone. "This is Lara Hicks. Please do what he says, or he's going to kill me. I can't leave my babies."

The kidnapper hadn't used the voice changer on her. I recognized her voice. Scott looked at Bishop and me. We both nodded.

"No cops," the kidnapper said. "I've got people watching your place. If they see any cops, she dies. Understand?"

We knew then the kidnapper worked alone. He wouldn't have made the call if someone had eyes on Cooper's ranch.

"No cops," Cooper said. "What do you want?"

"Five million, in unmarked bills," the voice said.

"It's going to take some time for me to get that."

"Make it happen or she dies."

"I'm the trustee. I have to go through a process to get the money. I need time."

"You've got twenty-four hours or she's dead."

Cooper's expression changed to panic as he fought desperately to keep the caller on the line.

Bubba jumped out of his seat flashing one thumb up at the team. One thumb up meant he connected the trace. Two meant he had the location.

Levy, Michels, and Jimmy stood behind him, watching the laptop do its thing.

"Okay," Cooper said. "Where am I meeting you?"

"You're not meeting me," the caller said. "Put the money in a black, nylon travel bag and at seven p.m. tomorrow, place the bag inside the Bell Memorial Park's concession stand number three garbage can. We'll be watching. If we see any cops, she's dead. Got it?"

"Bell Memorial Park," Cooper said. He scribbled the information down. "What concession stand?"

The caller repeated himself then said, "Got it?"

"Yes, I've got it," Cooper said. "I'm not sure I can get the money by then. It might take longer. What—how do we handle that?"

"Do it or she dies." The line went dead.

I dropped my head. "Damn it."

Bubba cursed softly. "Not enough time. He's using a burner phone, but I managed to narrow it down to a few blocks. It's something to go on." He eyed Scott. "We need to move fast."

One of the team jotted down the information and got on the radio with the SWAT commander.

Scott put a hand on Cooper's shoulder. "You did great, Mr. Cooper. We'll get her back."

Cooper nodded. "What do I do now?"

"It's likely the kidnapper planned for the trace," Scott said, "And they're going to be watching you."

"What happens next?" he asked.

"You'll have to go through the motions to get the money," Bishop said.

"And we need to wait for the next call," Scott added.

"All units," Jimmy said on the radio and then gave the general area of the trace. "SWAT is already in route." He explained that the drones were already heading to the general area. "It's not far from here," he said. "I want all units canvassing the area. I repeat. All units, canvass the area." He looked at Bishop and me. "Levy and Michels are already in route. Go."

I patted Cooper on the shoulder and rushed to Bishop's vehicle.

Bishop raced through the darkened streets of Hamby as the SWAT team's chatter crackled over the radio, their voices urgent and clipped. Bubba had traced the kidnapper's call to a one-mile radius of an industrial park on the city's border, and every second counted.

The SWAT commander's voice blared through the radio. "Team Alpha, proceed to the north entrance. Team Bravo, take the south. Acknowledge."

Both teams responded.

"All units, be advised," the commander said. "The victim is believed to be with the kidnapper." He described Lara Hicks. "Our objective is to apprehend the suspect alive. Repeat, we need the suspect alive for questioning. Use non-lethal force where possible and proceed with caution. Safety of the hostage is paramount. Acknowledge."

Both teams acknowledged.

"If I were in his place, I'd be in that industrial park. There are two warehouses unoccupied there," Bishop said. He spoke into his radio and repeated what he had just said to me and provided the location of the empty warehouses.

The SWAT commander acknowledged and dispatched one team to each warehouse.

I focused on the area as the park came into view. "Lots of places to hide."

Bishop skidded the car to a stop just outside the perimeter where SWAT units had already secured the area and set up the command post. Two slick sleeves stood beside it. Two drones buzzed overhead, their cameras scanning for any sign of movement.

"The first building is closest," Bishop said.

"Let's go."

As I hurried out of the vehicle, I let the teams know our destination.

Levy spoke next and said, "We'll cover the other warehouse."

Team Alpha had split into groups of ten. We joined the group surrounding the front of the building and moved toward the sides. We approached cautiously, noticing the busted security cameras outside.

A team member's voice burst through the radio. "Broken window on the south side of the building."

My heart pounded as adrenaline flooded my veins. We raced around the corner of the building as the team members sprinted past. They climbed through the window to enter the building.

With a swift, practiced motion, we hoisted ourselves through the broken window, careful not to make any noise. The warehouse was eerily silent as we moved slowly, methodically, sweeping our flashlights across the area.

The high ceilings and exposed metal beams turned the empty warehouse into an echo chamber. Dust coated the concrete floor, a clear sign this building hadn't seen much action lately. In the center of the front wall, a small section enclosed for offices caught my attention. A solid wall separated the area from the main warehouse, accessible through a single metal door marked Office. SWAT had already gone inside.

Bishop flashed his light in that direction as SWAT members from Team Bravo entered through the window. They spread out throughout the warehouse.

"Commander," one of the SWAT members said. "We found a cell phone in an office."

"Stay there," the commander said.

Bishop sprinted ahead of me.

"Copy that," the man replied.

"Team Bravo and the rest of Team Alpha, keep searching the perimeter. He couldn't have gotten far."

The warehouse cleared in a heartbeat. Bishop and I stared at the phone on the floor. Levy and Michels arrived.

"It's got to be the burner," Bishop said. "The rest of the place is clear."

Aside from the phone, the room was completely empty. Michels walked out and disappeared down the small hallway.

"Unless he just stuck her in an office, I don't think he was holding her here. He wouldn't have had time to clean up and leave."

"He knew we traced the call," I said. "He planned for it." I swiped a hair sticking to my forehead. "He's got her somewhere else."

Michels returned. "He broke the window to get in, and he had to exit the same way. The doors require a key to lock."

I snapped pictures with my cell phone.

"Team Bravo, report," the commander's voice crackled through the radio.

"Nothing on our end," came the reply. "Area is clear."

"Team Alpha, report," he said.

"Area all clear."

"Drones picked up nothing," a man said over the line.

"Teams return to command post."

I exchanged a look with Bishop. "We're missing something. He couldn't have just vanished."

Bishop nodded. "Let's walk the area."

Levy and Michels went the opposite direction. Bishop notified the teams of our plan.

The commander said, "Copy that. We're on the ready."

I moved cautiously, scanning windows on every building we passed. The minutes ticked by, each one stretching into an eternity. On the order of the commander, the drones continued their search, but the kidnapper remained elusive.

We scoured the area, looking for any clue that might lead us to Lara Hicks, systematically moving through the industrial park.

Levy's voice crackled through the radio. "Detective Levy. Need assistance at Evans Distribution. Located three buildings south of the warehouse, back side, facing the woods. No souls involved."

The commander acknowledged her request. We rushed over.

"It's a maintenance access," Levy explained. "I don't know for sure, but I think it leads to an underground utility tunnel. I dealt with these all over Philly."

"Most major cities have them," I replied. "I'm going down."

The SWAT lead stopped me. "We've got the tools, Detective. We'll take it from here."

"Is it big enough for a person down there?" Michels asked. "Is it even safe?"

"Yes," Levy responded. "The tunnel is typically constructed from reinforced concrete or steel for durability and to protect the utilities."

"There are multiple access points," I said. "Any manhole, access hatch—"

"And shafts," Levy added.

"Right. We need a team on the manholes."

"We've probably got several thousand all over the city," Bishop said. "Especially with all the new construction. We'll never cover them in time. They could have already climbed out somewhere nearby."

"Maybe the drones will pick them up then?" Michels asked.

"Maybe," I said. "The kidnapper planned this. They knew about the tunnel, so they probably planned where to exit."

"Hicks could be dead already," Michels said.

Bishop shook his head. "The kidnapper loses their negotiating power without her." He looked at me. "They're going to call Cooper again."

I got on the radio and reported that we were returning to the house.

15

I called Kyle on the way back to Cooper's ranch and updated him on the situation.

"Anything I can do to help?" he asked.

Bishop responded before I had the chance but said the same thing I would have. "Bring food."

He laughed. "I'll see you soon."

Bishop called Cathy and had a similar conversation, minus the food and appearance at the ranch.

"No calls yet," Jimmy said as we all walked inside the house. "I called the public works director. They can get Bubba a map of the manholes, but they need to print a map. It's not standard size, so they've got to wait until the UPS Store opens."

"The kidnapper won't stay in the tunnel," Levy said. "Too risky."

"Bubba could use the map to check street cameras," Michels said.

Jimmy shook his head. "He's got to be ready when the call comes in."

"What about Carl?" I asked. "Can he do it?"

He thought about that for a moment. "I'll talk with Nikki first thing. I'm sure she'll pull him off whatever they're doing for this."

Scott motioned for Jimmy to follow him to the kitchen.

I tried calling Rutherford again, but he didn't answer. "Call's going straight to voicemail," I said. "What about Daniel Watkins? He's been MIA."

"An obsessed fan kidnapping his obsession's spouse," Bishop said. "That's a stretch."

"It could be a John Hinckley Jr. thing," Michels said.

"But why kill the obsession first and then kidnap the wife?" Levy asked.

He was right. Logic, if there could be any in a psychopath's mind, would say kidnap the wife to manipulate the obsession.

"We've got this wrong. It's not Ryan he's obsessed with. It's the wife," I said.

Bishop's eyes lit up. "He wasn't stalking him. He was stalking her."

"And he killed Ryan because he had some delusional warped fantasy that she would be free to be with him," Levy said.

"Got it," Michels said. "He kills Hicks thinking that will endear him to Lara, but when it doesn't work, he kidnaps her."

"He's going to kill her," I said. "We need a BOLO out on him now."

"I've got it," Michels said and began the process.

"Ryder, get Nowak on the phone," Bishop said. "We need access to Watkins's phone records, financials, and to search his entire house."

"I'm on it," I said.

"I'll talk to Bubba about his social media accounts," Levy said.

Jimmy noticed us taking action and walked back over. "Did we get something?"

"We think it's Watkins," Bishop said. "His obsession isn't with Ryan, it's his wife."

"You have a reason for this theory?"

"He's been MIA since the murder."

"Good enough for me, but what about Rutherford?"

"Not sure yet," Bishop said. He tapped my shoulder while I talked to Nowak. "Let's get to Watkins's house."

"I'll get backup now," Jimmy said. He pointed to Levy and Michels. "You two stay here. Wait for the next call."

Bishop and I hurried to his cruiser just as Kyle arrived.

"Damn, he's bringing the food," I said. I rushed to his window and gave him the 411.

"Here," he said, checking a bag from the all-night Chinese place by our house, then handing it to me. "It's sesame chicken and rice."

"You're the best," I said and added, "Love you," as I climbed into Bishop's vehicle.

Thank God Bishop had to-go silverware from other restaurants in his glove compartment. Poor guy had to eat the sesame chicken with his fingers while he drove, but he didn't seem to care.

Watkins lived in an older part of Hamby, one still untouched by new builds. We rolled up to a completely dark house and a front porch he used for a storage shed, passed it, then parked down the street where three cruisers waited.

We stood under the eerie glow of the streetlamp preparing to search the home as soon as an officer arrived with the warrant.

"Watkins could be hiding inside," Bishop said, his voice a low whisper. "He's got a stalking history with the victims and could be agitated and paranoid. We don't know if he's got Lara Hicks with him, so proceed cautiously. Consider him armed and dangerous."

The three patrol officers nodded.

"We'll start with the exterior. You three take the right side and move to the back. We'll take the left and do the same."

"If there are no signs of occupancy, we'll try entering through the front, but it may be necessary to enter with force," I said.

Patrol officers carried rams and pry bars in their vehicles. Bishop did not. "Then we use one of your rams to gain entry. We need to be prepared for anything. This guy's dangerous, and we can't take any chances."

One of the other officers, Davis, adjusted the strap of his tactical vest. "I'll get my pry bar and ram."

As we spoke, another cruiser pulled up, its headlights cutting through the darkness. Officer Carter stepped out, a folded piece of paper in his hand. He approached us quickly, his footsteps echoing in the stillness. "Judge Nowak signed the warrant," he said, handing it to Bishop. "We're clear to enter and search the entire property."

"Great." Bishop took the warrant and read it over quickly before nodding. "That gives us the authority we need." He pointed to one of the other officers. "You take Carter and stay on the front of the house, instead of checking the perimeter. Be prepared for a possible exit by Watkins."

"Yes, sir," they said.

Just then, Nikki arrived in her van. She pulled up behind the cruisers and parked.

I walked to her side of the van. "You guys ready for me?" she asked through her open window.

"Just got the warrant. Stay here until we clear the place."

"Got it," she said.

"Do me a favor," I added before walking back to the team. "This guy could be armed. Take the van to another street. We'll get you on the radio when we've got the all-clear."

"Okay," she said and kicked the van into reverse.

"Ready?" Bishop asked when I rejoined the team.

I nodded.

"Yes, sir," the men said.

We separated, heading different directions in the event Watkins tried to run. The home's dilapidated state became glaringly obvious up close. We reached the edge of the property then waited until we saw the officers before we moved.

Finally, we moved cautiously around the left side of the house, the beams of our flashlights cutting through the darkness.

As we reached the back corner, Rob motioned for me to stop. "It's just the one floor," he said. "Most of these homes didn't have crawl spaces."

I peered through a window, but the home was completely dark. I pointed my flashlight into the room. The beam landed on a photo of Lara Hicks. I moved it an inch to another photo of her, then again, and again. Pictures of her—alone, with friends, her kids—caught mid-laugh, mid-life, clung to the walls. "Bishop. Look."

"Holy Mother of God," he said. "We're right."

"I'll take stalker on steroids for five hundred, Alex," I said.

"All clear," an officer said over the radio.

"All clear," I said. We regrouped at the front of the house.

"The guy's got a shrine to Lara Hicks in one of the rooms. No signs of anything related to the kidnapping, but that doesn't mean she's not being held somewhere else in the house."

Bishop said, "Alright. Let's do this by the book." He pointed to the officer who offered his equipment. "Get the ram and pry bar, please."

Davis eyed the junk on the porch. "We've got to move half that crap to access the door."

"There's a back entrance," I said. "Might be easier to go that route."

Bishop shook his head and pointed to two officers "You two secure the back entrance. Davis and Carter, you're on the door with us."

We moved enough of the clutter to allow a narrow path. After a quick examination, we decided on the ram over the pry bar.

After Bishop knocked and announced our presence twice, we took action. "Hold on," he said. "On my count," he paused, then added, "three...two...one...go!"

We rammed the door until it splintered under the force of the impact. One last ram and the door gave way, crashing open. We surged forward, weapons at the ready, as the darkness inside the house swallowed us whole.

16

The door shattered under our force, and instantly, that thick, coppery stench of blood slammed into us, unshakable and pungent.

Davis gagged beside me, his voice raspy with disgust. "What the hell is that smell?"

"Blood," I replied tersely. The scent clung to the back of my throat, so heavy and ominous I could taste it.

Bishop and I exchanged a quick, fraught glance—in silent agreement of what we'd find. "Start clearing the rooms," he ordered, his voice a low growl. "We'll take the right side."

I immediately contacted dispatch as we moved, our weapons drawn, the grip cold and solid in my sweaty palm. Our steps were soft but swift through the small, creaking rooms. I gave the location and knew we'd hear sirens in a matter of minutes.

"Clear," Davis's voice echoed from the other side of the house, each call adding weight to the building dread.

With each room we cleared, the tension twisted tighter, ratcheting up with the stark emptiness that greeted us. The only sounds were the suffocating silence and the eerie echoes of our own movements. My heart hammered against my rib cage, each beat a loud drum echoing in my skull.

"That's the room with the pictures," I whispered, pointing toward a door on our right, my voice barely audible over the thudding in my chest. We'd get to it last, but first there was one door in front of us.

I reached out toward the door before the one with the pictures, my hand shaking as I grasped the cold handle. It wouldn't budge. "It's locked."

Bishop assessed the barrier with a calculated gaze. "I've got it," he announced grimly. His boot slammed into the door once, twice, three times, the wood splintering with a violent crack on the final kick. The door burst open, revealing the horror within.

We froze, the sight unfolding before us draining the warmth from our bodies. A body lay submerged in a bathtub full of bloodied water with most of her head splattered over the walls.

"Son of a bitch," Rob breathed, his voice barely a whisper, his face ashen under the harsh bathroom light. He leaned against the wall, his hand pressing against the cool plaster as if to steady himself from the shock.

A fierce, painful turmoil boiled up inside me. Anger, sorrow—a tangled mess of helplessness and rage. "It's our fault. We shouldn't have tried to find him."

"It wasn't our call," Rob countered quietly, his own anguish barely masked by the steadiness of his voice.

I pressed the radio button, my hand trembling. "Dispatch, we need the coroner," I said, my voice steady despite the chaos whirling inside me.

Jimmy's voice crackled through. "Levy, Michels, and I are on our way."

Carter and Davis cleared the room with the photos and checked the rest of the house one more time.

"Damn," Davis said. "The room's full of pictures of the wife." The scene in the bathroom stopped him dead in his tracks. "Oh, my God. Is that her?"

"We think so," I confirmed grimly. "Secure the scene. Surround the property. No one but law enforcement and medical staff steps foot near this house. Understood?"

"Yes, ma'am," Davis replied, his voice resolute as they moved to secure the perimeter.

For a moment, Bishop and I stayed in the bathroom watching over her as if our presence could shield her in death—a protection we failed to extend in life.

"It looks like her," Bishop said. "What's left of her, I mean."

"It does." I noticed the diamond and emerald ring on her finger. "She's wearing the same ring she wore to the station." I realized then the blue stone diamond ring wasn't on her hand. She probably had a jewelry box full of rings to choose from.

He shook his head slowly. "We should have caught this sooner."

"Let's check that other room," I said.

The blood smell hadn't faded. I knew I'd carry that stench imbedded in my nasal passages and the forefront of my mind with me for weeks. Cops never got used to that smell, no matter how many times we smelled it. It was the scent of evil, one that clung to the skin and followed us home like a spectral reminder of the day's horrors.

"Bubba's looking for his family," Levy said. She'd arrived with Michels at the scene in record time, with the chief right behind them. "He's got to be close."

Bishop nodded. "Any known aliases?"

"He found two," Michels said. "Daniel A. Watkins and D. A. Watkins, but they're too close to his original name. He could have something completely off our radar."

"We've got a BOLO out," Jimmy said. "Fulton County is hot on this, both the locals and sheriff's office. Liz is already on the media. His photo is probably all over the internet by now. If he's still in the area, he won't go anywhere. Like Levy said, Bubba's looking into his family, but he's checking social media connections as well."

"He hasn't run. He's pissed. He'll call," I said. "He murdered the woman he thinks he loves, and he blames us. Had we not put him in this position, he'd be with her now."

"Cooper," Bishop said, his tone thick with worry.

"He's under tight security," Jimmy said. "No one's getting in or out of his place without the team knowing."

I hoped he was right. None of this should have involved Cooper, and I still felt guilty even though it wasn't our fault it had. Had we been quicker, figured things out sooner, Lara Hicks would still be alive, Cooper would be safe, and Ryan Hicks's kids would have at least one parent to get them through the tragedy.

"Agreed," I said to Bishop, my worry about Cooper reflecting his. "We should be at his place." I surveyed the area, knowing Nikki had it under control. "Where's Barron?"

"Vacation," Jimmy said. "Assistant coroner Mandy Simpson is outside now." He scanned our area then headed toward the room with Lara's face plastered all over the walls. We followed. He dropped a stream of cuss words as he rubbed his right eye with the palm of his hand. "How did we miss this?" He turned to the team. "He's been a problem for them for years. He should have been our first interview." His tone had escalated, which meant his temper was as well.

"Hicks never wanted to press charges," Levy said. "We tried to interview him, but he was MIA."

"Because he was in hiding," Jimmy said. "That should have been your first sign."

"We followed the money trail, Chief," Bishop said.

"We thought it was the right way to go," I said.

"What if it was?" Michels asked.

We all looked at him.

"Go on," Jimmy said.

"Rutherford found out Hicks banned him from his accounts and removed him as trustee. What if he knew Watkins obsession wasn't with Hicks, but his wife? He convinces him that killing Hicks will endear Lara Hicks to him." He paused for a moment and added, "Then he gets Watkins to kidnap her to gain access to the money. It blows up in his face, and Watkins has to kill her."

"Or," Levy said, "he could have framed Watkins for this and killed him so he couldn't talk."

The assistant coroner walked over to us. "We have a problem," she said. "I don't know who the girl in the tub is, but it's not Lara Hicks."

17

We followed her back to the bathroom.

"How do you know?" I asked.

"Lara Hicks is the poster woman for her plastic surgeon. She's all over social media talking about her implants." She eyed the body. "Our victim doesn't have implants."

"Nice catch," Michels said. He winced when Levy's elbow jabbed his arm.

"We'll need something from her home. A toothbrush or hairbrush are best. And let's get prints from something she'd touch often. Cell phone, maybe? Something I can compare to our victim's prints."

Jimmy nodded and asked Carl to find Nikki for him. "When you're done, we'll have our tech team get them."

"I'm done," she said. "I'll do the autopsy when the body arrives. Since there's no weapon on scene, I can say right now this woman didn't commit suicide."

We already knew that but understood how the process worked.

The coroner began explaining what she needed from the body to Nikki as we walked outside.

"This is a shit show," Bishop said. "If that's not her, who the hell is it?"

"Someone that looks a lot like her," I said.

"You think Watkins did this?" Levy asked the group.

"Anything's possible," Jimmy said. "Let's get back to Cooper's and regroup. Bubba should have something for us by now, and we need to be there for that call. Regardless of who it's from."

Cooper and Kyle sat in the matching leather chairs of Cooper's den. From the looks of him, you'd never guess Cooper's life had taken a jump off a cliff with no parachute. I assumed it was all a façade.

Surprised to see Kyle, I gave him a nod and hoped he read my silent thank you for being the human side of law enforcement Cooper needed.

"The Mrs. and our son made it to Texas," Cooper said. "She called about thirty minutes ago."

"That's good. How are you holding up?"

"I'm more worried about what happened to Lara and Ryan."

"Well," I said, sitting on the arm of Kyle's leather chair. "The good news is the coroner doesn't believe that's Lara Hicks in Watkins's bathtub. The bad news is the coroner doesn't believe that's Lara Hicks in Watkins's bathtub."

Cooper's mouth dropped open. I filled them in on the situation until Levy interrupted and said Bubba had something.

"His mother died six months ago. His father, long before that. No siblings. Chief said he'd bring any computers here for me. I'll look for emails or anything you all need."

"Thanks," I said, feeling the frustration of nothing making sense seeping into my veins. Our investigation had followed Cooper's life off that cliff, and I didn't have a clue how to proceed.

Bishop, Levy, Michels and I stepped outside to work through our thoughts.

"We're not looking in the right places," Bishop said. "If that's not Lara Hicks, then she's still out there, and she's either hiding or being held."

Levy paced back and forth chewing on her finger. Finally, she said,

"Rutherford's MIA, Lara Hicks, if that's not her, which we're pretty sure it isn't, is MIA, and Watkins is MIA. What if they're working together?" She bit her bottom lip. "What if Rutherford and Hicks planned this whole thing?"

"And what? Brought Watkins into the fold?" I asked.

"Or killed him and let us think he's a part of it."

Bishop said, "That's a stretch."

"Not really," she said. "Think about it. There were no out of the ordinary prints or signs of a struggle in Ryan Hicks's bedroom. No forced entry. Whoever did it got inside with a key. They had to have waited for Hicks to come upstairs, then shot him."

"In bed," I said. "That's a hard pill to swallow."

"Not really," she said. "Hicks found out about Rutherford's stealing and blocked him from the accounts." She looked at me. "One of you said something about Lara Hicks contacting Rutherford multiple times. What if she was in on it? She isn't getting the cash she wants. Her acting career, if that's what you'd call it, is dead in the water, and they both need cash. Rutherford takes Lara to the house and threatens to kill her. He gives Ryan a choice. Give them cash or she dies."

"Still doesn't explain how he ended up face down on the bed," Michels said.

"If you've got a gun pointed to the head of the mother of your kids, you'll do what the guy says," Levy said.

"The safe was empty," Michels said. "I assumed it was for the wife's jewelry, but maybe they got money from it?"

"Lara Hicks would know if there was cash in it," I said. "And Rutherford probably would too."

"Rutherford and the wife set this up," Levy replied. "She pretended to be the victim. Hicks, being a decent human being, followed instructions thinking he was saving his kids' mother, and Rutherford shot him anyway."

"And Hicks knew something was coming because he'd cut him off," I said. "How the hell did we miss that?"

"Where's Watkins in all this?" Bishop asked.

"Maybe he's not?" Levy said. "Rutherford would have known which of the two Watkins stalked. He could have taken him out and used him as a distraction for us."

"Which means we're not getting another call," Bishop said, "and he's taken off with Hicks."

I hollered for Jimmy.

He walked outside, stopped to talk to a patrol officer standing guard, and then came to us. After explaining our theory, he said, "Damn it. I pulled patrol from his place because of the kidnapping. Get a team over to Rutherford's now!"

Every wasted second shaved edges off our chances. We were prepped for a potential showdown with Rutherford—and possibly Lara Hicks, though any confrontation with her would likely be swift. Rutherford was the real threat; his intelligence and cold calculation demanded a full-throttle response. We needed to be ready to take him down, preferably alive, but dead if necessary.

As the pre-dawn gloom began to surrender to the first hints of morning, tension coiled tighter inside me. We approached Rutherford's estate, my hands tightening around the rifle, its metal cold and unyielding—an extension of my resolve.

Bishop turned sharply onto Rutherford's street, braking hard just shy of the property. He issued orders over the radio, his voice clipped with urgency. "No lights, no sirens. We approach this as a standard visit. He might think we're still in the dark about Lara Hicks, might even be inside pretending to be uninvolved. But if he doesn't answer, we breach. We're prepared for that."

"It's a steel door," I noted, eyes scanning the looming facade as Michels pulled the ram from his trunk.

I exited swiftly, aligning with Michels to assess the entry point while retrieving a pry bar from Bishop's trunk.

"The estate's mostly glass," Bishop's voice came through the radio, calm yet commanding. "Surround the house, teams of two. I want six on each side—front and back. Sweep the perimeter and stay low. Any sign of movement, I need to know immediately."

Acknowledgments crackled through the radio—sharp, concise.

The massive steel door stood before us, imposing and seemingly impenetrable. Levy and Michels positioned themselves discreetly to the side, their tools ready but out of sight. Meanwhile, I scanned for security cameras, signaling subtly to Levy and Michels the locations of two.

Bishop stepped forward, knocking firmly. "Colin Rutherford, it's Detectives Ryder and Bishop. We need to discuss an urgent matter with you," he announced, his tone authoritative yet measured to not provoke. "If you're inside and unable to come to the door, please make your presence known any way you can."

One after the other, the officers cleared their areas. The stillness thickened as we prepared to break the silence with force. Bishop gave a brief nod, the signal we'd been waiting for. He and Michels positioned themselves on the right side of the steel door, pry bars in hand. Their faces in expressions hard with the grim determination that this job demanded.

Michels, with a practiced ease that belied the tension in his muscles, wedged his pry bar between the door and the frame near the lock. Bishop mirrored him, their movements synchronized and precise. They looked at each other with a silent countdown communicated in a shared glance.

Then, in one fluid, explosive motion, they pressed their weight to the bars. The metal groaned under the strain. Michels adjusted his grip, his jaw clenched, and heaved again. Bishop did the same, the muscles in his arms standing out with every movement.

With a final, concerted effort, a sharp, rending crack broke the tension as the lock mechanism gave way. The door didn't swing open but stood slightly ajar, damaged but still defiant. Bishop nodded at me, a brief flicker of satisfaction in his eyes, before his gaze turned back to the task at hand.

"We're in," he whispered over the radio, his voice barely audible. He and Michels pulled the pry bars free, readying themselves for what might come next as they pushed the damaged door open to reveal whatever lay behind it.

Silence.

Guns drawn, we entered Rutherford's home as Bishop announced us. After calling for the man to make his presence known three separate times, we separated and moved to clear the home.

Bishop and Michels led the way through the front door. My heart pounded in my chest as my senses locked onto high alert. Levy followed right behind me, her footfalls mirroring mine on the pristine hardwood floors. Rutherford's home was immaculate, and a quick survey showed no one had disrupted it. The wall-sized windows made me hyper-aware of the potential for prying eyes outside.

"Levy, Michels, you two take the upper floor." He directed the two officers to take the lower level while we handled the main floor.

I whispered to Bishop, my voice barely audible over the thudding of my own heartbeat. "Got it."

We started in the kitchen, its sleek granite countertops and stainless-steel appliances gleaming under the rising sun's light.

"All clear," he murmured, his eyes meeting mine briefly before we moved on.

We entered the large living space next, an open space with nowhere to hide.

I scanned the room quickly, noting the strategically placed decor that could easily be disturbed in a struggle. Nothing had been moved. "Clear," I said.

A soft click on the radio in my ear startled me. Levy's voice came through, calm and collected. "Upstairs is clear. No sign of Rutherford or Hicks."

"Copy that," I responded, my voice low. "We're still searching the main floor."

Bishop and I moved to the open dining room, the long table set for a meal that clearly hadn't been eaten, but the room, like the others was clear.

We proceeded to the den at the front of the home. This room felt slightly more personal, with bookshelves lining the walls and a plush armchair facing a modern desk.

Bishop accidentally kicked a small wastebasket as he turned, the sudden noise echoing loudly in the otherwise silent house. We both froze, listening intently for any reaction. After a tense moment, I exhaled slowly. Nothing.

"Sorry," Bishop whispered, a note of contrition in his voice.

I gave him a tight nod, my eyes already scanning the room again.

We entered the hallway, pausing outside the full bath. I nudged the door open with my foot, weapon at the ready. No signs of anyone having been there recently.

"Clear," I said, and we moved to the next room at the far left side of the home, adjacent to the living space.

I wiped the sweat from my forehead and took a deep breath. A closed door. I forced myself to be calm, intent on opening the door until Bishop moved in front of me and did it himself.

An office. Heavy drapes darkened the room to midnight. Bishop flicked his flashlight around as we checked behind the door and desk. All clear.

I tapped my radio. "Main floor clear. No sign of Rutherford or Hicks."

A moment later, the two officers on the patio level echoed the same. "Patio level clear. No sign of movement outside."

I let out a slow breath, trying to quell the growing anxiety in my chest.

"No signs of a struggle," Levy reported, shaking her head.

"Same here," I replied, my mind churning. "We've got the warrant, let's see what we find."

Nikki didn't arrive until over an hour later, but we'd made sure to keep the home as neat as possible to make her job easier.

Rutherford's office was as sterile as an operating room, except for the open Apple laptop on the desk. I tapped the space bar, and his email popped up. "Bishop," I called. "Laptop's on and I'm in."

He was at my side in a heartbeat. "That can't be luck," he muttered.

I started scrolling through the emails. "He didn't clear his inbox. Maybe he left in a rush?"

He shook his head. "Doesn't fit. House is too tidy. Michels said he's got a full set of luggage upstairs, and his shaving kit is in the bathroom. He's planning on coming back."

"Check this out," I said, pausing on a gap in the correspondence. "Nothing from Ryan Hicks for over six months." I kept scrolling, looking for any breadcrumbs that might lead us to Rutherford or Lara Hicks. "He didn't wipe it completely. Just anything tied to Hicks."

"Keep digging," Bishop said as he rifled through a file drawer.

Levy walked in, holding a woman's ring with a large, square blue stone and diamonds dangling from her pen. "Found this under his bed. Pretty sure it's worth more than my car."

I stared at the ring, my mind clicking into gear. "That's the ring Lara Hicks wore to the police department." I blinked, processing the information racing through my head. "You found it under Rutherford's bed?"

Levy grinned. "Yep."

The puzzle pieces began to fall into place.

18

"No other signs of a woman," Michels said.

Nikki smirked. "A magician didn't put that ring under the bed. There's something here, but it's something I'll have to find." She headed upstairs with her bag and Carl, her eager intern hurrying behind her.

"She'll find DNA," Bishop said. "She took several items from Lara Hicks's condo. If Lara was in that bedroom, we'll know."

"That could take days," Levy said. "We have to make the assumption she was."

"But did she come willingly?" Michels asked.

"I'm thinking yes," I said. "It falls into what we said before."

"Which means the two are on the run," Bishop said. "Jimmy's got BOLOs out. Bubba's checking the airlines and trains, but they would have called if they'd found something."

"Does Hicks have a second home anywhere?" Levy asked.

"Hold on," Michels said. "I think I heard him mention a condo downtown in an interview once. Something about staying there after night home games so he didn't disturb his kids."

"Get Bubba on it," Bishop said.

∽

According to Jimmy, the negation team had packed up their things and left Cooper's house around four a.m. I envied their luck at going home to sleep, but a large cup of Dunkin' coffee helped keep my eyes open.

We all met back at the station, going through what we learned as we ate the breakfast Susan had ordered for us. I was so hungry, I downed an egg, bacon, and cheese bagel without breathing. I knew I'd eaten sometime in the past, but I couldn't recall when.

Jimmy arrived looking like he'd just been hit by a Mack truck that then backed up and ran over him again. He handed us each a paper. "Mandy Simpson is right. Our victim isn't Lara Hicks. Her name is Taren Levell."

"Why does that name sound familiar?" Michels said.

The corner of Jimmy's mouth twitched. "Maybe you've met her at her place of business?"

Michels expression went blank. "Where's that?"

"The Cheetah Lounge."

The room busted out laughing. The Cheetah Lounge was a popular strip bar in Atlanta.

"Oh," Levy said. "Ashley's so going to find out this little nugget."

"Bite me," he said. He pointed to Jimmy. "You just blew our cover."

Jimmy laughed.

"Oh," I said. "Is this the place you went for your bachelor party?" I eyed Bishop. "You thought I didn't know, didn't you?"

Bishop cleared his throat. "How did—Savannah."

Jimmy nodded. "I had to tell her, but I thought she'd keep it a secret."

"Anyway," Michels said. "In retrospect, I can see the similarities." He shook his head when he saw Levy laughing. "It's the hair, Levy."

"Simpson put a rush on the blood work and compared it to blood found in Lara Hicks's condo."

"We don't know if the blood in the condo belonged to Hicks," Michels said.

"Yes, we do," I said.

"How?"

"Female stuff," Levy said. "You want a detailed description?"

Michels's Adam's apple bobbed. "Nope. I'm good."

It would have completely disgusted him to learn she'd recently menstruated, but nothing was too gross for DNA discovery.

Bubba walked in.

"Perfect timing," Bishop said.

"Thank God," Michels said through a breath. "Subject change."

"Did I miss something?" Bubba asked.

Levy began to talk, but Michels cut her off with a, "Oh, hell no. He's too young for that."

"Uh, okay," Bubba said. "Good news. I made a connection with a former friend of Daniel Watkins. He's got a lot to say, so I told him to come now. I hope that's okay."

"We'll have someone talk to him," Jimmy said. "Anything else?"

"They asked for information on a condo Ryan Hicks owns." He set his laptop on the table and grabbed a breakfast burrito from the table. "I couldn't find anything in his name or his LLC, but I did find something listed with his and Rutherford's business name, HR LLC."

"That's creative," Levy said.

"Where is it?" Jimmy asked.

He gave us the address and then told us it was empty. "I contacted Atlanta PD, and they did a wellness check. Place is totally empty. No furniture, nothing."

"You contacted Atlanta PD and got a wellness check?" Jimmy asked, his tone showing his surprise.

"I went to college with their IT guy. He owed me a favor." He handed Bishop a piece of paper. "That's the officers that did the check. You can call them for information. Also, the condo was put on the market a month ago. I called the agent before coming here. She's got the listing on hold because she's still waiting for the key."

"Not sure she'll get that any time soon," Bishop said.

Susan knocked on the door and walked in. "There's a Brian Hanna here. He says he's supposed to talk to an officer about Daniel Watkins?"

Brian Hanna sat across from us in the interview room at the department looking like he'd rather be getting ready for surgery without anesthesia. The room felt brighter than the typical interrogation setup, featuring soft yellow walls and large windows that let in plenty of natural light. A couple of plants in the corners created a more relaxed atmosphere. We weren't there to intimidate Brian; we needed information, and his comfort level would determine how much he gave.

"Thanks for coming in, Brian," I started, trying to put him at ease. "We appreciate your cooperation."

Brian nodded, his hands fidgeting in his lap. "No problem. I just want to help."

"We're hoping you can tell us about Daniel Watkins," Bishop said. "You call him Danny, right?"

Brian nodded again, more vigorously this time. "Yeah, Danny. We've been friends since high school. He's a good guy, just a little strange sometimes, and complicated."

"What do you mean by complicated?" I asked, keeping my tone neutral.

Brian shifted in his seat. "Danny's always had this intense personality. When he gets fixated on something, he can't let it go. That's how he was with Lara Hicks, so when the guy from here called me, I realized this could have to do with him."

I exchanged a quick glance with Bishop. "Would you call his focus on Lara Hicks an obsession?" I asked Danny.

"Definitely. He believed he'd marry her one day. Claimed she thought it too, she just had to get out of her marriage to Ryan."

"So, he knew Lara?" I asked.

"He said he did, but I'm not sure it's true."

"Can you tell me about the relationship Danny had with Lara?" Bishop asked.

"He didn't really have a relationship with her, not in the way you'd think, at least not that I knew of. He was obsessed with her. Ever since he first saw her, he couldn't stop talking about her. He'd watch her, you know? Go to her house, follow her around. It was creepy, but he never did anything violent." He stared at the table. "I can't imagine he'd kill her husband."

"How often did he watch her?" Bishop asked, his voice calm.

Brian thought for a moment. "A lot, but I don't know how much. He got a little extreme lately. He kept saying he couldn't hang out because he had to take care of Lara. I figured he was bull shitting, you know? Living in his little fantasy, but now, I think he might have been blowing me off to stalk her or something."

"Did Danny ever talk about doing something to Ryan?" I asked, leaning forward slightly.

Brian's eyes flicked to mine, then away. "Not at first. But a few weeks ago, he started talking crazy. Said he was gonna make a lot of money from some private job. He said with the money, he could take care of Lara. I didn't think that meant killing her husband though."

He trailed off, and I filled the silence. "When did you hear about Ryan Hicks's murder?"

"On the news, the day after it happened," he replied, his voice low. "I didn't make the connection at first. Danny hadn't said anything specific about hurting Ryan. But then Bubba called, and that's when it clicked for me. Danny's obsession, the money, Ryan's murder. It all started to make sense."

"Did Danny ever tell you about this big job or who hired him for it?"

Brian shook his head. "No, he was secretive about it. Just said it was a big deal and he'd be set for life."

"Have you tried to contact Danny since Ryan's murder?" Bishop asked.

"Yeah, I've called him a bunch of times," Brian said. "He's not answering, and that's not like him. He always picks up or calls back."

"It's possible Danny could be hiding somewhere," Bishop said. "Just trying to keep low until everything blows over. Do you know where that might be?"

Brian sighed again, looking more worried than ever. "I don't know. He's got a few places he likes to go when he needs to think or be alone. There's a cabin up north his mom's brother owns, and he sometimes crashes at this old warehouse downtown, mostly after baseball games."

"Where's the cabin?" I asked.

"I'm not sure. His uncle doesn't let him go there, so he has to go when no one's around. He's been busted a few times, so I don't think he'd go there if he had to hide."

"Do you know his uncle's name?" I asked.

"No, ma'am. Sorry."

"That's okay," I said. "You're being very helpful, and we appreciate everything you're telling us, Brian."

"And the warehouse?" Bishop asked. "Do you know where that is?"

"Just that it's downtown. I didn't think of this before, but I bet it's close to the condo Hicks owns. He talked about that a while back."

"Brian, we need to find Danny before something happens," I said gently. "Anything else you can think of that might help us?"

He thought for a long moment, then shook his head. "I wish I knew more. I really do. Danny's my friend, but this is too much. I don't think I can be friends with him if he's murdered someone."

Bishop leaned back and said, "We don't know if he did, but we are concerned he might be in danger, so if you hear from him, you need to let us know right away. Okay?"

"Of course," Brian said, earnestness in his eyes. "I don't think I'll hang out with him anymore, but yeah, I don't want him getting hurt."

I nodded, satisfied we'd gotten all we could. "Thank you, Brian. You've been very helpful."

He managed a weak smile. "I hope you find him."

Bishop and I exchanged looks as Hanna left. We had more pieces of the puzzle, but the picture was still incomplete.

I nodded slowly. "Rutherford paid Watkins to kill Ryan Hicks, then made it look like he murdered Lara Hicks as well."

"What are the chances he's still alive?" he asked.

"Slim."

"Let's get Atlanta PD looking for that warehouse, stat," Bishop said.

"The incident report says a family member picked Watkins up at the station the first time he stalked Hicks," Bubba said. "It was a few years ago, and it doesn't say who, but Hicks was a pro ball player, right? Whoever brought Watkins in probably didn't forget much about the situation." He tapped on the keyboard of the desktop he kept in the investigation room. "It's Rick Pendley."

"I just saw him in the pit," Michels said.

I called the front desk to ask him to come by.

"This is good, Bubba," Bishop said. "You need a raise."

He smiled. "I'm all for that, but you have to convince the chief."

Rick Pendley walked into the investigation room a few minutes later. We discussed the situation and asked what he could tell us.

"You mean other than the guy's a complete nut case?"

"Yes," Bishop said, his tone completely serious.

"Yeah, sorry," Pendley muttered, clearly feeling as if he'd been scolded. "Hicks declined to press charges. His manager was pissed, and according to him, so was the wife, but he said Watkins was just an excited fan, and he thought it would look bad."

"Did he do anything other than peep?" Levy asked.

"Depends on who you're asking. The wife claimed he watched her sunbathe topless, but Hicks said that wasn't a big deal because she'd been doing that with the pool company there for months."

Michels cleared his throat.

"Was the maintenance company there at the time?"

"Just the one guy."

"How come he's not in the report?" I asked.

"He arrived after I did."

"When Mr. Hicks mentioned the pool guy, did you think to ask him about it?"

"We were already at the station."

"When did Mr. Hicks decline to press charges?" Bishop asked.

"He wasn't big on it from the start, but the wife and manager made him come here. He came alone, and that's when he decided."

"What about Mrs. Hicks? Did you ask her to press charges?"

"I don't want to sound disrespectful, but Ryan Hicks was an ass about it. He told his wife he'd cut her allowance in half if she did. He said it would be a slam to his career." He shook his head. "My wife would lose it if I even suggested she get an allowance."

"Mine too," Michels said.

"It surprised me to see Hicks get like that with his wife. He wasn't all that nice to her, and, honestly, it kind of ruined him for me."

"Understandable," I said. "Do you know who came to pick up Watkins?"

"Yeah, some older guy. Said it was his uncle."

Levy asked, "Did you happen to get his name?"

"No reason to."

"Is there anything you can tell us about him?" she asked. "We're trying to find him."

"The guy? Yeah, he wasn't happy to be there. Came in complaining that Watkins was going to end up in prison, and something about him screwing up his trip to the cabin."

"Did he mention where the cabin was?" Michels asked.

He shook his head.

"Did he say anything that might give us a hint to who he is?"

"He said if his brother was alive, Watkins wouldn't be such a pain in the ass."

The man had to be Watkins's paternal uncle. "Thanks," I said. "Anything else?"

"Just that I don't think Watkins cared about Ryan Hicks. I think he was more interested in the wife."

"Thank you," Bishop said. After Pendley closed the door, he added, "The uncle's the father's brother."

"That's what I think," I said.

Michels and Levy agreed.

"On it," Bubba said.

I called Rutherford again, knowing he wouldn't answer, but wanting to make him think we weren't onto him. I left him another message, letting him know I had something important to discuss with him.

The press had gotten ahold of the murder at Watkins's home, but we'd yet to give them the victim's identity. Mandy Simpson had informed Taren Levell's parents of her death, and they were on their way in from Savannah. Once they finished at the morgue, they'd likely come to the department, but Jimmy said he'd handle them.

The slight break wasn't much, and we would have rather been on our way to that cabin, but Bubba's work created a holding pattern for us.

"I'm taking a shower," Levy said.

"'bout time," Michels kidded.

"I'm with her," I said.

"Nice," Michels said. He wiggled his eyebrows.

I pointed at him. "Shut it, Michels, or I'm telling Ashley."

He nodded quickly, the landline ringing saving his butt.

"Investigation room," I said after hitting the speaker button.

"I have a Lieutenant Baker on the phone from the Atlanta Police Department. Line one."

"Thanks," I said and hit the button to answer the call.

They got a hit on a warehouse near Hicks's condo. The place was empty, but they'd found a mini-shrine to Lara Hicks, The Varsity food bags, and a sleeping bag. The food was old enough for maggots to appear, but that didn't give us much of a timeline. He did say the building's owner had replaced the locks and cameras three weeks before to stop the squatters, but there had been no sign of anyone trying to access the place since.

After we ended the call, Bishop said, "He hasn't been there for three weeks."

"He's got to be somewhere," I said.

"If he's alive, it has to be the cabin," Michels said.

I stood and opened the investigation room door. "Let's take an hour. I really need to scrub the past few days off me now."

19

The hot water cascaded over my shoulders, providing a much-needed reprieve from the tension coiled tightly within me from the past few days. I leaned my head into it, letting it run down my body, hoping it would relax me enough to think about something other than the investigation. Sometimes the best way to close a case was to walk away and forget about it. The epiphanies usually hit then.

But I wasn't going to have an epiphany because my brain wouldn't let it go.

Rutherford and Lara Hicks. The two names echoed in my mind like a drumbeat. Rutherford, I believed, was the mastermind. Were he and Hicks in love or were they using each other as a means to an end? He'd made a point of saying he didn't like her, that she was manipulative and cold-hearted, and he was cold to her on the phone, but that could have been an act. Looking back, it appeared convenient that he'd offered his opinion of her without us asking, not to mention dropping his list of threats and conference information all tied up in a neat bow.

Rutherford had somehow convinced Daniel Watkins to murder Ryan Hicks. Though we had no proof, we knew it. He'd told his friend he had a job that would pay big. Soon after, Hicks was found dead. It wasn't rocket science. Had the wife been involved then? Had she been the one to convince Watkins to kill her husband? Maybe she claimed she wanted to be with Watkins, but Ryan wasn't going to let them be together? Had she motivated Watkins to murder by trash-talking her husband? If Watkins was as unstable as we thought, that wouldn't have been a big leap.

I leaned my forehead against the cool steel, allowing the water to massage the knots in my neck. Bubba would get the uncle's name and a location for the cabin. Time wasn't on our side, but the fact was, if they'd planned to kill Watkins, which I suspected was the case, he was already dead. They wouldn't have sat on that. They could have told him to hide somewhere no one would find him. Had he known the warehouse wasn't an option anymore? If not, why wouldn't he go there?

Because someone took him to a 'safe place.' Rutherford and Lara Hicks. Could they have brought Watkins to the cabin then stayed there after killing him? An image of Lara Hicks flashed in my mind. Her perfectly styled hair, her designer clothes, her penchant for luxury. She wouldn't go somewhere without her comforts. She'd want to be somewhere she could blend in but still maintain her lifestyle.

"Think, Rachel," I muttered to myself. "Where would they go?"

The steam swirled around me as my mind raced through the possibilities. Even though I'd called Rutherford several times, they had to know we were closing in. They wouldn't stay local, would they? I scrubbed at my scalp to stimulate my brain into revealing the answer.

I closed my eyes, picturing Lara in various scenarios. A high-end hotel? Too obvious. A friend's place? Too risky. Then it hit me—Rutherford was meticulous, calculating. If it wasn't Watkin's uncle's cabin, he'd have a safe house, somewhere planned well in advance.

"An industrial area," I whispered, the idea forming in my head. "Another warehouse, maybe? They'd be perfect for hiding out. Enough space to stay hidden, easy access to transport routes if they needed to leave quickly. The more I thought about it the more it became no. Lara Hicks wanted to be treated like the princess she thought she was, and a warehouse wouldn't cut it.

Suddenly, I remembered something Bubba had said. "Hicks was a pro ball player, right? Whoever brought Watkins in probably didn't forget much about the situation." Bubba had mentioned this in relation to finding Watkins's uncle's cabin, but what if it also applied to finding Rutherford and Lara?

I turned off the shower, the water trickling to a stop as I grabbed a towel. My mind was racing now, pulling together threads of conversations, hints, and clues.

Rutherford was Hicks's business manager and attorney. Was being the operative word. Hicks had cut him off, but the divorce wasn't final, and he couldn't cut off his wife. We knew of one additional property they owned, but were there others, ones not in his name?

His kids. Could minors in Georgia own property or would it be held in the trust?

I wrapped the towel around myself and stepped out of the stall. "That's got to be it," I muttered, adrenaline coursing through me. Hicks had another property in his kids' names. Lara would have access to that. Right? Except it wasn't in the trust.

I dressed quickly, my fingers fumbling with the buttons of my shirt in my haste. If not a property of Ryan's, whose?

Lara Hicks had claimed to have taken her kids to Kansas City, but her parents said she never arrived. Did they have another property? Were they in on the scam? Lara wanted the money and the kids? Was that what it was about? I'd originally thought she didn't care about them, but maybe I was wrong.

"You okay?" Levy asked as I finished dressing. "You look worse than when you walked in here."

"Thanks," I said. "I think I've got an idea." I told her about the kids possibly owning property.

"I'm not sure kids can own property here," she said.

I explained my theory about her parents.

Her eyes lit up. "Oh, now that's good."

I dialed Bubba's number as I put on my shoes. He picked up on the second ring.

"Bubba, I think I've got something. Would you please check properties listed under the kids' names and then check for additional properties anywhere that could be owned by Lara's parents?"

"The kids' properties would be in the trust," he said. "I can ask Cooper about that,"

Bubba said, his voice instantly alert. "The parents should be easy to find. I'll check Lara Hicks's maiden name and get started."

"Thanks. I'll call Cooper and ask him about the trust." We were getting closer. I could feel it.

We ran into Michels and Bishop in the pit's kitchen.

Bishop had just dumped three sugar packets into his coffee. "Don't judge me. I can barely keep my eyes open."

"No judgment here," I said. "But drink that fast. I think I know where Rutherford and Lara might be hiding."

"Let's go," Michels said.

"We don't have the location yet," I said, "but I think Bubba will find it." All eyes locked on us walking through the pit as I explained my theory. It didn't go unnoticed.

Bishop cleared his throat.

In the investigation room, Levy said, "Nothing like a good stare down from the department."

"Let them take over the investigation," Michels said. "I'd like to see them do better."

"It's a tense case," Bishop said. "Hicks was everyone's favorite player. Most of the state is emotionally affected by his murder."

I fell into my seat. "No pressure." I called Cooper on the landline.

The PD's number must have shown up on his caller ID because he said, "We're all good. No need for the watchdogs on the property. The horses are already freaked out enough."

"What if it wasn't me?" I asked.

"You're the only one from there who calls me."

Good point. "Can you access the trust? We're looking to see if there are any additional properties for his children. Maybe something in the kids' names or even Lara's."

"I can call the attorney and check."

"Thanks. Can you tell them it's urgent? We need to find Rutherford and Lara."

"I'll call you back as soon as I know something."

"Thanks," I said and disconnected.

Bubba burst into the room. "Lara Hicks, formerly Lara Mason. Her parents own three properties. Their home in Kansas City, a place in Vail, and one in Ellijay." He handed us each a paper with the information. "I checked flights for Rutherford, Lara Hicks, and Lara Mason but couldn't find them. They could have fake IDs and flown under different names, but it would take a while to find that out."

"This is great," I said. "We'll contact the Vail and Kansas City PD's and see what they can tell us."

"I did run checks on credit cards under their names, Ryan Hicks, and Lara's parents. No airline tickets or gas station stops. If they went far, they'd need gas."

Bishop said, "They're in Ellijay."

"We'll need a warrant," Michels said.

I exhaled. "Nowak is in Italy. We can't wait for another judge to pull some strings." I eyed Bishop. "You play golf with any judges?"

"When exactly would I have time for golf?"

"What about Jimmy?" Levy asked. "He's the chief. He's got strings to pull."

I dialed his extension.

Susan answered. "He's in a meeting, but I can put in a few calls for him. When do you need it?"

"Yesterday."

"I'll do my best."

After cutting the call, I said, "We can't wait."

Michels smiled. "They haven't seen much of me or Levy. We'll pose as electric company workers."

"Lara Hicks has met me," Levy said.

"But only once. They've seen Bishop and Ryder multiple times."

"He's right," I said. "What electric company is out there?"

Bubba's fingers tapped on the desktop keys. "Amicalola AMC." He rattled off the number and a contact in their legal department.

"We don't need to call," I said. "Let's move."

Levy ditched her detective badge for electrician's coveralls and a tool belt that hung around her hips like she knew what she was doing. She topped it off with a fiery red wig that shimmered under the locker room's unforgiving lights.

"Wow. That wig suits you," I chuckled, adjusting the straps of my own bulky utility belt.

Levy smirked, checking her reflection in the locker. "It's got to look real, right? This might fool someone at a distance."

I fired off a quick update to Kyle, then pocketed my phone just as Levy and I were ready to roll out. We met up with Bishop and Michels in the weapons supply room, gearing up for anything that could happen.

Michels was another story. He had his jumpsuit zipped up to his chin and his hair slicked back so hard it looked painted on, and his mustache—God save us—looked like something straight out of a '70s skin flick.

I bit my lip to keep from laughing out loud. "You're killing that look, man," I managed, covering my laugh with a cough.

He grinned, all pride. "Touch it."

"What?" I backed up. "Not on your life, man. That's gross."

"It's just hair gel, makes it look thicker. Feels like a scouring pad. Come on, give it a touch."

When he looked to Levy, she backed up and said, "I'm good. Thanks."

"And you two think you can stop a killer," he said jokingly.

I tapped my weapon on my belt. "Want to test that argument?"

He smirked. "That's a hard no for me."

Just then, Jimmy found us, his expression stern. "Susan updated me." He eyed Michels. "What the hell did you do to your mustache?"

"Touch it," Michels said.

Everyone but Jimmy chuckled. Instead, he turned toward Bishop, shaking his head. "Unfortunately, you can't pose as the electric company without their approval and the approval of the Ellijay PD."

"Why not?" Bishop asked.

"It's against the city's policies."

"Even with a warrant?" I asked.

"I thought we didn't have a warrant," he said.

"We don't."

"I've got a call in to the Assistant District Attorney, Zach Christopher. He's coordinating with the Gilmer County DA's office on this."

"That's BS," Michels said.

"We need to find them," I said. "We're losing time the longer we stand around and argue about it. Are they going to do a wellness check?"

He shook his head. "They said you can go as religious solicitors. I'll contact Ellijay PD and let them know our decision, but remember this is just a discovery mission, not a pickup, alright?"

"What do you expect us to do if they're there?" I asked.

"If you want them now, we need a warrant and, like I said, local will need to be in on it. If you can wait, we'll keep an eye on them and grab them when they're outside city limits. I should have a warrant in a few hours either way."

So, waiting was the plan. That sucked. "They murdered two people. Rutherford stole money from Hicks, and Lara's somehow involved in that too. We need to pull them if we find them."

"Then we'll get Ellijay PD on the assist," he said. "After I get the warrant."

"Our goal is simple," Bishop said while checking the ammo in his handgun. "We're going to see if Lara and Rutherford are there."

"Good," he said. "Keep me in the loop." He eyed Levy and Michels. "Change into something that says religious solicitor, not electric company or cop."

"Like what?" Michels asked.

"You'll figure it out," he said and left the room.

We agreed to meet again in ten minutes. Levy had kept the wig but swapped her coveralls for something less conspicuous, her emergency set of regular clothing in her locker, and Susan, being her helpful self, lent her a cross necklace.

"Looks authentic enough," I noted as she added a swipe of mascara.

In the weapons room, Michels tried on a bulletproof vest, then tugged on a loose button down that hung limp over the vest. He had succeeded in looking more like a middle-aged pastor than a cop. "This is so not my look," he grumbled.

"You and Levy could be the poster couple for a church bake sale," I teased.

Bishop just checked his gun and smiled slightly, ready to blend into the background as always.

20

The home sat tucked away in a secluded, densely wooded area that even a seasoned cop would call a tactical nightmare. Visibility was crap thanks to thick stands of pine and oak trees, and the relentless downpour didn't help, turning the ground into a muddy slip-and-slide. Lightning flashed overhead, throwing stark, eerie shadows that danced across the forest floor. Thunder rolled, deep and ominous, mirroring the tension coiling in my gut. Chicago storms had nothing on the ones in Georgia, especially in the summer.

"This is going to suck," Michels grumbled as rain dripped off his hat.

"Just go with the plan," Levy shot back, pulling her raincoat tighter against the storm. "We knock, wait, and then hopefully make visual contact. If we don't, we'll pretend we're lost in the woods and walk the perimeter."

"Where we'll actually get lost in the woods," Michels muttered, "Or attacked by a bear."

I couldn't argue with the bear attack possibility. "You have a compass on your watch," I reminded him after a crack of lightning lit up the sky followed by a loud clap of thunder.

"The storm's close," Bishop said.

"There's a severe warning," Levy said.

"For once," I said, "the weather people were right."

"I've got a better idea," Michels said. "Let's grab these assholes and take them to Hamby."

"If only," I said.

"Bureaucracy is the boss," Bishop chimed in from beside me, his voice barely audible over another clap of thunder.

Michels just nodded, his face grim. "And a pain in my butt."

Scanning the woods, I noted the uneven ground muddied with rain and covered with a layer of pine needles and leaf litter that had quickly added to the muddy mess. Michels was right. The woods surrounded us for miles, an environment where anything could be lurking, and with the intense rain, that included swamp creatures. Yet, the area provided multiple options for Bishop and me to cover Levy and Michels.

"We'll take the east and west sides of the driveway just in front of the garage," I said. "The trees are thick enough there for us to hide, and even with this storm, we should be able to hear any conversations thanks to the echo. Plus, they give us a semi-decent view of the home's sides in case they try to run. Work for you?"

"Perfect," Bishop agreed, his voice steady despite the worsening weather.

Levy and Michels trudged up the stone path leading to the front door, their steps measured and cautious. Both carried a weapon in the back of their waistband, Michels with an additional one in his boot. With those, their vests, and Bishop and me close, they had a reduced chance of losing a gunfight, but we still didn't want it to happen.

Standing to the far side of the door, Levy popped open an umbrella and knocked, her posture rigid under the guise of a religious solicitor. My pulse quickened when Lara Hicks answered. There was something unnerving about watching from a short distance, knowing any moment could unravel our cover. Lara stood framed in the doorway, her face unreadable from my distance but her body language showed she was tense, guarded against the storm and the strangers on her porch.

I held my breath, praying she wouldn't recognize Levy, but she hadn't flinched upon seeing her, so the wig must have worked.

We were close enough to hear their conversation, as brief as it was. It carried over the sound of heavy rain hitting leaves.

"Ma'am," Michels said, projecting his voice over the noise of the storm, "We're with the First United Church of Reformists, and we'd like to talk to you about our program."

Hicks's eyes darted back and forth, flicking nervously behind her as if checking for an unseen threat. "I'm sorry. I'm not interested."

"Ma'am," Levy pressed, "it will only take a minute or two, and then we can answer any questions you might have."

She continued the talk hoping Rutherford would show up at the door, but he hadn't.

Hicks craned her neck to look behind her again, then quickly said, "I'm really not interested."

"How about your husband?" Levy asked. "Maybe you'd feel more comfortable if we talked to the two of you together?"

"No," she said sharply. "Please leave." With a swift motion, she slammed the door in Levy's face.

I watched the windows but saw no movement. Granted, I couldn't see straight in front of the door.

Levy and Michels turned and walked back down the path with feigned dejection. They leaned against the vehicle where Levy held the umbrella over Michels and he pulled out a map and pretended to study it. Bishop and I remained hidden in the event Rutherford or Hicks made a move.

"We need to contact Jimmy," I said to Bishop. "To get an update on the warrant," I added, already scanning the tree line for any movement.

"Give them a minute," he said. "They might—"

A sharp crack of a branch cut him off, snapping our attention back to the house. Michels was the first to react, his voice tense. "Movement at the east side of the house." He dropped the map and took off. Levy tossed the umbrella to the ground and followed.

I watched as Lara Hicks frantically darted through the trees and into the thick woods. At the same time, out of the corner of my eye, I caught sight of Rutherford bolting in the opposite direction through another set of trees.

Adrenaline raced through me. "Damn, they're splitting up!"

Bishop and I sprang into action pursuing Rutherford. The uneven forest floor littered with fallen branches and thick underbrush grabbed at our ankles as we ran. My foot caught in a root and dropped me to the ground. Bishop paused in front of me. "Keep going!" I screamed. I tasted blood. My ankle hurt, but not enough to stop me from running.

I dislodged my foot and took off, using every ounce of energy I had to pass Bishop. My heart hammered in my chest as I navigated the terrain.

Rutherford ran fast, but panic made him clumsy. He stumbled over a root as well, his curse loud in the quiet of the forest. We gained on him, the gap closing with every stride. Bishop was just ahead, his broad frame crashing through the underbrush like a bull. I pushed myself harder, ignoring the burning in my lungs and the sharp pain in my ankle. The chase felt surreal, the forest around us turning into a blur of greens and browns. We were so close, I could hear Rutherford's ragged breathing, even the desperation in each step he took.

Bishop shouted, "Stop! It's over, Rutherford!" But the forest swallowed his words. There was no response, only the frantic rustling of leaves and the pounding of feet against the earth.

Rutherford veered to the left, trying to lose us in the thicker part of the woods. He slipped on the wet ground and went down hard. Bishop and I seized the opportunity, cutting the distance between us and our target.

My ankle throbbed. I spit blood as my lip swelled. I swiped my hand over it, knowing I'd need stitches.

In the split second that Rutherford scrambled back to his feet, I realized something was off, something that didn't quite add up. But there was no time to ponder it. He was up again, running, but slower, each step more labored than the last.

"Almost there," I muttered to myself, urging my legs to keep moving. My mind raced with the possible outcomes, each one ending with Rutherford in cuffs. But something nagged at me, a small voice whispering that we were missing something crucial.

We burst through a dense thicket, our light cover from the downpour disappearing as the rain drenched me even more, and then we found ourselves at the edge of a clearing. Rutherford was in the middle, panting heavily, his back to us. Bishop slowed, lifting his weapon, but I kept moving, closing the final few yards.

"Rutherford, it's over!" Bishop shouted again, his voice echoing in the stillness. Rutherford didn't turn. He seemed to be waiting, and my sense of unease grew stronger.

Suddenly, Rutherford spun around, and my heart stopped. It wasn't him. The man facing us was someone else entirely, someone we hadn't anticipated. His eyes were wild, a twisted grin on his face as he raised a gun.

Bishop's reaction was instant. "Gun!" he yelled, diving to the side. I threw myself to the ground as Jerome White fired. The sharp report of the gunshot shattered the silence. I watched Bishop go down, clutching his shoulder, blood seeping through his fingers.

"No!" I screamed, the sound tearing from my throat. I fumbled for my own weapon, but White was already turning, disappearing into the trees once more. I scrambled to Bishop's side, my hands trembling as I tried to assess the damage.

"Bishop, stay with me," I pleaded, my voice shaky. He gritted his teeth, pain etched across his face, but he managed a nod. I got on the radio. "Officer down!"

"I've got it," he said. "Go!"

"It wasn't Rutherford," I said, my voice hollow.

"I know," he said. "Go!"

I studied the blood pooling under Bishop's shoulder, the severity of the situation sinking in. His eyes looked okay, clear and focused, urging me to go.

"I'll get help," he said. He muttered, "Radio," and told me to go again.

With a final, hesitant glance, I nodded and took off after White, my heart pounding not just from the chase but from the sheer weight of the responsibility I felt leaving Bishop behind.

I pushed through the trees, the rain beating down on me and clearing the blood from my face. The forest was a maze of shadows and shifting light. Every rustle, every movement, fooled me into thinking it was White. I had to be smart, had to anticipate his moves. I slowed my pace slightly, listening intently, trying to pinpoint his location.

A branch snapped somewhere to my right. I turned sharply, moving as quietly as I could. Every step was a gamble of noise and speed in the thick underbrush. I spotted a flash of movement up ahead and sped up, ignoring the pain in my ankle, the fatigue in my muscles.

White was fast, but not smart, leaving a trail of broken branches and disturbed leaves. I followed the trail, my senses on high alert. A sudden rustle to my left made me pause. I turned just in time to see White's figure disappearing behind a large oak.

I sprinted toward the tree, my breath coming in harsh gasps. I rounded it, expecting to see him there, but he had already moved. I caught a glimpse of him darting between the trees ahead, his dark clothing blending almost seamlessly with the forest.

"Jerome White, stop!" I shouted, hoping the command might slow him, might make him falter. But he kept running, not looking back. I pushed harder, my legs screaming in protest.

Suddenly, White emerged into another clearing, one smaller and bordered by dense, impenetrable thickets. He had nowhere to go. I slowed, raising my weapon. "It's over, White! There's nowhere to run!"

He turned to face me, his expression calm, almost serene, and pure evil. "You're too late," he said, his voice carrying a chilling certainty.

A cold dread washed over me. What did he mean? I took a step closer, weapon trained on him. "Hands where I can see them!"

White's smile widened, a grotesque mimicry of innocence that pissed me off even more. "You'll see," he said. He raised his hands, but instead of surrendering, he threw something small and metallic to the ground.

A flashbang. I recognized it just in time to shut my eyes and turn away, but the explosion of light and sound still disoriented me, sending me stumbling backward, my ears ringing, vision swimming. When I managed to blink away the spots and regain my balance, White was gone.

I cursed under my breath, pushing through the disorientation, forcing myself to move. I had to find him. The clearing led to another narrow path, and I took it, hoping I wasn't too far behind. My ears still rang, and my head pounded, but I couldn't stop.

The path twisted and turned, the trees closing in around me, the downpour making running hard. I could barely see a few feet ahead. Every sound amplified, every shadow a potential hiding spot. I slowed, moving cautiously, my weapon ready.

Finally, I reached a small, abandoned cabin. The door swung slightly in the breeze. Could White have been that stupid? Would he have hidden in such an obvious spot? I approached it slowly, my senses tense and paranoid from every sound and movement. I listened over my heavy breathing, but the place was silent.

Moving carefully, I cleared each room, but White was nowhere to be found. Frustration gnawed at me. He had to be close. I stepped outside, scanning the surroundings. A faint trail led away from the cabin, barely noticeable, but it was something.

I followed it, my mind racing. What was White's plan? What did he mean by "you're too late"? The trail led me deeper into the woods, the trees grew thicker but managed to reduce the rain pelting me.

Finally, the trail ended at a steep drop-off, a small creek running far below. I scanned the area, but there was no sign of White. He had vanished, leaving me with more questions than answers.

Levy's voice burst through the radio. Through jagged breaths, she said, "We got her."

"This is Sargent Parker, Ellijay PD. We have officers and an ambulance at the home. Can you provide your GPS Coordinates?"

Bishop's soft voice came over the radio with his location. After he finished, I asked Parker for assistance and gave him my GPS Coordinates, then, mouth bleeding, legs cramping, and ankle screaming in pain be damned, I ran back to Bishop.

21

The ambulance took Bishop to Piedmont Mountainside Hospital in Ellijay. He assured me he was fine and said if I went along, he'd request a partner change.

"To whom?" I asked him.

"Call Cathy," he said, trying to smile. "Tell her where I'm going."

"I will."

An EMT put a butterfly bandage on my lip and told me to get stitches immediately, and to have my ankle looked at. I promised I would.

I followed the team of EMTs out of the woods and back to the house. The walk didn't feel nearly as long as the chase, but the rain had slowed to a drizzle, which I assumed played a role in the intensity of the chase.

Levy and Michels waited near their vehicle with Lara Hicks inside it.

"All she will say is the red wig is hideous," Levy said.

I exhaled, patted my lip with my fingers and nodded. "She played us so she could escape."

"I can't believe we got that wrong," Levy said. "Jerome White."

"Where the hell is Rutherford then?" Michels asked.

I glanced inside his vehicle. "She knows."

Levy looked at Lara Hicks through the window. "Like I said, she's not talking."

"She will," I said. "Through her attorney." I walked over to the window and blatantly stared at her. She turned her head to the side. "Michels, can you drive Bishop's vehicle back? I think it's time for a little girl talk."

"Works for me," he said.

An Ellijay officer walked over. "Sargent Parker," he said. "Which one of you is Ryder?"

I raised my hand. "That'd be me." I should have been helping with the search, but deep inside me, I knew he wouldn't be found.

"We've got men looking for your suspect, but there's a road about a half mile from where he disappeared. We've got patrol searching there as well, but it doesn't look good."

He glimpsed Lara Hicks in the back of the vehicle. "She have anything to say?"

"Just that she wants her attorney," Levy said.

He nodded once. "We've got a BOLO out on your guy." He eyed my lip. "That needs stitches. I'll be in touch with an update soon."

I climbed into the passenger's seat and turned toward Hicks. With a big smile plastered on my face, I said, "You'll look good in orange."

"I want an attorney."

"Yes, ma'am," Levy said.

No one else spoke a word.

Levy dropped me off at urgent care because I did need stitches. I called Kyle and asked him to come because I'd need a ride back to the department. I wanted to be there for as much of Lara's experience as possible.

My badge got me into a room quickly. The physician's assistant tried playing twenty questions to gather intel on what had happened, starting with if it had to do with Ryan Hicks's murder. I played dumb and said I wasn't assigned the case.

Kyle showed up just as they wheeled me to x-ray my ankle. I'd wanted to walk. I'd already run a marathon on the thing, and I made it. I could make the walk down the hall.

"X-ray?" Kyle asked.

"Pretty sure it's a sprained ankle."

"You can wait in the room on the right, sir," the PA said. "I'll have her back in a few minutes."

Ten minutes later, I was sitting on the examining table staring at my stitched lip in a hand mirror when the PA returned. "Well, Detective, you really do know your stuff. It's just a sprain. Ice and heat with ibuprofen and acetaminophen every eight hours should do the trick." He cleared his throat and added, "I'm not going to tell you to stay off it, though you should, because I get the impression you won't listen."

"You've got a sixth sense," Kyle said.

I filled him in on the drive back to the station. At the turn into the lot, a familiar looking black sedan in the opposite lane slowed. "That's the car," I said. "Follow it!

Kyle slammed his truck into a tight U-turn, tires howling in protest against the asphalt. The abrupt maneuver hurled me against my seatbelt, and I groaned in discomfort. "Hold on, Rachel," he growled, his gaze riveted on the sedan now a few cars ahead of us.

I scrambled for my radio, the dispatcher's voice crackling through as I slammed the button. "Detective Ryder, we are chasing a black sedan heading east on Deerfield toward Windward Parkway. I'm in a black Ford F150. This vehicle is implicated in the Hicks investigation."

"Received, Detective. Is the vehicle in your view? Can you snag a tag number?"

"No. It's three cars ahead of us." The light flipped, and the sedan, ignoring the right turn, lurched left, nearly clipping vehicles turning left from the opposite direction. Kyle activated his lights and siren, halting the rest of traffic, and pursued the vehicle. A cruiser roared up from Windward, executed a U-turn, and claimed the left lane.

"We've got two squad cars on Windward, Rachel. They'll intercept them," the dispatcher confirmed. My grip on the radio tightened, the black plastic chilly and slick in my hand.

The traffic ahead bulked up, ensnaring the sedan. "Got you," I muttered under my breath. But our quarry was agile; he veered into a business center parking lot, tires skimming the curb as he blazed through.

"Stay with him!" I urged. Kyle nodded, his jaw clenched, eyes fixed on the target.

The sedan jerked to a stop in the lot, the driver's door swung open, and a figure clad in blue jeans and a black hoodie leapt out. He was nothing more than a streak of fabric and desperation as he raced toward the building's rear.

"That's him," I declared. I reached for the door to leap out, but Kyle shoved the truck into park.

"I've got this," he asserted. "Drive around and see if you can spot him."

Kyle lacked a radio, so the only way we could communicate was by cell phone—not an easy option.

I didn't protest. Sliding into his seat, I clutched the steering wheel.

"He's sprinting toward the back of the building that abuts the ramp onto 400," I informed dispatch, eyes tracking Kyle's vanishing figure with a surge of apprehension. After their acknowledgment, I confirmed that Kyle had launched pursuit on foot, clarifying he was DEA, not a regular citizen.

My hands trembled as I steered the car. My heart pounded fiercely. I raced to the back of the building, engine rumbling low. No sign of Kyle or the suspect. "Dispatch, I'm at the back. No visual on suspect or Agent Kyle Olsen. I suspect they headed north."

Circling the truck around, I drove back to the front of the building, eyes scanning for any sign of movement, any clue of where they might have gone. Then, screaming brakes and a loud crash boomed from the direction of 400, the sound of metal crunching against metal, chilling me to the bone. I froze.

Kyle.

22

The brakes screeched as I grabbed my radio. "Ryder here. We've got a multiple vehicle crash on 400 south near the entrance ramp." I took a breath. "Possible law enforcement involved. Send ambulances and additional units now!"

The cruiser that had tried to follow pulled up, brakes hissing as it came to a sharp stop. Officer Carter rolled down his window. "Get in. I'll get you there."

I didn't hesitate. I climbed into the passenger seat as Carter flicked on his lights and siren and then sliced through the chaos as we maneuvered past vehicles pulled to the roadside. My heart hammered in my chest, thoughts of Kyle caught in the maelstrom overwhelming me. We raced down the side of the road, nearly ramming into an idiot who'd pulled off to try to pass the accident and no one would let him in. Carter popped his siren twice. The vehicle slid to the left, bumping a vehicle in the right lane in the process. Carter raced past them.

We approached the accident site—a brutal tableau of twisted metal and shattered glass. Four vehicles had collided violently, each one smashed into the other. The front vehicle sat angled to the left, likely trying to avoid whatever was in front of it. *Dear God, don't let it be Kyle.*

Two others blocked traffic, one flipped onto its hood, the other a mangled mess, both smoking. People rushed from their cars, some charging toward the wreckage, others holding their phones above their heads. I opened my door as Carter skidded to a halt and bolted toward the front of the first car in the accident. The air tasted like smoke and gasoline.

A woman screamed, "He's not breathing!"

My eyes scanned the chaotic scene, each shout and cry knotting my stomach tighter. I held up my badge and pushed through the crowd, my gaze snapping from face to face, searching, praying he was okay.

Finally, I saw him. Daniel Watkins was lying in a crumbled heap on the ground, a dark pool forming under him.

I sucked in a breath, holding back the tears and conflicted because I was glad it wasn't Kyle.

Kyle stood near Watkins, his phone pressed to his ear and his face a mask of concentration among the havoc. Relief flooded through me. Relief so potent it nearly brought me to my knees. We made eye contact, and his face softened.

I approached him, my footsteps faltering as I took in the scene more fully.

"This is DEA agent Kyle Olsen. I need police and paramedics to a crash scene located on 400 south just past the ramp at Windward exit 11. Pedestrian hit, five vehicle wreck with injuries," he said, then ended the call. The blue and red lights painted his face, making his relieved smile glow.

"Why didn't you call me?" I asked.

He looked around. "I was a little distracted."

"You're bleeding! Are you okay?" I ran my hands down his arms, then his chest, turning him to check his back, but I couldn't find an injury. The blood wasn't his.

"I'm okay. It's Watkins's blood. He ran right into the traffic."

My gaze flicked to Watkins, then back to Kyle, the noise around us swelling like a storm. Sirens wailed in the distance, growing louder as they approached. The ground would soon vibrate under the onslaught of emergency vehicles as they approached. It was a feeling I knew all too well.

"I don't think he did it intentionally," he said.

"He ran into traffic, Kyle. This isn't your fault."

"No, I mean, the situation. They manipulated him."

"Let's get you checked out by the EMTs and then we'll talk about it, okay?"

"I'm fine," he said.

"I'm sure you are, but humor me, okay? Like I've gotten used to humoring you."

He smiled. "All right."

Fifteen minutes later, Kyle sat on the edge of the ambulance watching the scene. "I'm fine. I can help."

"We've got this," Jimmy said. He'd arrived shortly after the crew, then Bishop, Levy, and Michels showed up after.

"Jimmy," he said, "I talked with Watkins. Lara Hicks convinced him to help her and promised him they'd be together. She manipulated him."

Jimmy crossed his arms as he listened. "Did he say he killed Ryan Hicks?"

"He said he's innocent, and that there's more to the story than you know. I asked him about the woman at his home and the kidnapping. He acted surprised." He sighed. "That's when he said, 'This isn't my fault. They tricked me,' and ran into the road." His Adam's apple bobbed up and down. "They tried to frame him."

Jimmy pivoted from side to side, swearing under his breath. "She's in on it."

"She and Jerome White," I said.

"Then how's Rutherford in on it?" Levy asked. "And where is he now?"

"I'll call Assistant DA Christopher on the way back to the station. We'll offer her a deal she can't refuse," Jimmy said. "Let's go."

Kyle stood. "Jimmy."

Jimmy flipped around and motioned for him to follow.

~

I watched Lara Hicks inspect her manicured nails through the one-sided mirror. Like she didn't have a care in the world and wasn't just charged with a double murder and multiple other crimes. Her attorney sat beside her, scanning through a folder he had brought.

Christopher was en route but gave us the go-ahead to have a nice little chat, something I couldn't wait to do, but Jimmy wouldn't allow me to go in without Bishop. I had promised I'd behave, but he gave me zero odds of that happening.

"Bishop's coming in?" I asked. "I thought they'd keep him overnight." I wondered why he hadn't let me know.

"The bullet grazed his shoulder. He begged me to let him finish this."

"And you're going to let him? I'm surprised."

"He's been involved from the start, and I want this finished."

"You and me both."

Bishop slipped up beside me. "You ready?"

I studied him carefully. No sling, nothing. "Are you sure you're okay?"

He smiled. "Good as new. They stitched me up and told me to take it easy."

"You're a cop. That's not possible," I said.

"I'll be fine, and you can't go in there without me, so let's get this done."

"I need the files."

"Susan gave them to me on my way down here." He glanced into the interrogation room. "Can you believe that's Ken Keller? I thought a defense attorney with his reputation would be classier than him."

"The nerds are always the smart ones," I said.

"I wasn't a nerd."

"I know." I smiled.

He swung the door open for me.

After a brief introduction, Bishop and I sat across from Hicks and Keller. Bishop held the list of charges in his hand. He recited them aloud, his voice steady and unyielding. I watched Lara, my eyes never leaving her face, analyzing any flicker of emotion.

"Lara Hicks, you are being charged with the following crimes. Conspiracy to commit murder, in violation of Georgia Code § 16-4-8."

Her smirk didn't waver, but her eyes flicked to Keller, who gave her a reassuring nod.

"Accessory to murder, in violation of Georgia Code § 16-2-20," Bishop continued.

Her lips pressed together slightly, a micro expression of concern that she quickly masked.

"Attempted murder, in violation of Georgia Code § 16-4-1."

Her shoulders tensed, the first sign that the weight of her situation was finally sinking in.

"Kidnapping, in violation of Georgia Code § 16-5-40."

A brief flash of fear crossed her eyes, gone almost as quickly as it appeared.

"Fraud, in violation of Georgia Code §§ 16-8-3 and 16-8-4."

Her jaw clenched, the tension in her body intensifying.

"Obstruction of justice, in violation of Georgia Code § 16-10-24."

Her fingers clenched into fists, a subtle but telling sign of her growing anxiety.

"Theft by extortion, in violation of Georgia Code § 16-8-16."

Her nostrils flared slightly. She would break soon.

"Drug facilitation, in violation of Georgia Code § 16-13-30."

Her breathing accelerated just enough for me to notice.

"Conspiracy to commit fraud, in violation of Georgia Code § 16-4-8."

Her eyes scanned the room.

"And finally," Bishop's voice grew even more resolute, "Murder in the first degree, in violation of Georgia Code § 16-5-1. This charge could lead to life in prison, Lara."

For a moment, Lara's facade broke. Her eyes widened, and a flicker of panic crossed her face. But she quickly regained her composure. I noticed every micro expression, every crack in her armor. She might have been trying to hold it together, but it was clear the gravity of the charges struck her like a sledgehammer.

Ken Keller leaned over and whispered something in her ear. Her shoulders relaxed slightly, but the damage was done. She knew what she was up against, and no amount of legal maneuvering would change the fact that she was in deep trouble.

Bishop finished reading the charges and looked at me. I gave him a slight nod, then turned my attention back to our suspect. "These are serious charges, Mrs. Hicks. It's in your best interest to cooperate."

She stared at me, her expression once again a mask of indifference. But the fear was there, lurking beneath the surface. The confident smirk disappeared, replaced by a grim determination. She knew we'd backed her into a corner, and it was only a matter of time before she cracked.

"Detectives," Keller said, "while I appreciate your reminder of her charges, I'd like to discuss an arrangement between my client and the police."

I leaned back, trying not to laugh. "You want your client to get a deal?" I laughed then. "Did you listen to the charges, Mr. Keller? What kind of deal do you expect?"

He leaned in and whispered something to his client. She shook her head adamantly, so he whispered something else, and finally, she nodded. "My client is willing to accept most of the charges. However, she will answer your questions and tell you everything she knows to have murder one, accessory to commit murder, kidnapping, and blackmailing and fraud removed."

Bishop laughed. "You're kidding, right?"

"No, sir. We're completely serious."

"How can we be sure Mrs. Hicks will tell us the truth?" I asked.

"She has agreed to do that. You have her word."

I glanced at the woman and rolled my eyes. "She's been lying to us since day one. Now that we've got her on multiple charges, you expect us to believe she'll tell us the truth?" I shook my head. "Mr. Keller, your reputation speaks better of you than that."

"It is my understanding Mr. Christopher is on the way," he said. "We will wait for him to continue our discussion."

In cases with lesser charges, we would normally leave the room, but neither of us trusted Hicks nor her attorney not to plan something that could hurt the case. We stayed seated.

Bishop removed a comb from his sport jacket pocket and ran it through his hair. Two strokes and he'd finished. I wondered how much he spent on hair products compared to me.

Ten minutes passed, and Christopher finally arrived. We stepped out and filled him in on their laughable offer.

"They're not getting that," he said. "But I'm willing to take the death penalty off the table."

Levy, Michels, Jimmy, and Kyle stood with us listening to Christopher's options.

"If she gives us White or Rutherford," he added. "As well as everything she knows about the crimes."

"What if she doesn't?" Levy asked. "Can we set parameters for specific questions she must answer or the deal's off?"

"I'll give it a shot," he said. "If I were her attorney, knowing what I know, I'd jump at this. Life in prison without parole is my final offer, but I'll work with dropping the death penalty without dropping the charges first."

I had mixed feelings about the death penalty. Was it better to feed, house, educate, and medically care for someone with the taxpayer's money for what could be fifty years, or would taking their life, an eye for an eye, be the best route to justice? That decision wasn't mine to make.

Christopher opened the door and walked in. Bishop and I followed behind him.

He showed no emotion when he said, "Lara Hicks, you're a suspect in a double murder and the death of Daniel Watkins, as well as various other charges."

Mr. Keller acknowledged that, but Hicks stayed silent.

"It's my understanding you're looking for a deal." He talked to Keller, not Hicks. "Please share."

Keller reiterated his plea deal. Christopher sat there, watching the man speak, but showing no emotion.

When Keller finished, he said, "Your client has been charged with multiple felonies, two of which carry the death penalty. I can't make the decision you're suggesting without something from your client first."

"Such as?"

"Answer the detectives' questions."

"No," she said.

"Lara," Keller said as a warning. He leaned in and whispered in her ear.

She nodded. "She agrees to answer questions, but only under my advisement. If I tell her not to answer one, she will not. Is that acceptable?"

Christopher eyed Bishop and me. We both nodded.

I leaned in, my voice cold, and fired a hard question first. "Was this all your idea?"

Her stone-cold face needed a bitch slap, but that wasn't in my job description, and that was too bad. "Was what all my idea?"

Lara's eyes darted around the room, searching for an escape. "It wasn't any one person's idea."

"We're going to need a little more than that," Christopher said.

Keller whispered in his client's ear again.

She said, "Ryan found out I was cheating on him with Jerome White. He wanted a divorce and custody of the kids. I wasn't going to let him have that satisfaction. He could have the divorce, but not the kids, and I need money to raise my babies, but he didn't want to give me anything. I complained to Colin, and he said he'd take care of it, and he did, at first."

"That doesn't answer the question," I said.

"Yes, it does. I needed money. Colin made sure we shared temporary custody of the kids and convinced Ryan to give me $50,000 a month." She exhaled. "It's impossible to raise children and live my life on only $50,000 a month. I ran out in two weeks, but Ryan didn't care. He said I needed to manage my money better. I told him I managed my money fine, but that kids are expensive. He wouldn't budge, so I went back to Colin, and he said he'd take care of it."

"Did he?" Bishop asked.

"He claimed he and Ryan had a falling out, but he would fix it, and once he did, he'd get me more cash."

"Did you ask him what happened between them?" I asked.

She blanched. "Why would I do that? I just wanted my money." She cleared her throat. "For the kids."

"When was this?" I asked.

"A few weeks ago."

"Did he follow up with you?" I asked.

"Do you mean did he tell me he planned to kill my husband and steal his money? No, but I found out."

"Are you saying Colin Rutherford murdered Ryan?" Bishop asked.

She looked to her attorney, then said, "I don't know for sure, but it sure as hell wasn't me. A week passed. I needed money. Ryan refused to give me any, so I was forced to ask my parents." A tear slid down her cheek. "Do you know how mortifying that was? A woman like me, with the money I had, having to ask her parents for money? I've never been more ashamed in my life."

She hadn't earned a dime of that money, not as a wife or a mother. I had no sympathy for her. "What happened next?"

"I called Colin multiple times, and finally, I asked him what had happened, what they'd fought about. He told me then Ryan had accused him of stealing money."

"Did he admit to it?" Bishop asked.

"He said he took care of things Ryan couldn't handle. That was his job. He promised me I'd have all the money I wanted soon enough. I didn't realize what that meant."

"Go on," Bishop said.

"I saw Ryan a few times after that, getting the kids and picking up more of our stuff from the house. He was high each time." She looked at me. "I'm not heartless. I didn't want him falling back into drugs again, and I didn't want him around the kids like that, so I asked him about it. He swore he wasn't doing drugs and that just wasn't feeling right. I asked how long it had been happening, and he said about a week or so.

"That's when I realized it was Colin. Colin was feeding him drugs. I asked Ryan what happened between them, why they were fighting. He said Colin stole money from him. He said he cut him off and was done with him."

"How was Colin drugging him after their falling out?" I asked.

"Colin has a key to the house. I think he put it in the alcohol or something."

"Ryan drank liquor?" I asked.

She rolled her eyes. "He wasn't an alcoholic. He was a drug addict."

She said it like alcohol didn't alter the mind like drugs, like it wasn't a problem itself.

"Did you tell Ryan that?"

She nodded. "Of course. I didn't want anything to happen to him or the kids."

Maybe her soul wasn't completely black.

"How did Ryan react?"

"He said that wasn't possible because he'd changed the locks the week before, but the kids run in and out on the terrace level to get to the back yard. They're young. They don't think to lock the door, and I'm not sure Ryan realized that. He also left a key under a plant on the front porch in case the kids needed something while they were with me."

"Would Colin know that?"

"Colin knew everything, so I would imagine so. He could have copied the key or just gone in whenever he wanted."

"We have a verified alibi," Bishop said. "He was on a plane that evening. It would have been nearly impossible for him to get to Ryan's place around the time of the murder."

"I can't explain that. I'm just telling you what I know."

"What about Jerome White?" I asked. "Why was he at the cabin with you?"

"Why do you think?" she asked, rolling her eyes. "We're in love. We want to be together."

Or White wanted Ryan Hicks's money.

"Are you saying you're an innocent victim in all this?" I asked.

Lara hesitated, her eyes flicking to her attorney. "I went back to Colin. I knew he'd taken over two million dollars."

Bishop interrupted her. "How?"

"Because Ryan told me. He said he had proof."

"Go on," Bishop said.

"I went back to Colin and told him Ryan knew he took the two million. I told him I could convince Ryan he didn't, but I wanted half."

"Did he give it to you?" Bishop asked.

She shook her head. "He said he planned to get more. That's when he told me I wasn't going to be in control of the money if something happened to Ryan. I was angry. I had no idea he'd left it in a trust for the kids, and that I'd have to go to Colin every time I needed some. I deserved better than that. Colin saw how upset I was, and he assured me it would all be fine. He promised to make sure I got most of the estate if I would commit to giving him twenty-five percent."

"Did you?" I asked.

"Of course, but I didn't mean it. The bastard stole from my family and drugged my husband. He put my children in danger. I just let him think I was going along with it."

Bishop asked. "What did he tell you about his plan?"

"Nothing, and I didn't want to know. Then suddenly, the police are knocking on my door telling me my husband is dead."

"Did you go to Rutherford and accuse him?" I asked.

"Wouldn't you? He swore he didn't do it, but I didn't believe him."

It hit me then. "You blackmailed him, didn't you? That's why you've been calling him. You told him you would tell the police he killed Ryan if he didn't get you money."

"I think my client has answered enough questions," Keller said.

"One more," Christopher said, "Where are Colin Rutherford and Jerome White?"

"Give us our deal and she'll answer."

"I'm prepared to remove the death penalty from her murder charges, but I'm not dropping them."

"She didn't murder anyone," he said.

"Did I miss her verifiable statement?" Christopher asked Bishop and me.

We both shook our heads.

"I didn't think so."

"Even if my client had committed murder, there are no aggravating circumstances to put the death penalty on the table in the first place," Keller said.

"Mr. Hicks murder was especially cruel, Mr. Keller," Christopher said. "Given his celebrity, I suspect our jury will feel the same."

Ouch. Hit the man right in the gut.

We hadn't mentioned anything about the drugs in Ryan Hicks's system at the time of his murder, and Nikki hadn't found any sign of them at the home. "May I ask one more question?"

Keller and Hicks made eye contact. He nodded to me.

"Did Ryan drink before bed?"

"Only sometimes, if he had trouble sleeping or had a rough day."

"Is that enough now?" Keller asked.

Christopher closed his file folder and stood, said, "I'll get back to you," and walked out.

We hurried after him.

He took a breath and said, "Let her sit in lock up until her arraignment. I'm asking for no bail," then walked away.

"He's not happy," Bishop said.

"Neither am I."

23

Kyle walked into the kitchen. "Are you hungry? I can make some eggs."

It was late. My head hurt, and I'd lost my appetite seeing Daniel Watkins lying in pieces on 400. It hadn't returned. "Not even a little. I'm going to shower." I shuffled over to Louie's fish palace and dropped a few pellets in. He swam over, snatched one, gave me a side eye, and darted into his cave. "Louie hates me."

"He doesn't hate you."

"He gave me the side eye."

He chuckled. "He misses you."

I yawned. "You coming?"

"In a bit."

I walked over and wrapped my arms around him. Kyle compartmentalized work, he had to, but I knew what happened to Watkins hit him. "Want to talk about it?"

"I wish I could have done something to stop him."

"You can't do that to yourself, Kyle. You know that."

"I know." He pulled away and grabbed my hands. "Go to bed. I'll be up soon."

"Would you like company?" I asked.

He escorted me to the couch. "I'd love company."

I sat beside him, placed my legs over his thighs, wrapped my arms around him and leaned my head on his shoulder. "I love you. I'm so glad you're okay."

"Love you too."

Within seconds, I had fallen sound asleep.

The low, rhythmic thrum of Kyle's heart had been a steady lullaby, but the harsh chime of the doorbell sliced through my dreamy haze, jolting me awake. My eyes snapped open, the comfort of the couch beneath us no longer enough to keep the chill of alarm from creeping up my spine. Kyle stirred beside me, his own sleep shattered by the intrusion.

"I'll check," Kyle murmured, the words thick with sleep.

I didn't respond. Pushing off from the couch, I stumbled to my feet, the sprain in my ankle sending a sharp reminder of my aging body and dumb moves. I gritted my teeth against the pain, limping slightly as I walked to the door. Kyle, as much as his body had been through, didn't suffer any long-term consequences, and beat me to the door. Through the peephole I glimpsed a figure in jeans and a black hoodie, darting away from our doorstep.

"It's him, Kyle!" I shouted, not waiting for a response as I flung the door open and took off after the shadow rapidly disappearing down the street.

Kyle's voice, tight with concern, followed me. "I'll call 911!"

Adrenaline surged, dulling the ache in my ankle as I pushed my body to its limits. The cooler night air bit at my skin, but I barely noticed, my focus locked on the fleeting figure cutting through the quiet of our townhome community. He raced toward our small downtown where he could easily lose me.

"Damn it," I muttered. "Kick it into high gear, Ryder."

He ducked behind Duke's. I followed, my breath coming in harsh, ragged gasps. Anticipating his path, I veered around a break in the buildings, racing to intercept him. My heart hammered in my chest.

I skidded into the alley, spotting a broom against the wall. Snatching it, I brandished it like a spear. As he came into view, I thrust it across the path. He tripped, sprawling on the concrete. I pounced, pinning his hands behind his back, my knee digging into his spine.

"Stay down!" I snarled, fury and pain mixing as my ankle flared.

The door to Duke's banged open, and the owner stepped out, phone in hand. "Rachel? What the hell?"

"Call the police, tell them Detective Ryder has a suspect pinned. I need assistance ASAP," I said through gritted teeth, not taking my eyes off the struggling figure beneath me.

He grunted, his body tensing under mine as he tried to throw me off. "Get off me, lady!"

Sirens wailed in the distance, growing louder by the second.

"Not a chance," I growled back, adjusting my grip. I squeezed tighter, wishing I hadn't removed my belt upon returning home.

The pulsing red and blue lights spilled around the corner, as the police cruisers skidded to a halt.

"Detective Ryder?" one of them called out, recognizing me despite the chaotic scene.

"Yeah," I panted, relief flooding through me. "Take him to lock up. Keep him overnight."

"On what charges?" he asked.

"Being a pain in my ass for starters."

They cuffed the suspect and pulled him to his feet. My ankle throbbed painfully.

As they led him away, he turned his head towards me, a look of panic twisting his features. "I can explain. Please!"

I straightened up, ignoring the pain. "Not tonight," I shot back. "And tomorrow's going to suck for you."

The next morning, Nikki stopped me in the hall on the way to the investigation room to interrogate the kid from the night before. "Good morning, Detective. I finally heard back about the trace amounts of biological material on the exterior of the trigger. It is skin, but I didn't get a hint on it in the system."

"Thanks. I'm hoping we'll have someone you can match it to today." I sipped my coffee. "Did Carl get anything from the love letters?"

"He didn't email you?"

I shook my head.

She rolled her eyes. "No wonder no one brought them up. I can't say for certain, but I think they're from Colin Rutherford to Lara Hicks."

My eyes nearly popped out of my head. "What makes you think that?"

"The writer brings up money, getting what they deserve, things like that. Also, I have copies of letters and information from Rutherford to Ryan Hicks. Rutherford uses twenty-eight to thirty-two pound paper. It's thicker than most regular printer paper."

"The letters were on the same paper."

She nodded. "It's possible someone else uses the same paper. It's not uncommon for a professional looking for a higher quality look, but nothing else in Hicks's things is on that thickness."

"Like this?" I asked, removing the note the kid had left on my door. I handed it to Nikki.

She looked me in the eyes. "Yes. Is this from Rutherford?"

"I'm going to find out. Can you get me a letter and bring it to interrogation room one, please?"

"Sure. I'll get it now."

I rushed to the interrogation room where the kid waited.

I explained what I'd learned to Bishop before interrogating the kid.

"Why would the notes be at the house and not with her?" he asked.

"Because someone put them there to make Rutherford look guilty."

His eyes darkened. "Lara Hicks made it all up." He shook his head. "Get the kid to give us his boss."

"Jerome White," I said. As he hurried off, I said, "Get a BOLO on him!"

He waved his hand in the air as a yes.

"Benedict, right?"

The kid nodded. "Yes, sir."

"Benedict, what's your boss's name?" Bishop asked.

"Jerome White."

Bishop and I shared a look. That BOLO needed to come through for us.

"And what exactly did he hire you to do?" I asked, pressing him further, hoping to get him to give everything up.

"Don't I get a call or something?"

"You made your call last night. You're waiting for your arraignment."

"But I don't have a lawyer."

"You have the right to one," Bishop said. "You've been told that, yes?"

He nodded. "What happens if I tell you what I know? Will you let me leave?"

"Depends on what you tell us, but consider this," I said. "You're an adult now, so you won't go to juvenile detention. You'll hang with the big boys in a state prison."

Bishop smiled. "Those boys will love you."

His face paled. "I didn't do anything bad, I swear. I just deliver notes, followed some people, made sure they got the messages. That's it."

"Who else did you deliver notes to?" Bishop asked.

"That baseball player. The one that died." He sucked in a breath. "But I didn't kill him, I swear. He wasn't even home when I left them."

"Where?" Bishop asked. "Where did you leave them?"

He licked his lips, clearly nervous. "Jerome gave me a key, told me where to put them, and shit."

"Did you leave a stack of letters at Mr. Hicks's home?" I asked.

"You mean the love letters?" He nodded. "Yeah, I did."

"Did you write or type any of these notes?"

He shook his head. "Just delivered them. I had to do what he said. After I left the notes, he told me I was a part of it, and if I didn't do what he said, I'd end up in jail." Tears fell from his eyes. "I didn't know what to do, man."

"You could have come to us," Bishop said.

"I'm sorry, okay? I got freaked. I didn't want to die. My boss is psycho. I didn't know that until all this shit went down. I didn't know he'd kill anyone."

"What makes you think he killed someone?" I asked.

He shook his head. "No, I...I can't tell you that."

I sighed, frustrated but determined. "Look, kid, you're in over your head. If you help us, we can help you. Otherwise, like we said, you're looking at a long time behind bars with the big boys."

He looked down at his trembling hands. "He's gonna kill me. You gotta keep him from me. Please."

"We'll do what we can, after you tell us what you know," Bishop said.

"He told me what he did to the baseball player."

"What did he do?"

Benedict explained how Jerome White had used a key to enter Ryan Hicks's home, spiked a bottle of alcohol, and then forced Hicks onto his bed, face down, and shot him in the head. He explained that since he told Benedict, he was an accessory to the murder, and if he went to the police, he'd spend the rest of his life in jail. He promised him a bonus for the follows, the notes, and to drive him, in Benedict's father's car, to the industrial park where White made the ransom call. He said the black sedan wasn't his, and that he thought White owned it.

"Can I go home now?" he asked. "I've done everything you asked."

"Give us a minute," I said.

Bishop and I stepped outside.

"I know what you're thinking," he said. "You want to use him as bait to catch White." He shook his head. "He's just a kid, Ryder."

"I wasn't going to say that yet. First, we need to get Cooper off the ranch. If White knows we've got the kid, he may hit Cooper for money."

"Right," he said. He called Michels and filled him in, then suggested he get with patrol and get a team there, STAT.

"Thanks," I said, "Now, about the kid."

"No," he said.

"He's legally an adult, Bishop. All I want to do is ask him. If he says no, we'll figure out another way."

"He's not old enough to understand the danger in this, and I don't want to intimidate him into it."

"I don't either, Rob. Dear God, is that what you think of me? That I'd intimidate a young man to get what I want?"

He exhaled. "No, Rachel. I don't think that, but I don't want to use him as bait. It's not right."

"The kid is looking at—" I quickly did the math. "A minimum of fifteen years in jail. You'd rather take that risk than get the charges dropped with his help? All I'm saying is we give him the option, and tell him what could happen, in both cases. Let him choose."

He rubbed the stubble on his chin. "Do you even have a plan to bring in White?"

"I do."

~

"Cooper wasn't happy," Michels said an hour after Bishop called him. "But Jimmy approved OT for four officers. They're there now."

"We'll head over there in a minute," Levy said.

"Not yet," I said. "Benedict is going to help us grab White."

24

The oppressive darkness of the night clung to me, its weight amplifying every rustle and whisper around the dilapidated warehouse on the town's outskirts. White had chosen the forsaken place for the meetup—a perfect stage for our trap. We holed up inside the one beside it, waiting for our go call.

Sam Benedict paced a tight circle, his sneakers scraping the gritty floor of the warehouse. His gaze flickered like a cornered animal's, half expecting White to materialize from the shadows at any moment.

"Easy, Sam," I murmured, striving to mask the tremor in my voice. "Stick to the game plan, and you'll walk out of here alive."

Bishop narrowed his eyes at me.

He nodded, gulping down his fear. "I just... I just want this nightmare to end."

"We're right there with you," Bishop reassured him, his hand a steady weight on Sam's trembling shoulder. "He hasn't shown yet, but it's almost time."

The plan had come together easier than I'd expected. Benedict had managed to snag White's new number before we caught him. We convinced him to type out the message we'd scripted, the message had been bait—simple but effective, playing on White's paranoia. He told

White he had urgent, new information, something the man couldn't dare ignore.

Unexpectedly, White bit harder than we'd anticipated. His paranoia and nerves had gotten the best of him. We had listened in as Sam, coached by us, convinced him he was desperate to skip town but needed cash. It was a shaky conversation, but White finally fell for it, his greed and fear overriding suspicion.

White had picked the location and time. We scoped it out, setting up our team hours before their expected meet up. All we had to do was wait.

"And we're moving in first, right?" His eyes flicked to Bishop, searching for certainty. "You'll be close by?"

"We'll shadow you, out of sight," Bishop confirmed with a firm nod. "You remember the drill?"

Sam hesitated, then, hands trembling, pulled out his phone. "Can we run through it one more time? I don't want to screw up."

"You text him and let him know you're here. Just like he asked. When he walks in, tell him what we practiced," Bishop said. "We'll take it from there."

Sam nodded his agreement that it was time. "Once he shows, it's on you guys to take him down."

"Count on it," Bishop replied, his voice low but resolute. "Let's go."

Once the team outside assured us with an all clear, we entered the building in the back as planned.

"Send the text," Bishop said to Benedict inside.

Benedict's thumb hovered over 'send.' "Right now?"

Bishop nodded, then got on the radio and said, "We're getting into position and contacting the suspect. Remember, we want him alive."

Our team and SWAT members responded accordingly.

"When will he be here?" Benedict asked.

"Not long," I said. "He'll be close by watching the area. That's why we came hours ago."

"Won't he see everyone?"

I smiled. "We're good at our jobs. Don't sweat it."

He took three deep breaths.

I felt for the kid. "Count to ten slowly. It's what I do when I need to center myself or calm down."

He nodded. "Count to ten. Got it. One—"

"In your head is best," I said, smiling. "We need to stay quiet now."

"Oh, yeah. Okay."

I patted him on the shoulder. "You've got this, and we won't let anything happen to you."

"I know."

We positioned Benedict in the center of the space to give the snipers a clean shot, in case things went bad, then fanned out, each of us melting into the shadows as he sent the text. Bishop and I crouched behind the skeletal remains of old machinery, our weapons drawn and ready. Michels and Levy stationed themselves by the entrance, a promise of no escape for White. High above, SWAT snipers nestled against the cold metal of the industrial park's rooftops, their rifles trained on the ghostly outlines in the building.

Time stretched thin, every second ticking by with agonizing slowness. Our team reported sightings of the vehicle we'd found through his registration less than a mile away shortly after the text, until finally, a low rumble shattered the silence—the distinct growl of White's engine. The warehouse door groaned open and bathed Sam's silhouette in the weak glow from the single overhead light.

White stepped into the cavernous space, his silhouette more menacing than I remembered. "Sam?" His voice echoed, betraying a hint of caution. A gun hung loosely at his side.

With feigned calm, Sam stepped forward. "Thanks for coming. It's urgent."

White's approach was slow, deliberate, his eyes slicing through the darkness. "Out with it, then."

We tightened our circle stealthily, unseen yet omnipresent, as he drew closer to Benedict. Sam's voice was steady, betraying none of his inner turmoil. "It's the cops. They're onto the last job you had me do."

A flicker of uncertainty crossed White's face. "Explain that. Did they bust you?"

He nodded. "They caught me outside the detective's place. I stuck to the story, said I was working for Rutherford. They didn't buy it, though. They wanted his location, but I couldn't give it to them, and they arrested me."

Suspicion clawed its way back into White's gaze as he stepped closer. "And what then? They just let you walk?"

"They've got me on everything. Dad had to post bail—cost him big. I can't go to prison. I'll get eaten alive. Please, I need to get out of here, I need cash."

White paused, his voice dripping with skepticism. "You need my help?"

"Yes, or I'm a dead man walking." Sam's voice cracked, the strain of his role catching up with him.

White closed the gap, his intentions clearly darkening. "That's not possible," he snarled, a sinister grin spreading across his face. "Because Rutherford's long gone, and you're next." He stretched out his arm and pulled Benedict toward him.

That was our cue. Bishop signaled sharply. Lights blazed on, flooding the space with glaring brightness. White spun around, his weapon swinging up in a desperate pivot.

"White, drop your weapon!" Bishop's command thundered across the warehouse, his gun aimed with deadly precision.

Fear and fury warred on White's face. He wrapped his arm around the kid and pulled him close, using him as a shield. "Move and the kid dies!" His voice boomed with a harsh growl, the gun now pressed to Sam's head.

"Stand down!" I stepped up beside Bishop, my own weapon trained on White.

Tension crackled through the air, the next moments stretching into eternity as our team tightened the noose. Michels and Levy flanked him, closing off any remaining escape.

"You're cornered," Bishop's voice was a steel trap. "Let him go."

White flung Benedict to the side and raised the gun to his own head.

A bullet burst through the window and White went down.

25

White rolled on the ground, screaming, "Don't shoot! Don't shoot!"

Seconds later, Michels and Levy attempted to cuff him behind his back, but the sniper's bullet had hit him in the shoulder, so they yanked up his jeans and cuffed his ankles instead.

White cussed them out, yelling something about abuse and needing medical treatment.

Bishop stared at him sitting up on the floor. "Karma's a bitch, ain't it?"

I laughed.

Benedict stood there, sweat pouring from his temples, and so stressed out, his entire body shook. "Is it over now?"

"This part is," I said, walking him toward the door. "But there's still a long way to go, just not tonight. Let's get you checked out just in case, and then one of the officers will drive you home. We'll need you to come back first thing in the morning to give your statement, though, okay?"

"Is it safe for me to go home?"

"White's not going anywhere but jail."

He nodded. "Okay."

The next morning, while I took my second shower in six hours, Kyle prepared a sesame bagel sandwich with egg, cheese, and bacon, my favorite for me. I pulled on a pristine white Hamby PD polo, slipped into a pair of dark jeans, then slid on my Doc Martens. I ran a comb through my hair then blew it dry. I left the thick mess of waves dangling over my shoulders instead of pulling it into a bun for the first time in a while.

Kyle whistled when I walked into the kitchen. "I feel like a high schooler seeing the librarian with her hair down."

A smile stretched across my face. "We all know what happens next then."

He handed me a plate with the sandwich. "I'm not in high school anymore."

"Thank God because I'd be in jail."

He'd also made himself a bagel sandwich and bit into it. "I'll try to come by today, but we're trying to wrap up the investigation in Roswell today."

"So, you might not be home until late?"

He nodded.

"Be careful," I said. I removed my weapon from the safe Kyle had installed behind the poster-sized photo of Chicago a few weeks prior.

"Same to you," he said.

We kissed, and I wanted so bad to lean into it and keep it going, but that would have to wait. "Text me when you can." I headed into the garage.

I stopped at Dunkin' and grabbed two boxes of coffee with all the sides and then drove to the department. Bishop had pulled in right in front of me.

"How's your shoulder?" I asked when I stepped out of the Jeep.

"Hurts like hell. Your ankle?"

"Sitting at a pain level of five right now. I've got some ibuprofen in my locker. Want some?"

"Cathy already loaded me up with the stuff but give me a few hours and I might."

Two reporters and their camera people rushed over from behind a van.

The little blonde one from ABC shoved the mic toward Bishop after asking, "How did it feel arresting the man who murdered Ryan Hicks?"

"No comment," he said.

The other reporter, another blonde I'd never seen, asked me what happens next.

"We drink coffee," I said. "Now, please let us get to work."

We turned our backs to the reporters, knowing the cameras were still on us.

"Can you carry this to the investigation room?" I asked, holding up a box of coffee.

"Sure."

I handed it to him and grabbed the other one. We walked into the department and headed straight for the investigation room.

"Think that'll go on the news?" I asked.

"Hope not," he said. He turned around. "I wore my baggy pants today. No one could see my booty."

I laughed. "You always wear your baggy pants, and please never say the word booty again."

He opened the door and shook his butt as he walked in front of me.

I pretended to gag.

"Oh, bless your ever-lovin-heart," Levy said when she saw the boxes.

"What my what?" I asked, knowing she wasn't serious using the southernism.

She laughed. "Listen, I'm a southerner now. Can't walk the walk if I don't talk the talk."

"I'll break your arm if you call me ma'am."

"Good luck." She smiled and prepared herself a cup of java.

Jimmy walked in, and without saying a word, poured himself some Dunkin' and then sat at the head of the table.

We all waited for him to speak like a family waited at the dinner table for the father to take his first bite.

"Nice work, team," he finally said. "Liz is outside tackling questions from the media, and I need to get out there, but you need to know that White's got an attorney with him now. You know what happens next, right?"

Bubba raised his hand. We all looked at him.

He blushed. "Oh, you mean the detectives. Right."

"Finding Rutherford is our top priority," Bishop said. "Go. We've got this."

Once he left, I said, "I want Lara Hicks first."

Levy said she wanted to be a part of that one as well.

The tang of disinfectant and the underlying musk of despair seeped from the concrete walls of the jail as Levy and I walked down the echoing corridor. The attendant let us inside the women's section, telling us Lara Hicks had been crying most of the morning, and had just stopped.

"She'll probably start up again," I said.

He nodded. "It happens."

We stood in front of Lara Hicks's cell. "Mrs. Hicks," Levy said.

She stood up slowly, smoothing the front of her orange jumpsuit. Her eyes, usually sharp and calculating, held desperate hope.

"Can I go home now?" she asked, her voice soft but edged with a brittle cheerfulness that didn't quite reach her eyes.

"Go home?" Levy asked. "I doubt you'll ever see home again."

Her face fell, the mask slipping for just a moment before she regained her composure. "What about bail?"

"Your arraignment is this morning," I said. "And given we know you lied, I don't think you'll make bail."

"I didn't lie to you."

I leaned closer with my arms crossed, and my expression cold. "We've arrested Jerome White," I watched her closely. "And right now he's throwing you under the bus. Blaming everything on you."

"Everything," Levy said.

Panic flitted across her face. "That's not true!" she shot back, gripping the bars. "He's lying!"

I didn't blink. "Then maybe it's time you start talking, Lara. You can start with Rutherford. Did something happen to him? Where is he?"

She hesitated, her gaze darting between Levy and me as she wrestled with her options. Finally, resignation washed over her. "I don't know," she breathed out, sagging against the cold metal. "Jerome wouldn't tell me, I swear."

"Not good enough," Levy said. "Three people are already dead. If

Rutherford's dead, White's going to pin that on you too. Just tell us where he is."

"I'm not lying. I don't know if he's dead. Jerome said he was useless if he couldn't get the cash."

"Tell us something you haven't already," I said. "Something about your relationship, or the situation."

She blinked. "I don't understand."

"He'll know you talked. He'll tell us more that way."

She sucked in a breath. "The stripper. He was dating her when we first slept together. I knew about her and teased him that he'd had a crush on me first, and only dated her because he couldn't have me."

26

The interrogation room smelled like sweat. White sat there, his arm in a sling, his shirt entirely soaked with perspiration.

"My client would like a fresh set of clothing," his attorney said as I closed the door.

"That's going to have to wait," I said. "Right now, we need Colin Rutherford's location."

"Go to hell," White said.

"After you," I replied. "Listen," I said to his attorney. "We've got a possibly dead or injured man connected to this investigation, and your client knows where he is. Get him to tell us, and maybe we'll get him a shower and some fresh clothing."

White's lawyer leaned in, whispering something low and urgent into his ear. White's jaw clenched visibly, his eyes darted toward the lawyer before settling back on me, simmering with anger.

"We know about you dating Levell," I pressed on, watching his reaction closely. "Lara Hicks said you were only with her because you couldn't have Lara."

The mention of Lara Hicks stoked a fire behind Jerome's eyes. His fist tightened on the table, his knuckles whitened with the strain. "That's a lie," he spat.

His attorney murmured again, a low, persuasive statement that finally broke his client.

"Rutherford is up north," Jerome conceded. "He's lying low in a cabin by Lake Rabun."

Lying low? "He's working with you."

He looked at his attorney.

The attorney said, "My client has given you what you asked for. He would like what you promised."

"Not yet," Levy said. "We need an address."

Levy scribbled down the information as White said it.

We walked out of the room, then asked an officer to put him under the shower and get him some clean clothing.

Rabun County Sheriff's office provided an assist in apprehending Rutherford. We stood outside the cabin, the deputies flanking us, knowing their role was to secure the perimeter, but leave Rutherford alive if possible.

"Perimeter check," I whispered, my voice barely a breath as we encircled the cabin. Curtains covered the windows. Each team of deputies confirmed no interior visual.

Bishop told them to stand ready while Michels hurried back to his vehicle for his ram.

With Levy and Michels in standard position, covering me and Bishop, he knocked on the door. "Colin Rutherford, we know you're in there," Bishop called, his voice firm, authoritative. After no response, he added, "This is your last chance." Still no response came from within the still cabin.

He signaled for Michels to use the ram. Michels, muscles tensing, lifted the heavy tool. Bishop's shoulder wouldn't allow him to help, so two Rabun deputies assisted. The door burst open with a splintering crash, shattering the silence.

We entered swiftly, guns leading the way, but stopped.

"Blood," Bishop said. "I can smell it."

I doubted Rutherford was alive, but that didn't stop us from keeping our weapons at the ready.

Bishop and I took the first floor. The smell grew stronger as we approached the kitchen, but Rutherford wasn't there. As Bishop moved to open a closed door, immediately blood, gun powder, and lead smells hit us with brutal force.

He stood there, took a quick glance inside and then turned to me. "It's bad."

I squeezed between him and the door frame. "Damn it."

Colin Rutherford lay sprawled grotesquely over the tiled floor, his head and brain splattered over the walls and ceiling.

"We can't go in there," Bishop said. "We can't help him now."

Rabun County's coroner reminded me of Barron. Hefty, tall, but with a thicker southern accent. "I can tell you right now," he said, "this boy did it to himself." He'd dressed head to toe in surgical scrubs but was careful not to disturb the scene too much. He carefully moved Rutherford's shirt and touched his arm. "He ain't been gone long either."

Rabun County Sheriff Bobby Walton stood behind us. "Hate to sound greedy, but if it ends up doc here is right, we'll handle this one."

"Be happy to hand it over," Bishop said. "We're already dealing with three lost souls."

"Em, em," he said, shaking his head. "That's why I'm up north. Don't see much of that in this town."

A deputy interrupted us. "We found a letter on the bed." He handed it to Walton. He read it and nodded. "Looks like we're going to be here for a while." He handed me the note. "We'll do our due diligence and keep you in the loop."

I read the note, then handed it to Bishop.

After reading it, he asked if he could take a photo of it.

"Whatever helps," Walton said. "Let me get my boys updated. Y'all drive safely now."

Levy, Michels, Bishop and I stood outside the home.

"Where's the note?" Levy asked.

"Rabun County has it, but I've got a photo of it. I read the note out loud.

"None of it was my idea," I started reading, my voice steady despite the swirling emotions. "Yes, I had been stealing money. I admit to putting fentanyl in his liquor. I did it to distract him, so he stopped spending money on the school, and to take his money without him noticing. Ryan found out and confronted me at his house the day I went to convince him to give Lara more money."

Taking a slight breath, I continued, "Jerome White was there cleaning the pool. He overheard everything." I glanced up briefly to gauge their reactions. The lines of tension in their faces told me they were as caught up in the unfolding story as I was.

"White saw an opportunity," I read on. "He approached me at my office the next day, Lara Hicks by his side, claiming he knew a way to get the money but that he wanted a cut. He made up this whole kidnapping plot and used Daniel Watkins as a cover."

The weight of the next part made my hands tremble slightly, so I gripped my phone tighter. I almost felt sorry for the guy. "I felt trapped when I realized White intended to kill Ryan. I tried to back out, tried to warn Ryan. I left a message on his cell saying someone wanted him dead, and that it was serious. I know the police checked his phone. Ryan must have deleted it, but I believe that's why he left Detective Ryder the note. I should have told him it was Jerome White, but I feared White would find out and kill me."

"Damn," Michels said. "He tried to do the right thing."

"Too little, too late," Levy said.

I continued but only a summary. "He wrote that he didn't deserve to live, and that he'd die in prison, anyway." I lowered my phone, looking at my team. None of us wanted Rutherford dead. We just wanted justice for Ryan Hicks.

27

The small interrogation room felt more stifling than usual as Bishop and I sat across from Lara Hicks. Zach Christopher stood behind us. Lara's eyes darted nervously between the two of us, her fingers fidgeting on the table-top. "Did you find Colin?"

I cleared my throat and leaned forward, placing a photograph of the suicide note on the table. "We did."

She glanced at the note. "I don't understand. Is this from him?"

"Read it," Bishop said.

Ken Keller took the paper and read it first then whispered into Lara's ear.

Her face contorted from confusion into pain. She sobbed. "Oh, God! I didn't mean for any of this to happen. I'm so sorry!"

I slid the box of tissue toward her.

Bishop said, "Rutherford wrote this before shooting himself in the chin. We know most of what happened, but we need you to fill in the blanks."

Keller looked up at Christopher. "And the death penalty is still off the table, correct?"

Christopher said, "If she tells the truth this time."

"She will," he said.

Lara's eyes flicked to the note, then quickly away, as if the words burned her. Bishop nudged the photo closer to her. "Rutherford splattered his brains in an Airbnb rental, Lara. He couldn't take his part in what happened to Ryan. Can you handle your part?"

Taking a deep breath, Lara finally spoke, her voice barely above a whisper. "It's all true," she confessed, her gaze fixed on the worn surface of the table. "Jerome promised to just rough up Ryan, not kill him. At first Colin didn't know Ryan had removed him from everything. When he found out, he panicked. He wasn't sure he could get the money together."

"Is that when Jerome killed Ryan?"

She nodded. Her words tumbled out, laced with regret. "At first Colin was just going to steal a bunch of money. He'd split it between us, and he'd make sure Ryan didn't find out. I didn't know he was already stealing from him. Jerome went crazy when he found out Ryan cut off Colin, but he came up with a new plan. That's when Jerome suggested faking my kidnapping. He thought Ben Cooper would pay a ransom for me." A tear slid down her cheek. "I thought he would too, for the kids."

"Why did he bring in Daniel Watkins?" I asked, suspecting I already knew the answer.

"Jerome was there, at the house, when Daniel showed up to see me. He knew he was obsessed with me. He convinced me we had to make it look like Daniel kidnapped me because he wanted to keep us off the suspect list.

"I told Daniel I loved him and wanted to be with him, but I needed help in getting the money from Ryan. I hated doing it, but I was so desperate," she continued, her voice cracking. "Ryan had cut me off financially, just like he had Colin. I didn't know Jerome would kill the girl. Jerome said she was going to pose as me so that Daniel would think he saw me, that it had worked, I guess."

"When did he do this?" I asked.

"I'm not sure. He just told me it was all done, that Daniel fell for it."

"When did he tell you this?"

"A few days before Ryan was shot."

"And he murdered her because?" Bishop asked.

"Collateral damage, maybe?" She shook her head. "I don't know. I didn't know then that he'd planned to murder her." She buried her head in her hands and sobbed more.

We gave her a moment.

Finally, swallowing hard, she said, "I recognized the other detective when she showed up at my parents' mountain home. I wanted to say something, but I was scared. When they left, I told him the police were onto us, and I ran. He ran too," Lara finished, her shoulders slumping as if the weight of her confession was too much to bear. "I wanted to tell you the truth, but I was afraid. I don't want my kids to lose both their parents."

"You should have thought about that earlier," I said. "We have DNA to check. We'll need a DNA sample from you to verify it's not yours."

"DNA?" She looked at her attorney.

He nodded.

"One more question. We found love letters to you from someone at the house. Who wrote them?"

"Letters? What letters?"

Bishop excused himself. "I'll get them."

I tapped my pen on the table waiting for him to return. When he did, he handed her the letters. "These letters."

"Those aren't mine."

I opened one and compared it to the copy of Rutherford's note. "The writing isn't the same."

We read several of the notes Carl had tagged as referring to the recent events.

"That's Jerome's writing," Hicks said. "I have things in my condo you could compare it to. I've never seen those letters, I swear. Was he trying to set me up or something?"

"The paper is the same paper Colin Rutherford used for the note," I said. "It's possible White wanted to frame both of you."

"Do you have anything else you'd like to add?" Bishop asked.

She shook her head. "I don't think so."

I slid a pad of paper and a pen to her attorney. "Have her write it all down."

"But you're recording this. Is that really necessary?"

"She might remember something else," Christopher said.

We walked out and stood in the hall.

"That was easier than I expected," Bishop said.

"White isn't going to like any of this," I said.

"Wait on that, will you?" Christopher asked.

"Wait to interrogate him? Haven't we waited long enough?" Bishop asked.

"Let her finish her statement. Put him in a holding cell and then walk her by him. He'll know he's screwed then. It'll be easier to get a confession."

I smiled. "You're going old school." I nodded. "I like it."

An hour later, after updating the team, Levy and I won the coin toss to walk Lara Hicks past Jerome White. It took every ounce of composure for me to keep a straight face.

Christopher stood in the corner of the holding cell area, carefully watching us prepare to parade Lara Hicks past her former lover. The second Hicks saw White in that cell, she looked away and wouldn't turn her head toward him. We stopped and discussed a previous arrest briefly with the officer handling the holding cells, just to make it worse for White.

He couldn't contain his anger. "She's a liar! She planned the whole thing! She killed her husband! Ask Rutherford, he'll tell you it was all her."

Hicks sobbed, then finally turned toward him. "Colin's dead you son of a bitch!" Then, to our surprise, she stopped crying and smiled. "And he left a letter. They know the truth, Jerome. They know you murdered my husband and that stripper!"

"Let's go," Levy said. She nudged Hicks's arm forward.

White yelled an essay full of cuss words, promising he would kill Hicks for what she'd done.

We planned to wait another hour to interrogate Jerome White but never got the chance. His new attorney, Edward Vaine, met us in the interrogation room.

Christopher shook his hand, and asked how he was, signaling they had some form of a personal relationship. "We're ready for your client," he said.

"What's your offer?"

"My offer?" Christopher asked. "Eddie the guy murdered two people and is partially responsible for the deaths of two others. There's no offer on the table. We're going for the death penalty, and you know we'll get it."

He nodded once. "My client has agreed to forgo a trial and plead guilty to the murders if you'll take the death penalty off the table."

Christopher looked at us.

"What about the other charges?" I asked. "There are several."

He glanced at a paper in his file. "Those are open for discussion."

"Give me a minute," Christopher said.

We waited as he called the DA on his cell for approval. The answer was quick because the call only lasted a few minutes. "He'll take the offer," Christopher said. "Let's let Jimmy know."

The chief smiled at the news. "I want to hear this confession," he said.

EPILOGUE

It had been a long day. We'd sat in court to hear the verdict for Lara Hicks's trial, and then headed home to take a break before meeting again.

Lara Hicks told the truth. She hadn't murdered her husband. We'd taken DNA from both her and White, and White's matched the DNA Nikki found. Like White, Hicks received guilty verdicts on everything, but since Christopher had taken the death penalty off the table for her, she'd likely end up with life sentences plus. We'd know that in a few weeks when the judge made his decision. With Lara Hicks's testimony, White had racked up additional charges, but he had agreed to plead guilty to the murders and four of the other ten charges if Christopher removed the death penalty for him as well. He knew he was going down and had done his best to control for how long. Judge Nowak presided over sentencing. It took him twenty-four hours to give him two consecutive life sentences and a total of fifty-five additional years. White showed no emotion when he heard the sentence.

It felt good walking into Duke's. Normal, even. Kyle pressed his hand lightly against my back and followed me. If he had his way, he would have walked in front of me, checking the surroundings like an over-protective father, but over time, he'd learned I could take care of myself. He'd even begun opening doors and having me walk through first instead of checking for danger first. He did it under duress, and I appreciated it.

Bishop and Cathy sat at our usual table, a large wooden booth that could comfortably fit our entire group. They were deep in conversation, their hands almost touching on the table. I smiled, happy to see them so close, and slid in next to Bishop. Kyle sat beside me.

Garcia was back in town, playing it cool with his 'no big deal' girlfriend, but his eyes gave him away. I knew the guy well enough to know he was full of it. He was in deep, whether he admitted it or not.

Ashley and Michels—Justin, she called him by his first name—sat across from them, engaged in a slight argument. "I do not snore," Michels protested, shaking his head.

Ashley laughed, a light, carefree sound. "You do, and it's like a freight train. I don't know how I'll ever sleep through it."

Cathy chimed in, "Bishop snores too. It's like sleeping next to a bear."

"You snore?" I asked Savannah, throwing a smirk her way.

"Only when I'm dead tired," she shot back, her elbow finding Jimmy's side. "Ask him, he's the reason I'm always worn out."

Jimmy grinned, holding up his hands in surrender. "This is our last baby," he announced to the table, which set off another round of laughter.

"Done?" Bishop picked up on that, his laugh deep and genuine. "I remember that phase."

Michels looked a bit pale at the prospect. "That's our future, huh?" he said, half to Ashley, half to the rest of us. "My dad always said kids ruin a sex life." He smiled.

"Michels," Jimmy said. He swiped his finger in front of his neck while shaking his head.

Ashley patted his hand, her laughter light and easy. "We'll cross that bridge when we come to it, babe."

"Wait a minute," Nikki said. She stared at Jimmy. "You said this is the last one." Her eyes moved to Savannah. "Are you pregnant again?"

Savannah's eyes widened. "Dear God, don't curse me like that. I just got my body back."

Jimmy laughed. "We're done. Savannah cut me off. I mean Carter. He's the last one."

"That's disappointing," I said. "I wouldn't mind another niece or nephew."

"She cut you off," Bishop said. "I remember that, too." He laughed.

"So, how 'bout them Cubs?" I asked, hoping to distract the group.

"We're the lucky ones," Kyle said. He wrapped his arm around me. "Neither of us snores."

"Lucky indeed," I agreed, squeezing his knee under the table.

Nikki had shown up with Assistant District Attorney Zach Christopher —a new relationship I hadn't seen coming but I wished them well—along with Bubba as their third wheel.

"I'm not with them," he said. "It's not that kind of thing."

"Thank God," Nikki said.

Zach smiled. He still had to get used to all of us on a personal level, but he was getting there.

"I saw the news," Levy said. "I'm glad Dr. Burns decided to go through with the fundraiser auction. The school is more important now than ever and I'm glad the construction got back on track."

The waitstaff brought out our food—burgers, fries, and a variety of appetizers, and filled the table with the delicious aroma of grilled meat and seasoned potatoes. I welcomed the relaxed atmosphere after the busy few months we'd had.

"Who's going to the school opening tomorrow?" Savannah asked.

We all raised our hands.

"Ben Cooper will be there, and so will Ryan's parents," I said. "They're bringing his kids."

"I still feel terrible for those babies," Savannah said. "I'm glad Ben went ahead with the school though. He's taken on a lot since Ryan's murder."

"Handling sixty million bucks can't be easy," Michels said.

"And the 500 million he got for his last contract won't even start paying out until 2032," Bishop said. "I can't even imagine."

"Don't worry," Cathy said. "You work for the city. You'll never get close to that."

I laughed. "Wouldn't that be nice though?"

That's when Bishop stood, pulling the table into a sudden quiet. He had that look in his eye, the one that said he was about to change the game. He reached into his pocket, the small box in his hand catching the light. "Cathy," he began, his voice steady but filled with that deep, raw honesty that hit me right in the chest. "From the moment I met you, I knew my life had changed forever. Your strength, your kindness, and your unwavering support have been my anchor. I can't imagine facing a single day without you by my side. Will you marry me and let me love you for the rest of our lives?"

Cathy's eyes widened, tears welling up in her eyes as well. "Yes, yes, a thousand times yes!" she exclaimed, throwing her arms around him as the entire place erupted into cheers and applause.

I cried. I couldn't help it.

Savannah pointed at me and mouthed, "You're next."

I pretended not to see.

I looked at Bishop after the applause and cheering stopped, mock-pouting. "You were supposed to let me shop with you for the ring."

He grinned, sheepishly. "I already had the ring when we had that conversation."

Michels laughed. "Dude, you could have done it in a romantic, private setting," he teased.

Cathy shook her head, beaming. "I'm happy to have shared this moment with all of you. You're my family."

Trusted Lies
Rachel Ryder Book II

They built an empire from their pain—now it's under siege.

Welcome to the world of Battle Scars, an exclusive collective of divorced women who've turned their pain into power as successful businesswomen. But when new member Veronica St. James faces a terrifying home invasion and ominous threats, the group's solidarity is put to the ultimate test.

Initially skeptical, Detective Rachel Ryder's instincts kick into high gear when one of the Battle Scars women is found murdered in her own home. As panic spreads through the group, long-held secrets begin to surface, and trust becomes a luxury that no one can afford.

With her veteran partner Rob Bishop by her side, Rachel races to connect the dots before the killer strikes again. But in a world where success breeds envy and empowerment has a price, the list of suspects seems endless. Ex-husbands with grudges, rejected applicants with scores to settle, and rival businesses with everything to gain—everyone's a potential threat.

Rachel must race against time to uncover the truth before the scars they've survived split open into deadly wounds.

ACKNOWLEDGMENTS

I want to express my deepest gratitude to the incredible team at Severn River Publishing for their unwavering support and belief in my work. A heartfelt thank you to my amazing husband, Jack, for your endless encouragement and patience, and unwavering support. And a special acknowledgement to my expert of all things law enforcement, Ara, whose invaluable insights and expertise have been instrumental in bringing this story to life. Your collective contributions have made this journey possible.

ABOUT CAROLYN RIDDER ASPENSON

USA Today Bestselling author Carolyn Ridder Aspenson writes cozy mysteries, thrillers, and paranormal women's fiction featuring strong female leads. Her stories shine through her dialogue, which readers have praised for being realistic and compelling.

Her first novel, *Unfinished Business,* was a Reader's Favorite and reached the top 100 books sold on Amazon.

In 2021 she introduced readers to detective Rachel Ryder in *Damaging Secrets*. *Overkill*, the third book in the Rachel Ryder series was one of Thrillerfix's best thrillers of 2021.

Prior to publishing, she worked as a journalist in the suburbs of Atlanta where her work appeared in multiple newspapers and magazines.

Writing is only one of Carolyn's passions. She is an avid dog lover and currently babies two pit bull boxer mixes. She lives in the mountains of North Georgia as an empty nester with her husband, a cantankerous cat, and those two spoiled dogs.

You can chat with Carolyn on Facebook at Carolyn Ridder Aspenson Books.

Sign up for Carolyn's reader list at
severnriverbooks.com

Printed in the United States
by Baker & Taylor Publisher Services